"Beautifully written, Biz's story (of dark thoughts, grief and questioning her sexuality) is subtly revealed and immensely satisfying as she slowly unravels and puts herself together again."

—GIRLS' LIFE

"If you've read Anna Borges's story for *The Outline* 'I Am Not Always Very Attached To Being Alive,' you are perhaps already acquainted with the idea of 'treading to stay afloat' when living with mental illness. In *How It Feels to Float*, author Helena Fox tells the story of a young woman floating through life, struggling to hide her dark thoughts and a past marked by intergenerational mental illness."

—BUSTLE

"Teens who don't want to be labeled, who don't conform to checklists of attributes or fall into tidy boxes, will relate hard to this book about a girl who wants, very badly at times, to float away, but who ultimately finds herself . . . Full of life, resplendent with sensory details, lush descriptions, clever and witty narration, and a beating heart that will make yours swell with feeling."   —B&N TEEN BLOG

"A YA *The Bell Jar* with a ghostly twist, [and an] honest, nuanced portrayal of grief and life with mental illness."   —BUSTLE

"This book will explode you into atoms, put you back together, and return the new shape of you to earth. Alive with sensation and rich in thought and feeling, *How It Feels to Float* intensively explores what it's like to be here now."

—MARGO LANAGAN, AUTHOR OF TENDER MORSELS

"Impossibly beautiful, life-affirming, profound. This is not a book; it is a work of art."

—KERRY KLETTER, AUTHOR OF THE FIRST TIME SHE DROWNED

"Every now and then you pick up a novel and you know you've found something wonderful—a glorious voice, a character you adore. Helena Fox's novel delivers. It is exquisite. Read it."

—CATH CROWLEY, AUTHOR OF WORDS IN DEEP BLUE

OTHER BOOKS YOU MAY ENJOY

I'll Give You the Sun	Jandy Nelson
The Sky Is Everywhere	Jandy Nelson
As Many Nows as I Can Get	Shana Youngdahl
Things I'm Seeing Without You	Peter Bognanni
Darius the Great is Not Okay	Adib Khorram
Juliet Takes a Breath	Gabby Rivera
Look	Zan Romanoff
We Are Okay	Nina LaCour

how it feels to float

helena fox

PENGUIN BOOKS

PENGUIN BOOKS
An imprint of Penguin Random House LLC, New York

First published in the United States of America by Dial Books for Young Readers
Published by Penguin Books, an imprint of Penguin Random House LLC, 2019

Visit us online at penguinrandomhouse.com

THE LIBRARY OF CONGRESS HAS CATALOGED THE DIAL BOOKS EDITION AS FOLLOWS:
Fox, Helena, author.
How it feels to float / Helena Fox.
New York : Dial Books, [2019]
Summary: "Sixteen-year-old Biz sees her father every day, though he died when she
was seven. When he suddenly disappears, she tumbles into a disaster-land of grief
and depression from which she must find her way back"—Provided by publisher.
LCCN 2018058425 | ISBN 9780525554295 (hardback)
Subjects: CYAC: Mental illness—Fiction. | Depression, Mental—Fiction. |
Loss (Psychology)—Fiction. | Grief—Fiction. | Families—Fiction.
LCC PZ7.1.F686 Ho 2019 | DDC [Fic]—dc23
LC record available at https://lccn.loc.gov/2018058425

Penguin Books ISBN 9780525554363

Printed in the United States of America

7 9 10 8 6

For Anna

I

I

AT THREE IN THE MORNING WHEN I CAN'T SLEEP, THE ROOM ticks over in the dark and all I have for company is the rush of words coming up fast like those racehorses you see on television, poor things, and when their hearts give out they are laid on the ground and shot dead behind a blue sheet.

At three a.m., I think of hearts. I think of candy hearts and carved-tree hearts and hummingbird hearts. I think of hearts in bodies and the rhythm inside us we don't get to choose.

I lay my hand over mine. There it is.

It beatbeats beatbeatbeats skipsabeatbeatbeat beatbeatbeats.

A heart is a mystery and not a mystery. It hides under ribs, pumping blood. You can pull it out, hold it in your hand. *Squeeze*. It wants what it wants. It can be made of gold, glass, stone. It can stop anytime.

People scratch hearts into benches, draw them onto fogged windows, tattoo them on their skin. Believe the story they tell themselves: that hearts are somehow bigger than muscle, that we are something more than an accidental arrangement of molecules, that we are pulled by a force greater than gravity, that love is anything more than a mess of nerve and impulse—

"Biz."

A whisper.

"Biz."

In the dark.

"Biz."

In my room.

I open my eyes, and Dad's sitting on the edge of the bed.

"You need to stop," he says.

What? I squint at him. He's blurry.

"The thinking. I can hear it when you breathe."

Dad's wearing a gray sweatshirt. His hands are folded in his lap. He looks tired.

"You should sleep like you did when you were small," he says. He looks away, smiles. "Your tiny fingers, tucked under your chin. There's a photo . . ." Dad trails off.

Yeah, Dad. I've seen it.

"The one of us in hospital, after you were born—"

Yeah. The one just after Mum got her new blood and you fainted and they gave you orange juice. The one where Mum's laughing up at the camera as I sleep in her arms. Yeah. I've seen it.

Dad smiles again. He reaches across to touch me, but of course he can't.

That photo has been on every fridge door in every house I've ever lived in. It sits under a plumbing company magnet and beside a clip holding year-old receipts Mum can't seem to throw away.

The photo was taken an hour after I came bulleting out of Mum so fast she had to have a transfusion. In the picture, I look like a slug and Dad looks flattened, like he's seen a car accident. But Mum's face is bright, open, happy.

All the other photos are in albums on our living room bookshelf, next to the non-working fireplace. The albums hold every picture of me Dad ever took until he died, and all the ones of me Mum took until smartphones came along and she stopped printing me onto paper. I'm now partly inside a frozen computer Mum keeps meaning to get fixed, and on an overcrowded iPhone she keeps meaning to download.

And I'm in the photos friends have taken when I've let them and the ones the twins have taken with their eyes since they were babies. I'm in the ocean I walk beside when I skip school and in the clouds where I imagine myself sometimes. And I'm in the look on my friend Grace's face, a second after I kissed her, five seconds before she said she thought of me as a friend.

I blink. Dad's gone again. The room is empty but for me, my bed, my walls, my thoughts, my things.

It's what—four in the morning?

I have a physics test at eight.

My ribs hurt. Behind them, my heart beatbeats beatbeat-beats beatskipsabeat

beatbeat beats.

MY NAME IS ELIZABETH MARTIN GREY, BUT NO ONE I LOVE calls me that.

The Martin is for Dad's dad who died in a farm accident when he was thirty and Dad was ten.

I was seven when Dad died. Which means I had less time with Dad alive than Dad had with his.

There's never enough time. Actually, there's too much and too little, in unequal parts. More than enough of time passing but not enough of the time passed.

Right?

Ratio of the time you want versus the time you get (a rough estimate)—

1 : 20,000.

Ratio of Dad's time as the son of Martin : as the living father of Biz : as my dead dad, sitting on the edge of my bed telling me stories—

1 : 0.7 : ∞.

MONDAY MORNING, 7:30, AND IT'S SO HOT THE HOUSE FEELS like it's melting. Cicadas scream through the windows. The dog pants on the kitchen floor. I had a shower five minutes ago and already I'm sweating through my shirt.

"Ugh," I say, flopping over the kitchen counter, crumpled uniform on, shoes untied.

Mum reads my face and sighs. She's making breakfast for the twins. "Be grateful you get to have an education, Biz." She waggles a spatula. "Not everyone's as lucky."

I peer at her. "You might have read me wrong, Mum. Maybe I meant, 'Ugh. How I wish school lasted all weekend, I have missed it so very much.'"

I'm a month into Year 11, which is ridiculous because I am nano and uninformed but I'm still supposed to write essays about Lenin and Richard III and urban sprawl. Year 11 is a big deal. We are only seconds away, the teachers say, from our final exams. The teachers can't stop revving us up about our impending future.

This is a big deal! say the teachers of English, science, art, maths, music, geography, and Other Important Subjects in Which We Are Not Remotely Interested But Are Taking So We Can Get a Good Mark.

You need to take it seriously!

You need to be prepared!

You need to not freak out, then have to go to the counselor because we've freaked you out!

I open the fridge. "I'm going to sit in here, okay? Just for a minute. Let me squat next to the broccoli."

Mum laughs. She's making banana pancakes. Billie and Dart drool over their waiting plates. The twins have the morning off school. They're going to the dentist! They love the dentist—it's where Mum works, so they get extra toothbrushes, and as many little packs of floss and toothpaste as they can carry in their hands.

"Are they ready yet?" says my brother, Dart, six years old.

"Come on, Mum! I'm starving to *death*," says my sister, Billie, nineteen minutes younger than Dart.

"Give me a second," says Mum. "A watched pancake never boils."

She flips one over. It looks scorched. Mum doesn't love cooking.

I can't see how she can be anywhere near a stove in this heat. I grab some coconut yogurt and grapes out of the fridge.

"Did you study for your test?" Mum says.

"Absolutely," I say, and it's true, if you count watching YouTube videos and listening to music while reading the text-book studying. I don't know if I'm ready—there's the lack of sleep thing, and the not-having-spoken-properly-to-Grace-since-I-kissed-her thing, which makes today impossible and complicated before it even begins.

I hug Mum goodbye and smooch the twins' cheeks as they squirm.

I grab my bike from the shed, ride it for thirty seconds before I realize the front tire is flat.

Ah, that's right.

When did the tire go? Friday? No, Thursday.

Shit, Biz! You had one job.

A magpie laughs from a nearby tree. His magpie friend looks down, then joins in.

I could ask Mum to drive me but I know what she'd say: "Do I look like a taxi, Biz?"

I could skip school, but then I'd miss my test and ruin my impending future.

I shove the bike back in the shed. And start walking.

I LIVE WITH MUM AND THE TWINS IN WOLLONGONG, IN A blue-clad house on a street wallpapered with trees.

We moved here a couple of years ago, after moving to a lot of other places. We're one and a half hours south of Sydney. The city is not too big, not too small; it's just right for now, says Mum. The city sits beside the sea, under an escarpment. The sea pushes at the shore, shoving under rocks and dunes and lovers. Craggy cliffs lean over us, trying to read what we've written. The city is long like a finger. It was a steel town once.

There, that's the tour.

When I was seven, Mum, Dad, and I lived up north, near Queensland—in the Australian jungle, Mum likes to say. She says the mosquitoes were full on, but I don't remember them.

I remember frogs *click-clacking* at night in the creek at the bottom of the hill. The house was wooden; it had stilts. The backyard was a steep tangle of eucalypts and ferns and figs and shrubs.

You could see hills like women's boobs all around. I'd wake

up and hear kookaburras. Light would come in through my curtainless windows and lift me out of bed. I'd run in to Mum and Dad's room and jump on them to wake them up.

I had a puppy. I called him Bumpy.

Our street is flat now. It goes past a park where I walk the dog and he sniffs the shit left by other dogs. I can walk to school in fifteen minutes or I can walk straight past it and go to the sea. Or, if I want to be a total rebel, I can go the opposite direction and in fifteen minutes end up in a rainforest, under a mountain, gathering leeches for my leech army.

On the walk to school, the cicadas keep me company. They scream from one huge gum tree to another. I pass the community center. I pass the park. I get to the end of the cul-de-sac and wait under the bleaching sun to cross the freeway.

Traffic bawls past. I can feel my skin frying. I can feel cancer pooling in my freckles. I can feel the road tar melting under my feet as I scurry across the road.

Past the freeway there's a vet, a pub, and a train station. Every day I have to cross the train tracks to get to school. Every time I think, *What if the signals are wrong, and a train comes out of the blue and hits me as I cross?*

A woman walked against the signal once. Not here, but close enough it might as well be here. She was in a rush, they said; she ignored the ringing bells, the dropping barrier. She got halfway and thought better of it. She turned back. The train came.

Every time I cross the tracks, I think of her and try not to think of her.

I've traced and retraced her last moments in my head. I have googled her and I know the names of her family, the job she had, the music she listened to, and the last concert she saw before she died. I can feel the tightness of her skin when she saw the train, and how sweat sprang up a moment before the train hit—

step

and how our pupils widened

step

and turned my eyes to black

step

and in that infinite, molecular moment, I can't remember if I meant to cross, or have paused on the tracks and am waiting here—

"Hey, Biz."

I turn my head. Dad's walking beside me, barefoot, in his running shorts and KISS T-shirt.

"Do you remember your first train ride?"

No. I don't remember that, Dad.

"It was a steam train. You were four. We went through a rainforest! We went really high up a mountain, and visited a butterfly sanctuary. And you flapped around like a monarch. You were beautiful."

Is that right, Dad?

"You should flap around. Try it, Biz; it'll shake off the frets."

I look down. I'm over the train tracks and past the station. I'm on the path; it opens in front of me, green grass on both sides, the sun beaming.

I think of butterflies. I think of flying.

Dad laughs.

He's gone by the time I reach the school gate.

I WALK INTO PHYSICS JUST AS MS. HASTINGS IS HANDING out our tests. Ms. Hastings gives me a *young lady, you're late* look. I give her a *tell me about it and have you noticed I'm swimming in a pool of sweat* look. Ms. Hastings raises an eyebrow. I sit at my desk.

Ms. Hastings lays our tests facedown. She does the regular threats: "You must not look at anyone's work!" and "Put away your phones!" and "Your time starts now."

We flip our pages over.

Turns out, I am ready for the test. My brain fires up and the neurons make my hand move and the formulas come out like good little ponies at a show.

Most of my tests are fairly easy, which isn't me boasting; it's just a statement of fact. Mum says I might have a photographic memory, which is good for Mum because she often forgets her PIN numbers and passwords.

Mum could be right. All I have to do is look at something and it sticks. Sometimes, the image repeatrepeatrepeatrepeats, like a GIF I can't turn off.

The room fills with the buzz of numbers. Pi scuttles over our papers, theorems talk to themselves. Ms. Hastings looks at her phone—probably at some friend skydiving or snorkeling in the Bahamas, while she's trapped in here with us.

The bell rings.

"Time's up!" calls Ms. Hastings. We hand in our tests. Next class is English.

I don't chat or dawdle in the corridors; I slip between the crowds, a fish weaving. In fifty-five minutes I'll have to speak to Grace. *Just keep swimming, Biz.*

Mr. Birch stands like a flamingo in front of the class, one foot scratching the back of his leg.

"Okay, everyone," he says, "today we'll be writing about the ego. That is, your alter ego. Consider your readings over the weekend, and the work of Plath in this context."

A collective groan from all of us. We've done Plath now for three long weeks and no one is a fan. I mean, we all "feel" for her, but at this point we've read her and analyzed her and discussed her and it's like peeling an onion until there's no onion left.

"I want you to write a description of your alter ego, due at the end of the day," Mr. Birch says, ignoring our protests. In case we don't remember what he's just said, he writes it on the whiteboard, his blue pen squeaking. He then sits at his chipped desk behind his PC, doing paperwork.

We hunker down to do the assignment. That is, some of us do the assignment; some of us daydream. The new boy pulls out a book and reads it behind his laptop screen.

Fans *flick-flick* above us. A trickle of sweat moves down between my boobs. I stare at my computer.

I don't much like to write about myself. It's not my thing, discussing any part of me. Over the years, Mum has suggested we go see people because Dad is dead, but then we put it off. I did sit with a man once, when I was seven and a half, in a room with yellow-painted walls and framed cat pictures. The man had round glasses like Harry Potter. He laid out paper and blunt coloring pencils and said to draw, so I did. Then he hummed and ha-ed and said, "I'll just speak to your mum now, okay?" and when Mum came back out, her eyes were really red, so I didn't draw for anyone else after that.

The cursor blinks on, off.

I take a breath, and dive in.

My Alter Ego: A meditation/poem, by Elizabeth Grey

Consider the Ego / The ego is defined as a person's sense of self / Which includes but is not limited to self-esteem, self-worth, and self-importance / Don't we all think ourselves important, that we matter? / We are matter, this part is true / But do we? / And / Is it possible to have an alter self / I.e.: an opposite, matterless self?

No / Such a thing cannot exist / The universe is made of matter / And if I am alter or other, then I would be lacking matter or a sense of matter and as such cannot be in the universe / And if I am outside the universe, that makes me a singularity, a concept impossible to imagine / Therefore, my alter ego is beyond my capability for imagining / And thus, cannot be described.

The End

P.S. Some say God is a singularity, but people imagine God all the time / They think he looks like someone's white grandpa, or Santa Claus / God's Alter Ego is sometimes called a Dog / (Sorry) / It should be added that Dogs exist and have the potential to exist throughout the known universe / So it is possible that my earlier hypothesis is wrong.

I close my laptop, look up at Mr. Birch, who'll get to read this masterpiece tonight. What a lucky guy!

The bell rings.

"Please email me your essays by midnight!" calls Mr. Birch over the scrape of chairs, the shoving of laptops into bags, the clatter of our bodies beelining it to the door.

Now it's break.

At break and lunch, I always sit with Grace—and Evie and Stu and Miff and Rob and Sal. The Posse, they call themselves. I should say: We, as a collective, call ourselves The Posse. I am in The Posse. I am an integral member of The Posse, I think.

Grace and I have sat with The Posse since the first day of Year 9. We were both new. Evie saw us hovering uncertainly in the schoolyard, and decided we belonged to her. She brought us over to the bench under the tree by the fence. There, everyone interviewed us. What bands did we like? Did we prefer a day at the beach or inside? Had we read *The Communist Manifesto*? Had we seen *One Flew Over the Cuckoo's Nest*? Did we like it? Did we have a tattoo? If not, what would we get and where?

The group made the questions sound like conversation. But I could feel everyone marking us invisibly. Tick, tick, cross, tick, tick.

I let Grace answer first and watched everyone's faces. I crafted my answers the way their smiles went.

In the end it was okay. We could stay. But of course we could stay! *The Posse is inclusive! The Posse is Love Incarnate!*

We would have more people in The Posse, but most people are stupid, says Miff. We, The Posse, agree.

Before I came to this school, I was never in a group, so being in one—especially one with a name—was quite the novelty. It still is, because, I mean, I belong to six other people and they say they miss me when I'm not there. I've sat on the bench under the tree by the fence for just over two years now, laughing and saying things I think I'm supposed to.

And almost every second of every minute I'm with them, I feel like I'm seeing the scene from somewhere else. In front of a screen maybe, watching someone else's life.

I WALK TO THE LOCKERS. GRACE IS STANDING BY MINE.

"Hey," I say.

"Hey," she says. She smells like lavender—it's from the moisturizer she gave me for my birthday, then borrowed two months ago and forgot to give back.

I open my locker. I put in my books.

"Hey," I say again. My hands are actually shaking, which is stupid, because this is Grace, my best friend, who lives down the street and one left and two rights away from me. Grace Yu-Harrison, who knows all the songs from the Beatles' *White Album* (like me), loves *The Great Gatsby* (like me), and the art of Alexander Calder, especially his mobiles, which move when you blow on them. (We did this, one Sunday in Sydney, when the guard wasn't looking. The wires trembled at first, then danced.)

Grace lives with her mum and stepdad, who are workaholics. I'm not exaggerating; they literally can't seem to stop sitting in their offices, going to meetings and conferences and dinners with other workaholics, and coming home late. Grace has a lot of time to herself. Her dad lives in Wagga Wagga, which is so far from the sea it may as well be fictional. She has a pool and a hammock that fits two—we often swing in it after a swim.

Grace is also stunning, the kind of gorgeous most people try their whole lives to be. She has kissed five and a half guys. Half because one guy turned and vomited two seconds after their lips touched.

"It was disgusting," she said. "He nearly threw up in my mouth!"

I haven't kissed anyone else but her.

In the four-minute walk from the lockers to our bench by the fence, Grace usually talks. She says we should dye our hair, but not blue because everyone's doing that, so maybe silver? And she tells me about the drawing she did of her dream last night, and about Suryan in Year 12 sending her a photo of his penis, which she calls a dick, and which I say is unfair to all the people called Richard, and Grace laughs.

At least, that's what she said on Friday, when I saw her last, before I went over for a swim in her pool and she lay on the grass afterwards—her eyes closed, her hair glassy-smooth—and that's when something lurched inside me and I leaned over and put my mouth on hers.

"Hey," says Grace again, and I'm back, by the lockers.

We could do this all day, I think, but then she stands squarely in front of me, so I can't move. She pins me with her eyes.

"I'm sorry," I begin, which is what I said after I kissed her, and again, when she tried to say how she liked me but not *that* way, but I was so mortified I took off. I'm a thousand feet tall and when I run I look like a giraffe, so imagine me, hoofing it down my street in just my swimmers, school bag in one hand, uniform and shoes in the other, the neighbors gawking at me from their front windows. I must have been quite the sight.

"Biz," says Grace. She puts her hand on my arm. "Seriously, it's okay. It was nice, you know? I haven't been kissed in ages and you're not a bad kisser. I'm just not—" She pauses. And takes a long breath in.

I fix my eyes on the lockers, the floor, anywhere but Grace's hand on my arm.

She steps closer, so now we are just two pairs of eyes, floating. "So. Here's the thing, Biz. What I want—ah—what I'm wondering is"—another big breath in—"Biz, areyoubiorallthewaygay?"

I blink. "Sorry?"

"Bi? Or gay?" Grace asks the question like she's standing with a clipboard in a shopping mall, asking strangers for orphan money.

I gawp at her.

"Because," she says, "I was thinking over the weekend— which *sucked*, by the way—Dad called and I had to fly to Wagga for some great-aunt's funeral, did you get my text?—and we went to his girlfriend's *farm* for fuckssake—it's got no Wi-Fi, no signal, how's that possible?—and we ate lamb, which is seriously disgusting—and he kept saying how I have to get my shit together this year or I won't get into uni—God, that man's a nightmare—but anyway—*back to you, Biz*—I was thinking about who might be good for you instead of me, and whether guys are a no for you or still a possibility, because Evie said Lucas Werry might be keen—but if it's girls you're into, we can go in a whole other direction. That's cool. Like, unless—as long as you're not hung up on me, in which case"—she pauses—"that could be a tragedy of Shakespearian proportions."

Grace finally stops talking. She smiles, sort of, and waits for me to answer.

I can't speak. I can feel the pistons of my heart moving, feel my lungs filling, emptying, my pores clogging. I feel the movement of the stars and I can hear the echo of all the black holes consuming everything—

and then, just like that, my head clears.

It's Grace. Just Grace. (*Look, Biz.*)

Here she is, her hand still on my arm. My best friend.

(*Come down to earth, Biz. Everything is going to be okay.*)

I blink slowly, and feel myself waking.

"No," I say. "I don't think I'm hung up on you. As mesmerizingly beautiful as you are, Grace, I actually don't think you're my type." And as I say it, something untangles in my chest. Oh my God. It's *true*. I think?

I'm not. She isn't.

Right?

Thank God?

Grace looks hugely relieved. Which makes me laugh. And I keep laughing, and suddenly everything is fine.

Right?

Thank God?

"I don't actually know what I am," I say, and I think that's true. Am I bi? Am I gay? Am I something else? It makes my head fog to think about it.

"I mean, I wasn't planning to kiss you," I say.

She smiles. "I *am* pretty irresistible."

"You're the only person I've ever kissed, Grace. I'm seriously inexperienced. Maybe I should kiss more people to figure it out? Maybe we can line them up. Or lay them out on a tray like a taste test."

"So we can see if you're into pepperoni or anchovies," says Grace.

"Both are animal products, so therefore—" I begin, and then see Grace smirk. "Ah, *gross, Grace!*"

Grace laughs. She starts walking outside. I walk beside her. We head for the tree, the bench under the tree, The Posse sitting beside the fence. And Grace is already pulling her phone out, already texting Lucas-Werry-who-might-be-keen, and asking him over to her house for a swim.

Which will be good.

Right?

DAD SAW MUM FOR THE FIRST TIME ON A JETTY IN PALM Beach. He was swinging his legs off the edge, eating chips. She was fishing.

Technically, she wasn't fishing. She was standing on the jetty watching her boyfriend fish. The boyfriend was all: "Me strong. Me good at fishing. Me have muscles," and Mum was putting together the words she needed to break up with him.

So she broke up with the guy, right there, and as a parting shot she said, "Also. I don't like fishing. It's inhumane."

And the guy said, "They're fine! I chuck them back in!"

And Mum said, "Not before you rip out their insides with that hook."

And the boofhead said, "Ah, fuck off."

So she said, "That's not nice, Barry," and she took his fishing rod and threw it in the water.

Then the guy got all feisty, so she shoved him in too.

Dad watched the whole thing and thought to himself, *Get yourself a girl who can catch and release.*

That's how Dad puts it, anyway, when he tells the story. Most recent retelling: last Thursday night.

I was trying to study and Dad leaned beside the window saying, "And she marched off like Wonder Woman, Biz. And then I saw her at the bus stop waiting for the bus, and I went up to her, and said, 'Excellent technique.'

"She said, 'Thanks, I've had practice.' And then I said . . . Well, I couldn't speak, because boom, there she was, smack dab in my heart. We never looked back."

Dad grinned.

It was a great story. But I was distracted, trying to figure out a polynomial.

"That's great, Dad. Don't suppose you could be of use, and help me with my maths?"

When I looked around, he was gone.

I often think of a bubble when I think of Dad. He's sort of see-through, but when he talks about Mum, or me as a baby, his colors fill out.

It's kind of beautiful to watch. If I don't say anything, he'll totally float there for hours.

LUCAS WERRY IS NOT EVEN SLIGHTLY INTERESTED IN ME. I'M not sure where Evie got her information, but in Grace's pool on Friday afternoon he keeps paddling after Grace like she's catnip.

Afterwards, we can't help but laugh. Lucas heads home after the swim, clearly disappointed when Grace tells him he has to go. She says we're going out to dinner with her parents tonight (a lie), and they're taking us to an expensive restaurant in Sydney (also a lie), and he needs to leave so we can get ready (lie! Lie! So much lie! We are going to eat hummus and carrots for dinner and watch The Great Gatsby for the twenty-eighth time, and we might even study. This is what we call a party night).

"He wanted you, Grace," I say. "Did you see?"

"I felt it, Biz," Grace says, making a face. "He pressed it against me!"

I'm showering in Grace's bathroom when I realize nothing would appeal to me less than Lucas pressing any part of his body against mine. So what does that mean?

"Grace," I say when I go back to her room, toweling my hair dry.

"Yeah?" Grace bounces across her bed and looks up at me.

"I was in the shower and thought of Lucas pressing his penis against me and nearly threw up."

"Is that right? Lucas's fine body did not appeal to you in the slightest? Those abs? Those arms? That enormous, throbbing—"

"No," I cut her off. "But here's the thing." I lay the towel over the back of her chair and look at her. "I'm not sure I want anything pressed up against me. Boobs, penises, abs, vaginas. Not sure about any of them."

"Hmmm." She beams. "*Interesting!*"

Grace's project becomes "Solving the Conundrum That Is Biz's Sexuality."

The number of girls and boys she points out to me at school becomes a little exhausting. Before I even walk through the school gates, she's texted me a list of people to check out that day. I draw the line at some girl called Maddie in Year 8.

"I'm not Nabokov, Grace," I text her in English class.

"Sorry," she texts back. "I got carried away."

Her text arrives with a bright PING! just as Mr. Birch is telling us about an assignment we've got to hand in next Friday. Everyone looks up from their notes and swivels their heads—twenty-three owls noticing the rustle of a poor mouse who has forgotten to silence her phone.

Mr. Birch says, "Elizabeth, Elizabeth, Elizabeth." He shakes his head sorrowfully. After the alter-ego assignment, his ambitions for me must have significantly lowered. Mr. Birch walks over and holds out his hand.

School Policy: Use of smartphones in class is expressly forbidden, even when you're in Year 11 and should be permitted to self-govern.

Shit. I will now be without a phone until Friday. It's Wednesday morning.

I hand my phone over and see the new boy smile. The one who read a book behind his screen last week when we were supposed to be working—a full miscreant move, I might add. I'm not sure he even submitted his essay. I make a face at the new boy and Mr. Birch thinks I'm making it at him.

Turns out Mr. Birch has quite the temper. An anger management class would do that man some good.

Mum is not pleased. She thumps around the kitchen, opening and shutting cupboard doors, picking up saucepans and banging them down.

"Who gets detention in Year 11? Seriously? And your phone confiscated? This is some primary school shit, Biz."

"Mum!"

Mum keeps forgetting the twins are six and easily influenced.

"Shit!" says Dart, doing homework at the kitchen table.

"Mum said shit!" singsongs Billie, sitting opposite him. And the two of them start chanting, "Mum said shit! Mum said shit!" over and over until Mum burns her hand on the side of the kettle because she's distracted, and she swears again ("Mum said fuck! Mum said fuck!") and Mum slams the fridge door shut because there are no veggies in there besides one limp zucchini and a cauliflower with moldy patches, and her eldest is turning to the dark side, and the twins have mouths like fishwives, and *what did she do to deserve this?*

Poor Mum. I give her a hug. "Let's go get Thai food," I say.

She sniffs—a bit weepy—and agrees.

We go to the local Thai place and eat until the twins' bellies swell and we order too much satay, which is wonderful because we love leftovers.

And the ratio evens out.

Shit to Wonderful. 1 : 1.

MUM FELL IN LOVE WITH A MOVIE WHEN SHE WAS TWENTY. It was about a woman who caught a train and didn't catch a train. When the woman caught the train, she walked in on her boyfriend having sex with another woman. When she missed the train—doors sliding shut a second before she reached them—she didn't catch the guy having sex, and the universe split in two.

"It's the best," says Mum. "You follow Gwyneth in two lives, so it's all, *I wonder what happens if she catches the train; what happens if she doesn't? Will she end up in the same shitty life? Will she ever be happy?*"

"Mm-hmm?" I say.

I'm in the shower, back from a swim at the beach with the twins. Mum's on the toilet, peeing. Mum has told me about this movie before. We actually watched it years ago. Mum doesn't remember.

Mum's in a very good mood. She had the day off work and she's been having drinks with friends. Mum is pretty chatty at this point. I got home from the beach, stepped into the shower, pulled the curtain, and seconds later Mum opened the bathroom door, hopped on the toilet, and started talking. First I heard about her friend Jamie's haircut, then about the guy who tried to chat them up. Then, it was nonstop Gwyneth. Mum's been on the toilet a while.

I guess she watched the movie again this morning, after we went to school, before she went out for drinks. Mum has the DVD on the bookshelf, wedged in with the photo albums, the twins' art projects, and all the books stacked sideways so we can fit in more books.

"I love parallel universes," sighs Mum.

That she does. And she loves love. And fate.

"If it's meant to be, it will be," she loves to say. "Everything happens for a reason." I've even seen Mum cross herself. She can't run from her faith—it follows her no matter what.

Mum and I watched the movie together when I was thirteen. She sat on one end of the couch and I lay down with my feet in Mum's lap. I listened to Gwyneth's not-so-great British accent, saw her have steamy sex with a guy ("I forgot about this part! Look away, Biz!"), and I watched her die. At least in one universe. And when Gwyneth died, Mum and I cried so hard our eyes swelled almost shut.

I cried just as hard the second time, when I skipped school a few months later and saw it again.

Dad sat on the edge of the couch, watching with me. He popped in to see the part where the Gwyneth of the other universe doesn't die, where she wakes up in hospital and tries her hand at living instead.

He said, "I took your mum to that movie. She had a cold and

said I shouldn't kiss her but of course I did, and of course I got sick too."

I squinted at Dad through puffy eyes.

"I cried so hard when Gwyneth died," said Dad. "Even though she had to. I couldn't stop myself. Your mum too. We were the only ones in that place, thank God, so we could bawl in peace. That's when I really knew," he said, doing his faraway smile.

That you loved her, Dad, right? I wanted to say. *That you'd be with her forever. That you would stay till Death wrenched you apart, right, Dad? Isn't that what you promised?*

"'I'm going to make you so happy,'" said Dad. "Best line ever said to a dead woman. Heartbreaking."

Dad sat on the edge of the coffee table, in his patterned socks and dressing gown. He said, "Shall we watch it again?"

So we did.

THE NEW GUY'S NAME IS JASPER ALESSIO. HE IS TALL AND narrow. He has a strange gait, a limp, like his right leg is too slow to keep up—a stubborn dog not done with its walk. He has longish hair like everyone else. It goes over his eyes. Jasper fiddles with it when he's thinking hard, usually in maths. He bends over the paper. He frowns over the little x's, the tiny n's. Doesn't he know they can fend for themselves? They are everywhere—the unknown owns us. But Jasper taps with his pencil. He fidgets and scribbles. In English he doesn't seem to care, but in maths, Jasper frets.

Jasper appears to not have friends. No one has claimed him yet. The group at the top won't. They are beautiful and have no physical impediments. Not even pimples. So even if Jasper is funny, even if he can play guitar *and* drums, even if he's had sex with exactly the right number of people, it's the leg.

The next group down might take him, but it all depends on Jasper's personality. Is he clever without being up himself? Is he the right kind of funny? Does he keep the teachers on their toes?

He has only a little time to prove himself. He has to make his move soon.

I don't care, except I mentioned him to The Posse and Evie made a face.

"He's kind of creepy," Evie said.

Miff nodded.

"What makes him creepy?" I said.

"He breathes really weirdly in chemistry," said Stu. "When he's measuring out the hydroxide."

I looked at Grace and she shrugged.

"And what do you think is up with his leg?" said Sal.

"Have you seen it?" Evie asked me.

"I haven't," I said. How would I have seen it? Jasper wears pants every day, even when it's boiling. He doesn't do sport; none of us do. He doesn't look like a surfer. He doesn't look like a gamer, or stoner, or drama head, or nerd, or anything really other than a boy, tall and narrow. He actually looks a bit like a smudge—like, if it wasn't for his leg you might pass right by him, like he's a part of a wall you've needed to repaint for years but can never find the time.

"Well, he seems like a bit of a dick," said Grace.

It's true. He hasn't made the best first impression. He could be a dick and only a dick. But he also seems a bit lonely.

The Posse started speculating on the cause of The Limp. As Jasper would not be getting an interview, they had to figure out his story themselves.

I find myself thinking about Jasper and not telling Grace I'm thinking about Jasper.

What does he do when he's daydreaming in English? Where

does he go? What makes him fret in maths? What happened to his leg? Was it a tractor tragedy? Was he riding a John Deere through the family farm and did he stop for a huddle of mice snuggling in the wheat stalks? Did he step out to save them, and the tractor, mind of its own, ran him down? Thirteen surgeries later, three steel pins, and five hundred staples, Jasper can finally walk again.

Or is he in fact an arsehole, and did he run over an old lady with a stolen motorbike? Jasper: buzzed on drugs, tattooed and merciless, just released from juvenile detention. Was he a second away from offending again?

I can't help but wonder.

Mum always says "Answers are your friend." Maybe all Jasper needs is a kind face. I'm sure I can put one on.

I wait for Jasper outside school on Tuesday. He is walking down the steps, tilting a little from side to side, a sailor in a storm.

I go up three steps to meet him and say, "Would you like to go for a walk?"

He stops, startled, and stares at me. "Sorry?"

I say—slowly, because maybe he's a bit thick, maybe this is why he breathes loudly in chemistry, maybe this is why he frets—"I said, would you like to go for a walk?"

"Are you taking the piss?" Jasper frowns.

"Sorry?" I lean forward.

"Are you asking me because you think I can't walk? That's a pretty shitty thing to do, if you are."

I'm so surprised, I step backwards and stumble off the step, banging my leg on a railing. My eyes flash with tears. I bend over to hold my ankle. I've probably broken it.

"That's karma, I reckon," Jasper says, and then he walks off.

o ° o ° o

Turns out, Jasper *does* ride a motorbike.

He hoons off on it, passing me on the front school steps where I'm sitting, nursing my broken bone. And anyone looking at him would have to agree, empirically, that on his bike, Jasper doesn't look at all like a smudge.

DAD SAYS, "IS IT BROKEN, BIZ?" HE'S ON THE STAIRS, JUST above the stairs. You can see an inch of air between his feet and the concrete.

I don't know, Dad.

"Have you checked? Should you walk? Should you get an ambulance? Maybe you should get an ambulance." Dad is pacing. He looks gray. Like he's been hung on a wall in direct sunlight and has been left to fade.

I don't need an ambulance, Dad.

"Just to be sure. You might make it worse. It could be splintered in there. You could get gangrene, Biz."

I turn my body towards him. He's in his pajamas. The ones he was wearing when he died.

"Dad. I'm just going to go home, okay? Mum will fix it. Relax."

He looks at me for one beat. Two. And then he blips out.

AFTER I LIMP HOME, AFTER I ICE MY ANKLE AND WATCH THE dark bruise rise, Mum comes back from work. I'm in a chair on the veranda, floating in the twilight. A cluster of mosquitoes circles my head but I've smeared myself with repellant, so the mozzies are cranky and whining. The twins are in the living room, watching TV and punching each other.

Mum plonks her keys down on the kitchen counter and sighs. I can hear her; she can't see me.

"Hi, Mum," I say.

Mum jumps. Peers out the window.

"Biz?"

"Outside."

"Why?"

"Because," I say.

Mum never goes out in the garden. She rarely goes onto the back veranda. The garden overwhelms her, she says. All the undergrowth and overgrowth and grass and dog shit.

But I like the mystery of it. Somewhere in this foresty jumble is a swing set the twins still use, running a narrow path to it through the high grass. There's also a jacaranda tree, limbs twisting—it drops flowers every season and turns the garden purple. The twins have laid out toys at the tree to lure fairies. Also here's the dog, who likes to snuffle for lizards and lilly pilly berries. Right now, Bump is dozing at my feet.

Mum creaks open the screen door. She's already poured her first wine. Another day done for Mum. She works too hard. Mum wanted to be an artist once. Now she's a dental assistant. She looks in a hundred decaying mouths a day. Her boss asks her in for extra shifts all the time because Mum always says yes.

"You okay?" she says.

"Broke my ankle," I say, gesturing to my foot.

"Really?" Mum steps out. Already she's got that note in her voice. The *I don't think so, Biz* tone. You could make a song of that sound, after all the stories I've told her.

"It's the size of a basketball," I say.

Mum stands over my foot, looks at it. "That's a nasty bruise," she says.

"See?"

"Can you move it? Can you wiggle your toes? Can you bear any weight?" She's leaning over it, touching my ankle, and already it's better, just for the touching and looking.

They say observation affects reality, that it can pin an electron into place. Until then, the electron is just a possibility, just an idea. Until it's seen, it might as well not exist.

Mum has pinned me all my life. I've tried to dodge her sometimes, but she has me. And I've had her. Two electrons eyeing each other, moving wherever the other moves.

I think Dad was harder to spot. He always went so fast, Mum said. He hardly slept. He'd be up before five, making to-do lists, drinking coffee, pulling on his sneakers, and heading out the door for his morning run.

He had so many plans. They were always traveling—job to job, town to town, house to house.

Mum would say to Dad, "Shall we stay here?"

And Dad would say, "But what about *there*?"

Dad worked as a carpenter, a gardener, a fishing boat mate, a youth worker, an office assistant, and a teacher's assistant, and Mum looked in mouths.

Were they happy?

I've asked Mum more than once.

She says, "Yes, Biz. Lots of times we really, really, really were."

Mum has me tilt my foot, up and down, all around. Turns out, it's probably not broken. I hobble inside and she straps it, her hands moving around my ankle until it's giftwrapped.

We eat flavored tofu on soggy white rice for dinner, with a few stalks of broccoli planted hopefully on the sides of the plate. The twins go and get tomato sauce from the fridge and turn their dinner into lava.

I persuaded Mum to go vegan from vegetarian a few months ago, but I don't think her heart's in it. Nothing much has changed in the nutrition department. Dinner used to be some kind of cheese with some kind of carbohydrate with some kind of vegetable. Our new meals are not so much a step up, as a step sideways.

Sometimes I think about making a better, brighter meal and surprising Mum. I think about it and I go to my room after school, open my laptop, and fall into the Internet. I look up, and three hours have passed and Mum is home, making dinner. We sit and eat: something boiled, something gray, something green.

I move the food around my plate. The twins gobble it down. They talk and talk, and Mum nods and laughs. Sometimes I wonder if she's really listening. She looks like she is, but maybe every time we're having dinner, half her mind is here and half is in Tahiti.

My mind is almost always elsewhere.

How can Jasper's parents let him ride a motorbike? Aren't they worried he'll die? Does he even have parents or is he with caregivers, having just left kid prison? Is he hungry? Is he homeless? Is he holed up in a cardboard box right now, shivering and gnawing on dumpster bones?

After dinner and washing up, I go to my room and look for Jasper online.

He barely exists. There's almost nothing to pin him down, just a shadow-self on Facebook. That's it.

I almost send him a friend request; I have my arrow pointed on the button and my finger ready to click, but wait—what are you doing, Biz? He's a dick, isn't he? And what makes you think he'll even accept? He thinks you're a bitch.

I move the arrow away. I take my hand off the keyboard.

In his profile picture, Jasper is a silhouette against some kind of sunset. His cover photo is a windmill in a field. The photo is beautiful; he could easily have stolen it from someone else (who probably stole it from someone else).

Maybe Jasper steals everything. Maybe his motorbike was pilfered from a front yard, with some biker out looking for it, furious and weeping. Maybe Jasper's bag and books and phone and clothes are all stolen. Maybe his limp is fake. Maybe Jasper is a lie.

I'M AT THE BEACH WITH A BUNCH OF HOOLIGANS. Everyone's drunk. I think I'm also drunk? I had three ciders and then something from a bottle, which burned. It was whiskey; I think it was whiskey. And then we did tequila shots out of medicine cups, which was funny.

Grace is here and Stu and Miff and Evie and Rob and Sal. We are "The Intoxicated Posse" hahaha. Other people are here too. We are all together. The youth are congregating. We are the Church of Youth. Let's pray.

The ocean looks enormous and inky. You can see the white of the waves where they break. You can see our feet where the firelight touches them. You can see our bright, happy faces.

Someone's playing guitar and everyone's singing along. Everyone's shouting all the swears in the song: *Fuck! Fuck!*

Why is shouting the word *fuck* so satisfying?

It just is.

It. Just. Is.

I've got my head in Grace's lap. Grace is kissing theguywhosentthedickpic. I can hear their tongues slapping around in each other's mouths. Grace twists to mash her face closer to his. Her knee keeps bouncing my head.

I can feel the ciders and whiskey and tequila swirling around in my stomach along with the two hash browns from McDonald's. The food and liquids aren't loving each other.

"I'm gonna throw—" I say. I get up. Grace isn't listening. Whatshisname has his hand on her boob, under her shirt.

I go to the dunes where the bushes and rabbits are. The rabbits must be covering their ears right now because we, the youth, are too loud. I bend over a bush and decorate it. I step two steps to the left and decorate another.

Lucky bushes. They will look like Christmas trees in the morning. Hash brown baubles on the branches and maybe some of Mum's dinner too, noodle tinsel—that's funny but also my head hurts. I step down the dune, away from the bushes and rabbits and back towards the fire, but the fire hurts my eyes and the singing too (why are they singing the same song over and over?) and the sight of Grace with her tongue down whatshisname's throat, and Evie, who is flopped over some guy called Tim, and Stu, who is all heart eyes at Jamal, who's in Year 12 and plays rugby and is super talented, Stu says. Everyone's all tongues-down-throats-and-drinking-and-wanting-and-singing. They're all mouths open, laughing at jokes they won't remember, and no one cares that I've gone.

I go down the beach away from the fire and the noise and them.

I stand at the edge of the water. I look out at the white of the waves and the dark of the ocean. I imagine all the sleepy fish. I imagine how warm they must be.

The water's at my ankles and it is warm; those fish aren't wrong.

Then the waves are at my knees and they're having a chat.

"Sigh," sigh the waves. "We've been waves for so long. We get so bored, rolling and rolling. What's it like to be a girl?"

"Not bad," I say, but that's not true, and I don't want to lie to the ocean. "Actually, it is bad sometimes," I confess. "Sometimes it's been very bad."

The waves nod. "We thought so. We see all sorts of things."

"I can imagine," I tell them. The waves are at my hips now; we're having a lovely time.

"We've seen sharks and drownings and shipwrecks and plastic. Ratio of sharks to drownings to shipwrecks to plastic, 5 : 2 : 1 : 1,000,000," say the waves at my waist.

I shake my head sorrowfully.

"That's so sad," I say.

"It is sad," the waves say from under my boobs. "Why don't you do something about it, Biz?"

"Me?" A wave slaps at my chest.

"Yes, you, Biz, what the fuck are you doing just scrolling the Internet when the sea is suffocating?"

Whoa. The waves are getting stroppy. The waves are at my shoulders, whapping. They're yanking at my arms, tugging at my chest and hips, grabbing my knees and ankles and feet.

"No need to be like that," I say, or try to say, but a wave shoves into my mouth and slops around trying to see why I can't be bothered to get the fuck off my chair and save the ocean.

I choke. I try to twist away but the waves have me gripped. They're whooshing into my eyes, my open mouth. My tongue tastes only salt and wet.

I wish I could save the ocean; I want to tell the waves that, but they've pulled my words away. I wish I could save the oceans and the glaciers and the rhinos and I want to save the rainforest and the Pacific islands and Dad. I want to tell the ocean how useless I've been, but the waves already know. The water sees everything.

You can wish as hard as you want for something to stay,
but it will slip right through you,
drift to the bottom of
you
as you stand, watching,
watery, logged,
bleating bloated blubbering,
doing and holding nothing.
Look at yourself, Biz.
Do you see?
pushandshoveandslap
How useless/stupid/hopeless you are?
Of course the waves should take you.
Yes.
Of course.
They should.

But now here's Jasper.

Here's Jasper, in the waves with me.

He has his arm under my chin and armpit and he's grabbing me back from the sea. He's dragging me back to shore, his face grim, and the waves are saying, "Oi! She's ours!" but Jasper isn't listening.

He pulls me onto the beach and I want to say something but I am full of water.

He leans me on my side and I'm coughing and coughing and the water is seriously pissed off because it was happy inside me.

I heave and choke and the waves are a jumble now, angry words and shouting, but as I lie on the sand, I only hear one line, over and over—the waves saying,

"Fuck you, Biz. Fuck you. Fuck you. Fuck you."

I take in a ragged breath.

Cough. Breathe. Cough. Sit up.

My hair is tangled. My shirt is ripped. I've lost a shoe.

Jasper sits back on his heels. He looks exhausted.

Where did he come from?

I suck in another breath.

"Thank you," I say.

Jasper nods.

None of this could possibly be true.

People only come out of the blue and in the nick of time to save someone's life in stories. Therefore, I am a story.

And Jasper is a story. And the blazing youth with their tongues in each other's mouths and their singing and their fire and the clump of them sauntering over and saying "What happened?" is a story.

We try to tell them.

Jasper tries to explain and I try to explain but they take us in—our wetness, my ripped shirt, my lack of shoe—and pin what happened with their eyes. And that is a story.

They think we've been groping each other. They think we went for a swim and made out and maybe had sex or tried to, and I breathed in water instead of breathing in Jasper.

They don't listen to me when I try and tell them about the waves talking.

They don't hear Jasper when he says, "I was just walking and I saw her."

They see us together in a rumple on the sand and the way we are both red and flushed. "Nice work," they say to Jasper. Me, they ogle, because they didn't know I had it in me. And yet, they did, because Evie says it's "just like" me to open my mouth and take in the sea instead of a boy.

It *is* just like me.

I look at Jasper, who is being pulled up by someone and invited to have a beer. I look at Evie, who's yanked me up too and is walking me back to the fire with her arm around my waist, talking about something something something.

I look at the waves. They're silent now.

I look at Dad, standing by the waves, a gauzy cloud against the water.

He's silent too.

Dad just saw how useless I am. Or maybe he already knew?

I HAVE NEARLY DIED A THOUSAND TIMES.

Okay. Maybe ten.

Okay. Maybe six.

There was the time I fell off the slide when I was five. From the edge of the playground, Dad saw me climb the slide to the top and stand up. Why did I stand? Maybe I was thinking of flying. Maybe I thought I was on a mountain? I don't remember.

I teetered, and Dad started to run, but no one could run that fast, not even Dad.

You could hear the crack of bone when I hit. My hand flipped all the way back and slapped my arm. Then I screamed.

Dad drove me to the hospital. He kept saying, "Fuck! Fuck! Fuck!"

I lurched sideways when the car turned corners. I threw up in my booster seat. I remember Dad saying, "Why'd you stand up, Biz?" and, me crying and saying, "I don't know! I don't know!" and Dad saying, "You could have died, Biz; if you'd landed on your head you would have *died*."

There was the time I came roaring out of Mum in a wave of goo and blood. I was so slippery the midwife could have dropped me, Dad said. It's a miracle she didn't.

There was the time before Dad died when he couldn't sit still. He kept pacing through rooms, out the back veranda, out the front drive, up and down the stairs. Mum said then he was just restless, that his legs were restless.

She said, "Go for a run, Stephen," and he said, "I can't."

I showed him how to run with Bump. The dog and I went up the long drive so fast we left Dad behind, and when we got to the road, we almost forgot to stop and a yellow car drove past us so fast it made my body shake. Bump barked and barked. When we came back to the house, Mum said Dad was so tired from watching us run, he'd gone to have a nap.

There was the time I walked into the sea and the sea almost took me, but a boy pulled me out and didn't speak to me afterwards, not once.

There was the time I was seven and saw my father in that room, in that wooden house on stilts, and I took off down the stairs, onto the back veranda and down the steep slope, tumbling almost over, almost splitting my crown like Jack or Jill.

I bolted over the creek and up the other side, scrambling to the little paddock with the brown horse and the big fig tree, and the tree's arms lifted me up and up until I was at the top and I wrapped my legs and arms around the big branch and shut my eyes until night came. Then Grandpa stood at the bottom of the tree and called my name.

I could have fallen from that tree. It was tall. I could have flown and fallen. I could have broken my neck. And the last thing I would have seen was the sky with its blinky stars. Or the broad leaves of the fig tree. Or Grandpa's wrinkly face. Or Dad, with his eyes widewidewide, so sad to see me go.

So it turns out I have almost died somewhere between six and ∞ times.

I am dead in infinite alternate universes. I am mostly and most likely dead. I am dead, now, here. All doors opening, all doors closed.

JASPER HAS FOUND A GROUP TO SIT WITH. HE SITS WITH A bunch of guys—surfers, stoners, Suryan, who sent Grace the dick pic, and Tim, who Evie likes and is the school cross-country champion. They're all quite hot but also stupid.

Jasper hasn't spoken to me since I died in the waves. Almost died. Died in an alternate universe in the waves.

He hasn't looked at me once all week, even though I've looked at him, pointedly, in class. I've also lingered when leaving English and maths but he's walked right past me like I'm not there. I've counted how many times he hasn't spoken and hasn't looked. It's going into the triple digits.

Well, fuck Hero Jasper, who can't be bothered to say hello to the girl he saved. It's not like I asked him to do it. I could have swum myself to shore. I am no damsel.

When I pass the stupid boys they look at me with new eyes—they move over my face, arms, boobs, legs, the space between my legs, the space they picture under my dress.

I tell Grace by the lockers. "They're stripping me *as I walk,*

Grace. Arseholes. They think I was doing it with Jasper in the ocean. They think I'm about to have sex with them, which is seriously the most revolting—"

"I'm sure they're not thinking that, Biz." Grace is digging through her locker, searching for something.

I raise my eyebrows. "Seriously?"

Grace's voice is muffled; she's got her head deep in the locker now. "Biz, they don't think you were having sex with Jasper in the ocean."

"How do you know?"

Grace comes out of the locker, holding up her calculator. "Ha! Found it!"

"How do you know, Grace?"

Grace won't catch my eye. She crouches over her backpack and tries to cram the calculator in.

"Grace?"

"I told Suryan and Suryan told them," she says, finally. She zips up her bag. She straightens and looks at me.

"Suryan. Penis photo guy?"

"Yeah."

"You're talking to him now? So the thing at the beach was an actual Thing?"

"Yeah," Grace says, and shrugs.

Grace heaves her pack onto her back. Our bags weigh a thousand kilos. I've got mine on and I can feel my bones bending. We both have four assignments due next week. We haven't had a break from homework in months, and I don't understand why the teachers don't talk to each other and space all this shit out, or why Grace is talking to Suryan, who sent her a photograph of his wrinkled penis. She's *talking to him* and the kiss at the beach wasn't just a kiss at the beach, and now that I think of it, she wasn't standing with Evie and the others when I was flopped on the beach, mostly dead.

We walk out of school together. It's Friday. Every Friday we go to Grace's house. We swim, study, eat.

"Grace," I say.

"Mm-hmm?" says Grace, looking around the car park.

"Is there any information you want to share with me?"

Grace smiles, and I think she's smiling at me because she has to be kidding—she must be about to tell me she's joking—but her smile is directed past me, at someone leaving the car park with his arm out the window. It's Suryan, Penis Guy. And Jasper's in the back too, looking the other way, and the boy driving pulls out onto the road with a squeal, which the teacher on car park duty doesn't like at all.

TURNS OUT GRACE AND SURYAN ARE THE REAL DEAL: boyfriend and girlfriend.

Lovers.

Turns out Grace didn't come and see me die on the beach last weekend because she was having sex with Suryan in the dunes.

"Did he use a condom?" I ask her after our swim, over Doritos and dried apricots and guacamole.

"Of course," says Grace, nibbling on a chip.

"Oh my God, Grace," I say. I shove an apricot in my mouth but it tastes wrinkly, which makes me think of penises, and I have to spit it out into the bush next to Grace's pool deck.

"Gross, Biz," says Grace. "And also, a waste of a perfectly good apricot."

I stare at her. "You seem very calm for someone who had sex in a *dune*."

"I was ready," Grace says. "I wanted to see what it was like."

"What was it like?"

"A bit pinchy. He was kind of awkward, and it was fast. Like, it was over in maybe a minute, so there's room for improvement." Grace smiles, clearly reminiscing.

"So it hurt?"

"A bit, but Biz, that's how it is the first time."

Already Grace sounds a trillion years older than me. Jesus, I must sound like a child. *Did it hurt?* Of course it hurts. You're ripping something open that will never come back together again. All the king's horses.

"And now you're going out with him," I say, my voice flat.

"Yeah, and it turns out he likes anime, Biz, and he likes the same music and he's even read *The Great Gatsby*."

"Did he like it?"

"Well—he preferred the movie."

"DiCaprio or Redford?"

"DiCaprio."

We both make a face, and then we both start laughing because, *really?*

Grace shoves at my shoulder and I shove her back and for a second we look like an old photograph of us from a month ago, when we were whole and untouchable and nothing at all had changed between us.

I study at Grace's for about an hour after our swim and then she gets a text from Penis Guy. She looks up at me, already guilty.

"Biz," she says.

But I know where she's going with this, because she's been surreptitiously texting him all afternoon and she keeps laughing at the things he's written but not saying them to me and it makes me feel like I'm floating, like I'm one of those balloons people let go, even though that balloon is going to fall in the ocean and kill a turtle.

"Yeah?" I say.

"It's Suryan. He doesn't have to work tonight."

"So?"

"He wants to see me."

"Is he taking you to a movie? To dinner? Ooh, nice," I say, sarcasm dripping because Suryan is too stupid to think of either of these things.

"He's saying we should go down to the beach again. A bunch of people are going. He says he misses me."

It's only been three hours since school finished.

"Aargh," I say.

"You can come. You're invited."

I try to arch a single eyebrow, but end up lifting both.

"Really," says Grace. "They said to come. And Jasper's going to be there," she adds, as if this changes anything.

"So much no to that request, Grace," I say, and I stand up.

Grace makes more noises to convince me to come, but I am not interested. When I go, I can tell she's already thinking about Suryan. Her goodbye sounds like someone calling from a train as it leaves.

MUM AND DAD MET WHEN SHE WAS NINETEEN AND HE WAS twenty-one and the first time they made love, she cried. From happiness, she said, but he kept apologizing. "Did I hurt you? Oh, God, did I?"

Mum had had a bit too much wine when she told me this story. I was eleven years old. I don't think she remembers telling it.

Dad loved poetry, and the Beatles, and Escher's drawings. He always wore patterned socks. He could juggle.

Dad was also a surfer. At least, he was sort of a surfer. He became a sort-of surfer when he moved from the country to the coast. He'd paddle out behind the break but then forget to catch any waves. Mum said he'd float with his feet dangling, considering the universe, the ocean rising and falling like it was breathing.

Once, a shark brushed by his left leg. Just a whale shark, just bumping, he told Mum, but he was rattled. And then after I was born, Dad said he wouldn't surf again.

Mum and Dad would walk along the beach with newborn me, near their flat in Sydney. Dad would watch the break and Mum said he looked at the sea like it was a woman he couldn't touch. She cried then and told him to go back in. But every time he went out with his board, he came back a bit more rattled—like a crack you see on a windshield, a split that starts tiny and just keeps growing.

That's what Mum said, anyway.

This was glass four, the bottle almost empty. Mum never, ever talked like this.

Mum's boyfriend had just left us three hours before—ditched Mum, the twins, who'd recently turned one, and me. I heard him tell Mum he was done being her bloody shoulder to cry on, so fuck her, fuck your kids (forgetting, I suppose, that two of them were his), and fuck *him* (meaning of course, Dad, who wasn't there to defend himself but I'm sure was listening).

The boyfriend had already packed his truck, so all he had to do was say his piece and shove out the door. It slammed behind him, which made Mum flinch and the twins start to cry.

Mum sat on the couch with the wine bottle all evening. I fed the twins, gave them a bath, and got them into bed. Then I went and sat beside her.

What else, Mum?

"Your father had a softness inside him that went gooey after you were born," she said. He looked the same, but parts of him had loosened. You can't reconstruct a man like him, she said. You can try. He did try.

"He tried and tried," Mum said. She went to pour more wine, but the bottle was empty.

Dad would get up every morning, go to work, come home, and try to keep moving through the world the same as before. But in his dreams, Mum said, he'd look at his hands and see blood. He'd be out past the break and be holding me, and think, why did he have his baby out past the break, when I was so tiny? He'd see sharks swimming, circling. They'd push at his feet. I'd howl in his arms.

In his dreams, he told Mum, he'd stand over my crib and I'd be wailing. He'd lift me, take me to the change table and undo my little clothes to change my nappy. But I would disintegrate in his hands. All he could see was water.

I'm sure Mum doesn't remember this conversation. If I asked her, she'd say, "No. I didn't say that. That can't be true."

Mum only says good things about Dad to me. I'm like the opposite of one of those worry dolls. I'm the one you tell only happy thoughts to.

That one night with the wine is the only time I remember Mum ever talking about a different Dad, one with cracks. And I was tired and I was young, so maybe it wasn't true?

Maybe I dreamed it?

It's hard to tell, because I don't have a recording. All I have is the look on her face, as she said I was the reason Dad turned sad. It printed itself onto me, in the dark as she spoke.

THREE WEEKENDS LATER, I'VE SUCCUMBED. I'M AT THE beach with most of the stupid boys and Grace and Evie and the others. We seem to have amalgamated so now we are The Posse Et Al, and I'm so drunk I can barely see.

It's the end of school holidays and we're drowning our sorrows with beer and liter bottles of vodka. I've hardly seen Grace during break because she's been having sex all over her house with Suryan while her parents are at a conference. Normally when her parents are away, I sleep over; normally Grace and I stay up all night watching bad '80s rom-coms. Normally, normally, normally.

The boys are squidges, making sounds like farting bears and wrestling in the sand. They offer me something else to drink and another. I drink everything I'm given. I'm impervious to harm—alcohol poisoning, drownings, grief. Nothing can take me down.

"Maybe it's time to go home, Biz," says a shape that is probably Grace, but I'm not going to listen to her. I'm laughing too loudly. I can hear my voice kicking the rabbits out of their homes. The stars are turning their faces away. The waves are disgusted. I'm loud and my laugh is loud and my laugh is ugly and I'm ugly. A bit of sex will sort me out. I'll be just like Grace, who's done it, and Evie, who'd love to do it, and Miff too and all the women in love who do it and the women not in love who do it.

I'll be a woman: split inside but so whole.

I whisper in the ear of one of the stupid boys. "Let's have sex," I say.

He looks at me and grins.

"*Okay!*" He slaps his knees.

"Yeah. Let's get this shit done," I say. Do I say that out loud or do I just think it?

The boy nods and pulls me up. We don't look at anyone. We just go. We stumble up to the dunes and lie down and scrabble around for a while.

And then suddenly I'm not sure because I look closer and I see it's Tim—cross-country Tim—and wait, isn't he the one Evie likes? And suddenly everything feels so messy and maybe painful too, although we haven't done it yet, and I say, "I'm not sure."

And Tim says, "Ah, come on,"

and I say, "I don't know. Um. No."

And he says, "Come on, Biz,"

and he's yanking my underpants down and his hand goes between my legs

and I think, *No,*

and the feel of his hand and the sand on my bum is cold, cold, cold and I say, "No!"

I push him away and he flops over like a toy off a bed, which would be funny,

except it's not.

And then I sit up and puke all over him, which is actually hilarious and not at all hilarious, and I can't stop laughing and crying because of the look on his face, and I pull up my undies, stand and push down my skirt and run away from the beach, to the bike path and along the sunless streets. And I know Tim's back on the beach, sitting by the stupid fire, telling a stupid story about stupid Biz and how I handed him my virginity on the dunes before I threw up everywhere like a dickhead and went home.

I know this, because the stars are telling each other in shocked, hushed voices.

Did you hear?

I did!

Gosh!

Can you believe?!

God. They're so disappointed.

The night is close and thick. Dad's running alongside me, but he isn't talking. He's in his running shoes and dark blue shorts. He is moving beside me. He stares ahead like I'm not even there.

And it's so clear how far I have fallen. How far I am from where the stars are.

IT IS SIX A.M. MONDAY. FIRST DAY BACK AT SCHOOL AFTER the break.

I count to one thousand eight hundred and ninety-three and then I go back to sleep.

I wake up. It's seven a.m.

The wind whirls and clatters. The sun arcs over the sky. The dog woofs outside. Somewhere in the house, a toilet flushes.

I lie in bed and don't get up.

Billie and Dart run up and down the hall. They are arguing over a dinosaur, a card game, a lost shoe. The sun tries to fight its way into the room.

I smell coffee. Toast.

Any minute, Mum's going to come and check on me. When she does, I will flatten my body so she can't see me. She'll think I've gone out. Perhaps to jog or buy bread or donate my clothes to charity.

I am going to lie here for the entire day. I will sleep and get up only to pee and then crawl back inside my cave. I will slow down my breathing until it is barely perceptible. I will spend autumn and winter here and come out with the spring flowers.

If I come out.

It is ten to eight.

Dart and Mum come into my room and look at me. My mother frowns.

"What's up, Biz?" Mum says.

"Yeah. What's up?" says Dart.

"I'm sick," I say to them.

"What kind of sick?" says Mum.

"Yeah, what kind of sick?" parrots Dart.

The kind where everyone thinks you had sex with hot, stupid Tim on Saturday night and your best friend hasn't texted and neither has anyone else and Jasper hasn't spoken to you since you died in the waves four weeks ago and the earth is being poisoned and will one day be swallowed by the sun.

"Cramps," I say. "Like knives, Mum. Feel like I'm going to throw up."

Dart looks confused. Mum looks sympathetic. Woman to woman. She knows how terrible blood can be.

"Maybe you have too much poo," says Dart. "I get cramps sometimes when I need to poo."

I look at Dart. "Yeah. Maybe, Dart. There is a whole lot of shit inside me."

"Biz!" says Mum.

Dart sort of laughs. Have I ever sworn in front of him before?

He leans over the bed and pushes his face close.

"I love you, Biz," he says, his breath warm in my ear. "Get better soon."

Billie yells from somewhere. Dart kisses me, then rushes out. Mum touches my hair. "Want a hot water bottle?"

"No. I'm good."

"Panadol?"

"Just took some."

"Okay then."

Then I am alone except for Mum's deodorant smell floating in the air, and the imprint of Dart's wet kiss on my cheek.

The twins slam out the front door for school. Mum backs the car down the drive. And the day turns into a syrup of Netflix movies and checking my phone and nothing and silence and birds looking in at me with their sideways eyes.

Dad doesn't visit. He doesn't sit by the bed or the window. There are no stories for me.

The next day I tell Mum I am still sick.

Mum frowns.

A sloppy kiss from Dart. A quick hug from Billie.

Silence in the house.

Nothing from Grace. Nothing from The Posse.

I check our group chat. No mention of me. It's like I've become a particle.

Why the fuck aren't they writing to me?

And the whole day slides away—from light to dusk, to dark.

The next day, Mum opens the curtains. She says, "I'm worried about you, Biz. Shall we go to the doctor?"

I make a face. "No."

When she leaves, I shut the curtains.

o ° o ° o

Next day, Mum opens the curtains. She says, "Please leave these open for the day, okay? Biz? And if you're not better by tomorrow, we are going to the doctor."

Fine. "Okay."

The day passes.

The trees outside look in.

It's cold today. The trees look chilled. The trunks are shivering. The leaves are curling inwards. Birds cuddle on the branches and clouds clank against each other muttering, "Blimey, it's bloody freezing! Isn't it freezing? Too right."

I watch the clouds parade in bunches. They gather, building into and onto one another until they fill the sky. The trees flick back and forth. The air roars. Lightning spears, in long, electric flashes. And down comes the rain.

It beats on the house.

The thunder splits everything open. Splits me.

The thunder looks inside and sees: how I lay down in the sand, how I opened my legs to the boy, how I threw up on the boy, how I ran home, how no one is saying a word to me, how I am invisible.

The thunder laughs and laughs. "Hahahahahahaha!" it says.

Fuck you, thunder.

In the beat between booms, I hear something crashing outside, and three shrill barks.

God. The dog.

He must be terrified.

I push off the blanket, get up, and go onto the back veranda. The storm is a whole-body howl out here. Bump is panicking; he's trying to push his way out the side gate, hurling himself hopelessly against the wood.

"Here," I call. "Here, boy!"

He bolts to me, his body twisting sideways with relief. I crouch and he presses himself against me, his tail whapping.

I bring him inside. He's soaking wet. I find a towel to dry him. I rub his fur. I speak to him, "It's okay, boy, it's okay, it's okay."

I croon over the slam of rain and over the thunder and through the split of the sky. I rub and rub, Bump trembling and whining. He licks my hand over and over again.

The next morning, I get out of bed. I go to the kitchen for breakfast.

Billie and Dart look up from their cereal and grin.

"She's better!" Dart says.

"Yay!" Billie says.

My mother claps.

Everyone is so happy. A marching band comes in and marches through the living room. A cheer squad cheers. All the fireworks explode at once.

I have a shower after breakfast. I think I have bed sores. I try to see my bum in the mirror but then I don't want to look at myself. What did Tim see, what did his hands feel? I wrap myself back up in the towel.

I put on my uniform. I go to the kitchen to hug Mum goodbye.

"So you're okay?" she says.

"Of course!" I say. Too brightly.

Mum measures me with a look, tries to see in. "You sure?"

"All is well, Mum," I say.

Is it? Is all well, Biz?

I kiss Mum and off to school I go.

And it's another normal day.

See?

Look at me walking down the road.

Sun is shining. It's warm again today. That's how weather works; it changes in an instant, nothing to be alarmed about. Life is absolutely normal. Here I am, just a girl on her way to school with assignments overdue and nothing to show on her phone—no texts, no chats, no messages.

I walk down the road, under the trees.

I cross the freeway.

I cross the train tracks—*thewomanfrozeandturnedbutitwastoolate*.

I walk down the bike path, along the school fence. I go in through the gate. Everyone's a shape with eyes, watching me. The bell's about to ring.

I walk out the side gate and down the bike path to the beach. I sit on the top of the dunes. I tuck my feet under my knees. I huddle into my jacket.

The waves roll in, out. They say nothing.

I sit at the edge of the sea and cry.

DAD SITS BESIDE ME ON THE DUNES. HE LOOKS AT THE water, glances over at me, then down at his feet. He doesn't speak for a minute.

"Remember how you hated the sand, Biz?" he says, finally.

I sniff, wiping my nose.

"We took you to the beach one time, when you were maybe a year old, just starting to walk. And you suddenly decided you didn't like the sand on your toes. You kept lifting your feet up every time I put you down."

I turn and stare at him.

Dad's wearing a pair of board shorts and a Rage Against the Machine T-shirt. I've seen the shirt and shorts before—Mum keeps them in a drawer along with a bunch of Dad's other clothes. She asked me once if I wanted to wear any and I said no. She kept them, all the same. She says maybe Dart or Billie will want them someday, so she doesn't throw anything out.

I found Mum smelling a blue button-down once, when I was almost nine, just before Mum's boyfriend came into the picture. Mum told me she was checking whether it needed to be washed. She said it was hay fever that was making her eyes go wet. But I knew it wasn't true, because Mum's a terrible liar.

Two weeks later, Mum went out on a date—her first since Dad died. I was left with some neighbor called Doreen who smelled of hair spray and bacon. Doreen wanted me to sit on her lap when we watched TV.

"I am nearly nine," I told her politely. "I don't sit on laps."

"Oh, gosh," said Doreen, "aren't you quite the grown-up!"

We watched TV until Doreen fell asleep on the couch. I kept watching Doreen's murder show until I heard the car drive in. Then I scooted to my room. After Doreen left and Mum went to her room, humming, I hopped out of bed to see her.

"Did he kiss you, Mum?" I said, standing at the door.

"Oh!" said Mum, turning. "What are you doing up?" She was unzipping her yellow dress, a new one.

"Did he?"

"That's none of your business!"

"Yeah, it is," I said.

Mum's zip was stuck. She flailed a bit, then dropped her arms to her sides. "Can you help me?"

I stood on the bed and Mum backed up. I unzipped Mum's dress. It flopped to the ground like an empty banana.

"Thanks, sweetie." Mum pulled on her nightie. She looked like Mum again, thank God.

"So?" I asked.

"What?" Mum went to the bathroom to brush her teeth. I followed her.

"Did he kiss you?" I said.

Mum waved her toothbrush vaguely in the air. "Maybe," she said, and smiled.

"Was it gross?"

"No." She looked at me through the mirror. "It was strange. And nice. And strange. It was my first kiss in a long time."

In other words, it was Mum's first kiss since the last kiss she had with Dad.

I wanted to crawl inside her body and feel what she was feeling. "Do you love him?" I asked, and Mum burst out laughing.

"What do you think, Biz?" she said. She looked at me, toothbrush close to her mouth, eyes on mine.

"No," I said.

"Exactly," she said, and began to brush.

But three months later the man she didn't love moved in with us, and four months after that, she was pregnant with the twins.

Now Dad's here on the beach staring out over the water. And like so many times before, I want to ask him questions. Like, did he see the kiss that first night, between Mum and the boyfriend? Did he see the second kiss? The third?

Dad showed up for the first time on Mum's sixth date, just after Mum said, "I'm starting to really like Brian, Biz."

Maybe Dad had been watching us. Maybe he'd been floating close by in some unfixed form, watching Mum get all smiley when the boyfriend rang, when the boyfriend asked her out, when the boyfriend kissed her. Maybe it broke his heart so much Dad popped back into being. Maybe he stepped into his old clothes and came to find me—Biz, who would never love anyone as much as I loved him.

"Dad?" I say.

I want to know: How did he feel, watching Mum fall in love? Did he die—again, even more—inside?

"I remember you cried when the sand touched you," says Dad, staring hard over the water. "You said, 'Off! Off!' and we had to lay down a towel just to get you to sit."

"Dad?" I want to ask him a thousand questions. I want to tell him about The Posse not talking to me. I want to ask him how heartbreak feels. I want to know what it's like to watch and not be seen, because I think I already know, but is it different for him?

Dad says, "I remember your mum saying, 'She'll like the sand, give her time.' And guess what? She was right." He tries to smile.

"Dad?"

"You ended up loving the beach, Biz. I remember the first time you ran on the sand. It was like you'd never been happier in your whole life, like the past had never existed, like you'd never been afraid. Have you seen that photo?" asks Dad. He wobble-smiles again and reaches out a hand.

I reach out mine.

"Yeah, Dad, I've seen it, but—"

And poof! He's gone.

I GET A TEXT FROM GRACE AT LUNCHTIME. I'M STILL IN THE dunes.

I've peed behind a bush. I've eaten my sandwich. I can't bring myself to go anywhere—school or home or on a plane to Istanbul—wherever, whatever, I can't move.

The sun squints at me from behind a cloud. A family of rabbits have inched out from their hidey-hole, noses trembling, and had a meeting, nose to feathery nose. They've agreed I can stay, seeing as I haven't moved except for peeing and eating and sniffing and wiping my eyes.

I am Elizabeth Martin Grey: invisible girl, zero threat.

The sun's overhead, a blur behind the clouds. The clouds are hovering and lurching when my phone goes *PING!* for the first time in days.

It's Grace.

Biz! Where the fuck are you?

Huh. An interesting opener.

I don't know what to say. So I don't say anything, just stare at the text, and this is when I realize I might actually be invisible; maybe I am a ghost and I can't text back because I don't have fingers or a mind that functions and even though I can physically see myself maybe I'm 100 percent a lie.

My phone goes *PING!* again.

They've said to freeze you out. But fuck it, Biz. I don't want to.

I hold the phone up to my eyes because this makes no sense. The phone jiggles and I can see my fingers actually trembling like in those books where it says "Her hands shook," just as the heroine is about to be shot or see her true love ride off into the sunset with someone else.

My hands have gone fuzzy. I look at them from very, very far away.

I poke at the silly box with my silly fingers and words come out:

Who? What? Freeze? What?

PING!

GRACE: Suryan. Tim. Evie.

BIZ: Evie?

GRACE: Says you're a slut.

BIZ: But I didn't have sex with him.

GRACE: Tim said you did. And he said you went crazy afterwards and told him you'd tell everyone you didn't say yes. He says you're a mental case. So Evie said we should freeze you out. Until you tell the truth and apologize.

BIZ: But I haven't told anyone anything!

GRACE: Suryan said we can't text you. Everyone's gone mad. I held on as long as I could but then I thought, What the fuck? I'm no gladiator. I'm your fucking best friend.

Bile rises in my stomach and grinds up my throat. I've

heard about this kind of thing happening—I've seen it from a distance, girls turning their backs on girls, laughing as the girl walks away, guys spreading shit, girls spreading shit, everyone copy-pasting, everyone baa-baa-baa-ing—but I've floated outside it. And I've been held in a Posse bubble and a Grace bubble so long I didn't know this could happen to me.

I stare at the phone.

PING!

GRACE: I'm so sorry, Biz.

. . .

. . .

PING!

GRACE: Where are you?

. . .

GRACE: Biz. Come on. Where are you?

. . .

BIZ: Beach.

GRACE: Our spot?

BIZ: Yeah.

GRACE: I'll be there in ten minutes.

. . .

GRACE: I love you.

. . .

GRACE: I'm really sorry.

. . .

GRACE: Fuck everyone. We'll burn the place down.

In ten minutes the cavalry will come. Grace, who's going to be prime minister one day; Grace, who feels so lonely some nights she asks me to talk to her on the phone till she goes to sleep. Grace, who never bends, never lets you down. Grace, who hasn't texted or spoken to me for six days because her boyfriend told her not to.

I stand up. My knees crack. The rabbits scatter. I pick up my bag and go home.

IN THE STORIES, THE BEST FRIEND CHOOSES THE BOY AND doesn't look back. In the stories, the best friend is disloyal and untrustworthy. In the stories, the best friend doesn't come over and bash on the door and scream your name when you bail on her and don't meet her at the beach.

Grace is a storm at the door. Grace is shouting so loudly I'm sure the police will be called. Grace won't leave until I send her away.

I open the door. I find Grace standing there in her uniform, raising a single, furious eyebrow.

"Sorry," I say.

"Uh-huh," she says, and shoulders past me.

"It's just—"

"You didn't want to see your best friend." She stands, arms crossed in my hallway, filling it.

"*Best* is a tenuous term at this time, Grace."

"But I texted you!"

"Six days late."

"Hmmm." Grace peers at a nail. Nibbles it.

"Because dick boy said so."

"True," says Grace.

"What kind of an arsehole—"

"Yeah. Yeah, yeah, yeah," says Grace. She moves forward and wraps her arms around me. "Okay. I messed up, Biz."

"Yep," I say, and my voice feels like glass in my throat.

Grace leans into me and I can feel her boobs on me, her arms tight around me, her breath on my neck, her heart radiating its beat to me. She starts to rock, so we lean back and forth, like two statues, wobbling on our tiny pedestals.

"Okay. I promise. Enough fuckery from me," Grace says, finally. She leans back, gathers me up with her dark eyes, and kisses me on the cheek. "It won't happen again."

"Good," I say, and I wipe away whatever is in my eye.

"I think we need some fortification," Grace says.

She goes into the kitchen. I follow.

She opens the fridge and starts rummaging. She shakes her head.

"Abysmal," she says, holding up a flaccid carrot.

Then I hear the clink of glass and she's pulled two beers out of the fridge.

"Time to make a plan," she says. "World domination in three-two-one."

I smile for the first time in approximately six days, or a month, or ever. Something inside me shifts, opens. It makes way for the possibility of something good.

IF ONLY IT WERE THAT EASY.

Turns out rejecting a friend group is a bit like detonating a school-sized bomb.

Grace and I tell The Posse we are leaving and Evie's eyes turn to slits. "You aren't *leaving*," she hisses. "You are actually not welcome here."

No one else says anything. Stu focuses on his sandwich. Rob coughs. Miff looks at me, then at Grace, then sideways at the air beside us. Sal sits with her lips pinched.

Evie crosses her arms, lifts her eyebrows, and that's that. Our joyous, inclusive, delightful Collective has made its decree: We can't quit. We're *fired*.

How is it possible that Tim's lie has smeared itself over them so easily? When I've sat with them for years and not made a touch of trouble? When I've been a good lump on a seat and nodded and smiled and drunk and sung and linked arms and swapped notes and agreed with everything I needed to agree to?

Turns out it takes almost nothing at all. Just me + Tim + a dune + his hand in the wrong underpants + a lie + Grace siding with me + our clear lack of remorse. You'd think it would take something bigger, but I guess this is how it works? Things change in an instant—one minute a mountain, solid and immoveable. The next, the land drops out. Trees collapse and tumble. The landscape slides into a mess of scars.

The lie oozes around the school, all the way from the Year 9s to the Year 12s. The younger years are oblivious, which provides exactly no comfort.

I *am* a slut. Everyone agrees. Their eyes slide off me when they see me.

(Except for Jasper, who never looked at me anyway and doesn't seem to be anywhere at school.)

I *am* mental. Everyone has always suspected. *Have you heard about her dad?*

No!

Well, Evie says. . .

I *am* a bitch. Everyone has heard what I did to Tim, who's, like, gorgeous and can surf.

(Where is Jasper? I don't know, because literally no one but Grace is talking to me. Has Jasper left school? Did he hear what I did and he thought, *I'm not going to school with a slutbitchho like her?* Most likely.)

I deserve everything I'm getting. Everyone is 100 percent sure. It is a single, inalienable truth.

And Grace—beautiful, smart, funny Grace? What did she do?

Did you hear what she did?

With Suryan?

Yeah!

And he says—

Grace too. Grace deserves it.

Grace Yu–Harrison and Elizabeth Grey, those two slut bitch fuckinhoes.

WE SIT ON GRACE'S COUCH. IT'S FRIDAY EVENING. WE HAVE a pile of food, and Grace is crying over it.

"Everything is so stupid," she says, chugging a Red Bull liberally laced with her mother's vodka. What number is that, her fourth?

"I'm a slut because I had sex with Suryan but *he's* not? And you, Biz, you're a slut for having sex with Tim even though you never did and he's a hero for having sex with you and saying you said you'd say you never said yes?" She shakes her head. "What the living fuck? Where's the logic?"

Grace drinks and eats and weeps and rages.

Poor Grace.

Suryan has dumped her, by text. Everyone has dumped us. We are now not just Ex-Posse, but Ex-Every-Group-That-Exists-in-Every-Corner-of-the-School.

Grace has never been a social outcast before. She's really too beautiful for this kind of shit.

Dad says he doesn't know how to help.

He sits on the edge of Grace's couch and watches Grace weep. Her hair flops over her eyes, and I'm sure Dad wants to smooth it back, just like I want to, but we can't—Dad because he's dead, and me because Grace isn't up for anyone touching her. She's too angry.

Dad's wearing a suit today. It's dark blue. He's wearing his patterned socks, gray and blue diamonds. He's wobbling in the air, like he's being steamed.

"I wish I knew what to do," he says, wringing his hands, helpless.

I nod. He looks so sad, like he's walking into Grace's water and dissolving.

"The suffering of a child," he says, and tapers off. "You want to keep them safe—" he says. He shakes his head. "Those arse-holes. I'd bash their heads in if I could."

"Violence isn't the answer," I say, and Grace's head whips up.

"Sorry?"

Dad blips out.

"Just saying, uh," I start.

"But violence is the answer, Biz," Grace says. Her eyes gleam. "That's exactly what it is." She swigs down the last of her drink. "Time to fuck up some shit."

GRACE IS ON A BENDER. GRACE IS ON FIRE.

Which looks like this:

I try to talk her out of it—I grab the car keys from her hand—
I pull at her clothes, but she's out of the house and running
and I'm running after her—it's crunchy with cold and thick
with dark, but we can see over the roots of the trees and the
lumps in the driveways because we know these streets—these
are our streets—and Grace runs so fast—she has won prizes
for her running—has her mother ever come to the awards?—I
don't think so and even though I've got giraffe legs I'm not
much use, because I'm not a runner and Grace could be in the
Olympics—and she's at Suryan's house before I realize where
we are, because how would I know what his house looks like,
except Grace is shouting his name and she's throwing a huge
rock through his front window—whoa, Grace, Jesus, where'd
you get that?—and she's shouting, "Arsehole stupid shithead
motherfucker!"—and Suryan's parents are at the door, clutch-
ing each other and Grace is wild, wild, wild—and I'm pulling

her away into the slurping dark—we're ghosts going back into the shell—we're leaving—"We're leaving, Grace, come on, shit, shit, shit," I say—and I'm running with her back down the street as she totters and bumps into me, snot dribbling as she cries—and we're almost home, we've almost made it to her house and our books and our boring, good-girl lives when the police pull up beside us, and their lights go around and

around and

around.

THE YOUTH LIAISON OFFICER WEARS A NAVY-BLUE UNIFORM, a yellow badge, and a red, tired face.

Her pinched ponytail hair is bottle orange. You can see the brown roots. She is older than Mum. She is short.

We sit at a gray table, on gray chairs, in a gray-walled room.

When the Youth Liaison Officer sits down opposite us, the buttons strain on her uniform.

She says, "You girls know what you did wrong, I'm guessing?"

I don't know what to say. *Yes? No? Everything? Nothing?*

The officer doesn't seem to need an answer. She flaps open a notepad.

"Okay. Here's how this is going to go," she says, huffing her breath. Her cheeks go out like a squirrel's. Is she tired? It's almost midnight. Does the officer have kids? Is she glad we aren't her kids? Is she there thinking, *Jesus, if little Mike did this, he'd be in deep shit?*

Most likely.

She squints at her notebook. "Sounds like you got drunk and broke some poor bugger's window? Is that right?"

She peers at us. We don't nod or move or speak. Should we nod? Should we speak? The officer sighs.

"You're going to tell me what you did," she says. "You're going to tell me, 'Officer, this is exactly what we did and we are very sorry.' Then I'm going to give you a caution. It will sit on your record until you're eighteen, so you'd better not stuff up again. And then you're going to go home and stop being dickheads."

Grace and I look at each other.

Grace leans forward. She's been crying for so long her eyes look like two marshmallows.

"Biz didn't do anything," she says.

"Sorry?" says the officer. "Who's Biz?"

I raise my hand.

The officer looks at her notes and reads out slowly. "Elizabeth Martin Grey." She looks up at me. "And this translates to Biz?"

"You can call me Elizabeth," I say.

The officer raises her eyebrows. "Ah, a smartarse, hey?"

"No," I say, "just—"

"Listen, kiddo. You and this one"—she thumbs over at Grace—"were both in front of that house, maliciously destroying a living room window. In someone else's *home*. There were three witnesses. You could have killed someone. And you're bloody lucky you're getting off with just a caution."

Grace palms her hands on the table, leans forward again. "No. *I'm* the one who got drunk. I'm the one who ran to that fuckwit's house. I'm the one who broke the window. Biz did nothing wrong."

Seriously, Grace? Still on fire. What the hell?

I start to speak, but the officer is shutting her notebook. She's standing up.

"Looks like you pretty things need some time to cool off. How about I show you to your accommodation?"

Shit.

Grace's face sets and I feel my insides go liquid.

We meekly stand and follow the officer down the hall. We go past the empty-eyed windows of all the other interrogation rooms. We pass a row of benches. A man lies asleep on one, his mouth open in a snore. He smells like urine. We turn right, we turn left, left again, and she opens a door.

It's just like a movie and way, way worse than a movie.

Inside: two bare beds. No window. A toilet.

It smells of bleach and loneliness and old vomit.

Ohmygod.

THE BEDS FEEL MADE OF CONCRETE.

The walls have deep scratches on them.

The police have taken our phones. So all we have is the room and each other.

Grace can't stop crying.

"I'm so sorry, Biz."

"Yeah," I say. "You said that already."

Grace wails. "It's all gone to shit. Everything! What's Mum going to say? That fucking Suryan. That bitch Evie. What about uni?"

"You only broke a window, Grace."

That's all she did. Right? And somehow I did too.

"But someone could have *died*," she says. A sob heaves itself out of her and flaps on the floor. Which is when it hits me.

Someone could have died.

We could have killed someone. Grace with her rock and me with not stopping her.

Who might have died? A two-day-old baby lying on the other side of the window?

A cat on a couch? A grandmother, knitting?

Or Suryan. Or his brothers. Or his mum and dad.

I stare down at my hands. I can see blood pooling on the palms. I see blood on the caved-in heads of Suryan/the two-day-old baby/the grandmother/the children/the parents/the people. Their eyes are open, wide wide wide wide wide.

When the officer comes to get us, I can't breathe. I walk, not breathing, as she brings us back to the interrogation room. Mum's there, and Grace's mum and stepdad too.

When the officer looks at me and asks, "Did you do the thing?" I nod.

I say, "Yes, I did. I did that exact thing," even though Grace is interrupting and saying, "But she didn't! Biz didn't do anything!"

I shush her away.

I say, "I did it. I did the thing."

I sign the papers. I agree to the terms and conditions. I tick the box that says: Biz is terrible. She has blood on her hands. All the heads are caved.

Grace looks at me. She stares into my body, sees all the holes. She shakes her head slowly. She signs the paper. She doesn't look at me again.

All her fire is out.

DAD SITS ON THE EDGE OF MY BED.

What were you thinking, Biz?

Mum paces back and forth. She's been raging for about an hour. I don't even know what she's saying; it's a swirl of fury and fear.

I look at Dad. He's in his blue suit but it's rumpled and filthy. It looks like he's been crawling through vines, like he's been pulling himself out of a hole.

Mum says, "Did you hear me, Biz? You're in so much shit, do you understand?"

I do understand. I *am* in such shit. I've been in shit for longer than I can explain.

It started when I was small. I want to stand up and say, "When I launched myself out of your vagina, Mum, when I ripped you, and Dad fainted, that's when it began."

I know Dad would agree.

Dad doesn't speak. He doesn't look at me. He sits on the edge of my bed. Sadness oozes out of his eyes. He's almost completely see-through.

o ° o ° o

Grace and I have been released to our parents, and two days later, in an impressive turn of events, we are also suspended from school—for two whole weeks, pending further inquiry. The principal is appalled. *Such a shock,* he says in his email to Mum. *So promising, so disappointing.*

Grace's mum is apoplectic.

When she came to pick up Grace from the police station, she looked like she'd been sucking on an exhaust pipe, her lips pinched, her face ash. Grace's stepdad just stood at the door of the interrogation room, jiggling his keys. The whole station rattled with his rattle.

Grace's mum had already heard from Suryan's parents. She'd heard everything Grace had done before she heard a word from Grace.

"But, Mum!" Grace tried to explain.

"Don't even start with me, Grace," said her mum. So Grace didn't even start.

Three days after the Incident, Grace is withdrawn from school. Five days after the Incident, Grace is sent to Wagga Wagga, four whole hours and a world away, to live with her father.

I'm not allowed to see her. Mum gets a single message from Grace's mum to let me know Grace is leaving. I am not permitted to text Grace, or email, or call.

Grace doesn't text me.

Grace doesn't email.

Grace doesn't call.

Grace doesn't say goodbye.

I am sent away to exactly nowhere. I get to continue my life at home, in my house, with my brother and sister and mother and dog and dead dad.

Mum says I could have gone to jail. Which makes sense, because I nearly killed someone. Which is exactly the same as: I killed someone.

I didn't throw the rock, but I let Grace throw it.

I didn't drink four Red Bulls with vodka, but I watched Grace drink them.

I didn't sleep with Tim, but told Tim I would sleep with Tim.

I didn't walk into the ocean with Jasper, but I walked into the ocean and Jasper followed me. He could have gone under; he could have been slapped and dragged and choked and drowned.

I didn't ask to be friends with Evie, but I was friends with Evie, even though I was never friends with Evie. I never said, "No, Evie. I can see directly into the molecular arrangement of you. It tells me you are a future bitch, so I won't be your friend."

I didn't ask for Dad to die, but I am why he was sad.

I didn't ask to see him in that room *eyeswidewidewide*.

I didn't ask to be born.

But here I am.

Good riddance, slut, say the text messages.

Such a fuckup, says the group chat.

And then I'm blocked.

It's so easy, isn't it? For everything to change.

On/off. Love/hate. Alive/dead.

What did I do? What didn't I do?

I didn't speak the way I was supposed to, walk the way I was supposed to—bright and smiley into a future where I was more agreeable, smaller, blinder, legs wide open, letting everything that wanted to, come in.

And the thoughts come sauntering, like they've been waiting in the wings all this time.

You know, Biz, you could just leave.

All you have to do is stop.

All you have to do is swallow.

Or cut.

Or step.

Come on, Biz. No one will miss you if you go.

One moment, a mountain. The next, the land slipping out. A mess of falling trees and scars.

DAYS CRAWL BY.

Work comes from the teachers. I'm supposed to be studying. Squeaky assignments scurry themselves into piles.

But I can't get out of bed.

I scroll the Internet endlessly—round and round—until Mum takes my phone away.

Mum says, "Get up, Biz," but her voice sounds like scratches and I can't move. Someone has taken my legs away.

I don't hear from Grace and I don't hear from Grace. I send her messages I'm not supposed to send. I don't hear from Grace.

The twins come in. I stare at them. I'm a ghost; they're ghosts. They kiss me with their paper lips. Billie leaves me a homemade card, a red heart looped around my name and hers, and the words:

"Get bettar Soon BIZ I luv U"

○ ° ○ ° ○

The sky grinds overhead. I can hear the clouds clacking. I can hear the movement of the secret stars, the ones you never see because it's day.

I wait in bed. For time to pass. For life to stop being bad/ worse/worst. For the thoughts to stop sauntering in.

It's not hard to go.

You don't have to stay, Biz.

Come on, Biz.

Just leave.

Dad floats on the edge of my bed. He's a blur.

And it's like I'm seeing him through a window and the rain outside is falling so hard everything is indistinct, unreal.

He's squidgy and vague. His face is like a door, closing. I hold my hand out to him, but just as I'm about to touch . . . he fades out. Leaving only the idea of him. The idea of his eyes, staring, before they vanish.

I don't see him again for a very long time.

II

GRIEF FEELS LIKE THIS:
    an okay day and a good day and an okay day
    then a *bad*.
    Bad that follows and empties you.
    Bad like a sinkhole.

It feels like
    an unrelenting urge to lay your head down on the table,
    wherever you are, whomever you are with.

It feels like
    a night of vivid dreams, and when you wake,
    all day you hold one dream close
    because in it
    everything was back to how it once was.

o ° o ° o

It feels like

you've fallen overboard.

You are swimming to get back, but the boat moves steadily away. You can see the lights; you can hear the laughter and the music on the decks.

You try to follow. The boat moves away.

It feels like

missing.

You miss her. You miss him. You miss belonging.

You miss the bench by the fence. You miss the walk from the lockers. You miss the talks by the pool, in the hammock, at night, on the phone, the screen winking blue light. You miss the stories on the bed, by the window, beside the desk, on the dunes. You miss his voice. You miss her smile. You miss and miss and miss and miss and miss.

And all you want to do is walk into a forest and cover your-self with leaves.

I HAVE NOT BEEN TO SCHOOL IN A WHILE.

To sum up: I dropped out.

Due to illness. A chronic, debilitating inability to get out of bed.

I have been in bed so long, barnacles have had to be scraped off my bottom. I gathered moss in my belly button. I grew mushrooms on my tits.

Mum told me I shouldn't say "tits" in front of the twins, but it seems I was incapable.

Mum sent the twins away for a while to her sister's house. My aunt Helen lives on the Gold Coast right by the beach, in one of those units with a view. She fed the twins dough-nuts for breakfast. And bacon and egg rolls. Which the twins loved.

On the third week of not going to school—after my suspension was over and I was clear to return and be a good girl again, but did not return—the doctor came for a visit. I lay under my pile of blankets. He asked me questions; I blinked answers with my eyes. He took my temperature and looked into my throat. He checked my wiring and my oil and the air in my tires and my water levels. He listened to my history and frowned.

He said, "She needs medication." He ripped off a piece of paper with words on it. I squinted at the prescription. He'd written medical words and a signature that looked like it had gone through a mulcher. But all I saw was: *Elizabeth Martin Grey is a fuckup and should probably not exist.*

The doctor said I also needed to see a psychiatrist and a psychologist. Another piece of paper and another. *Rip. RIP.*

Mum's eyes went watery. She nodded. After the doctor left, I heard her making hushed appointments in the next room.

That night, she cried. I could hear her, even though she was trying to be quiet. I heard weeping over the scritching of the possums and the tapping of the frogs and the trees easing their roots out of the earth.

I saw a psychiatrist who put me on half a pill and asked me the next week, *So, how are you going? Feeling better? Sadder? Stranger? Any headaches? Itchy?*

I was no better, sadder, stranger. No headachier, no itchier. Same same same same same same same.

But a bit sleepier.

Definitely more sleepy.

After two weeks, he put me on a full pill, and sent me off.

I have rich dreams; I see the edges of them when I wake up.

I'm running. The jungle is filled with flowers. I'm riding a bus and everyone is wearing yellow. I'm in a gallery—the colors creep out of the paintings. I don't know where I'm going. I'm lost. I'm asking for help. I'm drowning.

I have been sent to a clinical psychologist and she has asked me other questions. Not: *Are you itchy or are you sleepy or are you getting fat or sad or thirsty.*

More like: *Elizabeth, how are you feeling?*

Where do I start? Because it's the wrong question, I think.

I don't feel. There is no feeling here.

Ratio of questions my psychologist has asked me to the ones she has not—

1 : 1,000,000.

How are you feeling, Elizabeth? :

> *Oh, you're not feeling? You don't feel? Please can you explain this, the not feeling? Scientifically, is that possible, not to feel? Because are we not made of nerve endings and impulses? Is that not our biological makeup? So is it possible, Elizabeth, that you are wrong?*

So your father passed away? :

> *He's dead? Oh, he's only mostly dead? Not really dead? What's that, he sits with you on the end of the bed at night and sometimes in the day? Is he here right now?*

Ah, he's missing? He's been gone how long? Is that hard for you, Elizabeth?

Have you spoken to Grace? :

Has Grace spoken to you? Has she texted or written or messaged or flown letters to you via pigeon? Has she left you, abandoned you, forgotten you? Do you hate and love Grace in equal measure for the leaving and the not writing or calling, and for loving you so much she threw a rock through a window?

Do you wish you'd kissed her more? Less? When Evie claimed you both on that first day, do you wish you had turned and walked across the courtyard to the termite bench no one sits on and do you wish you'd set up a Biz Compound, with bars and guard dogs to keep everyone out and you in? Do you wish you'd walked out of the school gates and to the sea and all the way into the water so you didn't have to love or lose anyone ever again?

How do you feel about what has happened? :

Have you felt so sad you couldn't breathe? Has your throat hurt, your chest hurt, your bones? Is this why you have become benumbed? Are you still obsessed with death with deathwithdeathwithdeath? Do you still feel alone in spite of being surrounded by almost eight billion people including twins who come into your room and kiss your face and a mum who brings you warm soy milk when you can't sleep and a house with walls and a roof? Why are you so sad and empty when you have a house with walls and a roof and people who love you?

Elizabeth?

Why are you so ungrateful?

Elizabeth?

Why is it so hard for you to be happy?

"WHAT DO YOU WISH FOR, ELIZABETH?"

It's Wednesday. I'm in the psychologist's office. It's our third appointment. I have been a non-functioning sad person now for almost two months.

My psychologist's name is Bridgit. She wears seriously upmarket scarves. She sits in a room stocked with chocolate-brown armchairs and light blue cushions. The room always seems hushed, like she's painted the walls with padded paint. Lamps sit in the corners and glow.

Bridgit has kind eyes. I've told her one thing, then another. Somehow, Bridgit has eased words out of me—maybe because she seems nice, like someone's sensible friend, and she hasn't asked me to draw. I've told her about Dad being dead, Mum's boyfriend leaving, our years of moving house and moving house, Evie being a bitch, Tim being an arsehole, Jasper saving me from drowning (and then disappearing), and Grace being in Wagga with her new life that I can't see, because I am blocked, barred, binned. I've also told her about the sauntering thoughts.

Bridgit has taken a lot of notes.

Bridgit is very calm. Bridgit is like a meditation video. Bridgit is an excellent listener. But Bridgit also wants me to get my arse into gear. Bridgit wants me to think of my present and my future, so I can imagine myself living. Beating on. Orgiastic green light all over the place.

"What do you wish for, Elizabeth?" she says. She says it gently, like she's coaxing a kitten out of a box.

I keep it simple.

I say, "I would like my dad to come back."

This feels like an uncomplicated answer: Once upon a time, I had a dad and now I do not, and wouldn't it be nice if he returned?

Seeing as every action has an equal and opposite reaction, it creates an uncomplicated response in my psychologist: Bridgit looks sad for me.

Of course. Here I am. The sad girl. This is sad. My dad is dead. People are sad when people are dead. So here I am, sad and grieving because, look, my dad died. Totally normal. Couldn't be normal-er.

"It's very normal to want that," Bridgit says. "You are not alone. It's important and necessary to grieve. I can help you through those feelings. And then, at some point, I can help you honor him, by living."

Clearly Bridgit doesn't understand.

Of course Dad is dead and of course it's sad. I missed him and cried about him being gone for exactly one year and 335 days, until, just after my ninth birthday, he showed up in my room wearing a plaid shirt and his old jeans.

Mum was out with the boyfriend. I was ignoring Doreen the babysitter and reading *Watership Down* in my room when Dad appeared and sat on the end of my bed.

"What's up, Biz?" he said. Very casually, like he'd just been out in the kitchen and thought, *Hey, I'll go chat to my little girl who I haven't seen since I stopped being alive.*

I screamed.

I couldn't help it: the sound just came out.

Dad's eyebrows went up! His mouth opened. His eyes went wide and—

Pop.

He disappeared.

I screamed again. I looked around my room. Was he really here?

Dad?

Dad?

Doreen flew in.

"What's happened? What is it, pet? What?"

I was kneeling on the bed. Was I shaking all over? I was shaking all over.

Doreen's arms went around me. She smelled of popcorn. I didn't want her touching me. I shook her off and she flew like confetti, a hundred little pieces of Doreen, pink face and purple shirt and green cardigan Doreen.

And the sound of me filled the room.

I don't remember much else.

Mum came home, and I slept in her bed that night. And the next and the next and the next.

The second time Dad came to see me, he appeared slowly over my desk, like the Cheshire Cat in reverse. I was sitting in my pajamas, drawing a picture of an upside-down town.

He said, "Biz, remember the first time you swung on the swings?"

My mouth dropped open, just like in all the cartoons.

"You were wild with happiness. Every time I pushed you, you laughed," Dad said. "Your face was like a book I wanted to keep reading. You were sunshine, the whole way through. You couldn't stop squealing. I took a photo." Dad smiled. "Have you seen it, Biz?"

"Yes," I said. "I've seen it. But, Dad, how—?"

Which is when he left. Gone again, a bubble bursting.

Every time the same. Years of Dad floating over beds and desks and couches, talking. *Did I remember? Had I seen?*

Blipping out if I spoke.

I learned not to ask questions. Just be glad when he came.

I should probably tell Bridgit all of this. All the years with Dad, all the time-not-time with him.

But I'm tired.

I want Dad to come and explain it. I want Dad here, hovering over the edge of the chair while I talk to Bridgit. I want him on the end of my bed, on the arm of the couch, beside the sea, with me. Telling me stories in fragments, putting my past together like pieces of sea glass. I want him here, whole, pinned into place. I want him to not be disappointed in me. I want his eyes not to go widewidewide. I want him talking, being; I want him dead or alive.

I'm fairly certain if I tell Bridgit, she won't understand.

So I nod when she says, "Elizabeth, I can help you."

And she suggests, very gently, that we talk through the day he died.

To which I say no.

She tries the following week.

"Shall we talk about—"

No.

"Elizabeth, I'm thinking it would be good—"

No.

No.

No.

The next session, she gives up—"Let's focus on now, shall we?"—and we move on.

Seeing as I have opted out of school, cancelled my subscription to Year 11, moved on to quieter things, Bridgit suggests we find a gentler, simpler Learning Experience for me.

Bridgit gives me pamphlets: classes I can take, workshops I can work at, communities I can commune with. Choir. Soccer. Photography. Painting. Et Cetera.

She and I lean over the pamphlets, heads bobbing forward.

Here is the picture of us.

She: handing over the colorful seeds.

Me: pecking dutifully.

Look at me. Aren't I a good little bird?

THE PAMPHLETS FROM BRIDGIT ARE FILLED WITH HOPE: OLD
men and children and women in nylon blouses, leaning over
macramé and car parts, laughing with their bright, white teeth.

They splay over my desk.

Here, Biz!

Take a class!

Knit with metal like a Viking!

Big-nose cartooning!

Tablet weaving—experiments with Egyptian diagonals!

How to give yourself a fashion makeover!

Find the colors that suit you!

Forensic facial reconstruction: facts and fictions!

Clutter clearing!

Lawn maintenance!

French!

Film—the liveliest art!

Black-and-white photography!

Perform CPR!

Getting started with emails!

Getting started with Facebook!

Getting started with your life, Biz, because look, your arse is covered in barnacles!

Getting a life, any life!

Getting the fuck up!

Come on, Biz!

Get the fuck up!

Biz!

Biz!

Biz!

I AM AT THE INDOOR POOL. I CAME HERE TO DO LAPS AND have ended up on my back, limbs out in a star. Bridgit said to do exercise—"It'll make a world of difference, Elizabeth"—so I'm doing my best. I've done three laps and I'm having a rest.

I've got the pool almost to myself. Because I'm not at school, or at work, or at anything at all, I get to swim with almost no one else. Today a hairy, thick-necked man walks slowly up and down a lane, recovering from some heart bypass/footy accident/ladder fall. A lifeguard sits in her office, reading the paper. Doesn't she worry we'll drown? Shouldn't she be at the pool side, gauging our moods, making sure we don't pass our tipping points and submerge?

I suppose she thinks we're fine. Two large humans—one walking, one on her back like a dinghy—both dull, lazy, and completely reliable.

Water's crinkling in my ears. I'm soaking and thinking about floating, thinking about water, thinking about being water, when something flicks inside me—OFF to ON, or would it be ON to OFF?—and I leave my body and turn molecular.

I rise up. I'm above the water, above the roof of the pool, above the gym complex, above the neighborhood, the roads, the city, above the escarpment and the sea.

I'm above the earth. I'm in space, moving away. I'm going fast and the earth is receding, and *all I feel is bliss.*

Ohmygod. It's beautiful.

It's a crystal feeling, a *ding-ding-dinging*—everything coming into focus. Suddenly, I get it: who I am, what I am, where, and why. I am everywhere. I know everything. I *am* the universe. I have always been. How funny to think I was anything else? I never want this to end.

Here is everything. Here I am—

and a kid laughs.

I open my eyes, and a toddler cannonballs into the pool.

My body-not-body rocks in the water. My face drips from the splash.

I am back.

And not at all back.

Here I am, in borrowed bones, in makeshift skin, looking out of eyes that are a construct, breathing with lungs that are only a step—a basic rearrangement—away from leaves. How funny, to have a body when I am not a body? How funny to be inside when I am outside?

I walk out of the pool and go to the showers. I stand in the shower and fall from the showerhead onto myself. I pour into the drain, under earth, out into the ocean, spilling.

I turn off the shower. From light-years away, I rub the strange thing that is my body with the strange thing that is a towel. I pull on clothes and they are the strangest things.

People walk out of the gym and they are such funny

creatures, aren't they? But I am them, so here we are, in between death and death, all of us spinning through space a trillion miles an hour. We are going so very fast.

I stand at the bus stop. Wind whistles past, cold and slick. The bus comes. I ride the bus. It starts to rain, and water glides into water on the glass.

I walk from the bus stop to my house, water inside, water outside. I am the rain. I will be the rain. I will be dead and I will be ash and I will be thrown into water and taken by the sky.

The feeling of wanting to leave comes so suddenly, I can't stop it before it hits.

The thoughts are loudloudloud:

If you are already the universe, why not just become it, Biz?

Why wait?

If we are a blip between non-existences, why bother staying?

Come and be the universe, Biz. Come. Please.

I stand in front of my house. Bump sees me through the side gate. Starts barking. Barks and barks.

I can't go in. I can't—

I sit in the hollow of the willow tree in the front yard. I twist into the space between the lifted roots, knees up. I try to find myself, but I'm a second away from leaving and I've already left.

If I tried to explain this to anyone but Dad I don't think they'd understand.

Dad?

Dad?

What's it like?

Is it good?

Dad?

Not to be here?

I'm under the tree and I'm in the tree I climbed after Dad died and I'm in the room Dad died in and I'm in the chaos of the moment before he left and I'm in the part of him that decided to leave.

Come and see, Biz.

It's so beautiful.

Come.

But he's not here. It's not Dad talking.

It's a man, standing by my front fence.

"Mate? Are you okay?"

I slam hard back into myself.

I stand up. The ground drops and the tree shrinks. I'm Alice after the Eat Me cookie; I've shot up so fast my head has hit the sky.

"Uh, yeah! I'm fine!" I say, too brightly.

The look on the man's face makes my skin ache. He doesn't think I'm fine. He's probably thinking, *What the fuck is she doing? Fuckin' giraffe-looking girl. Why the fuck isn't she at school?* This man is not my friend.

But here he is, saying, "Mate, you look sick. You all right? Need help getting in?"

I shake my head, but he comes round the fence and under the willow. He helps me out from under the tree, onto the front veranda, to my door. And he waits while I fumble in my bag for my keys and he says, "Want me to call your mum?"

How does he know Mum?

I squint at him. And he turns into Matt, the guy two doors down who comes and fixes the fence when it falls over in the wind. Matt, the guy who works at the car dealership downtown, who got us that great deal on the 2008 model Subaru last year. Mum was so happy.

"No," I say. "Don't call her. That's okay, don't worry. I think I was just hungry. Big swim, you know?" I flex my arms like I'm Popeye, and he sort of laughs and I fold into myself and die of embarrassment.

He pats my shoulder and says, "Okay, then. Take care of yourself, Biz."

And I say, "Oh, yes. I will. Thanks!" so brightly the corona of my immense positivity almost burns us both to a crisp.

I will take care, thank you, yes, that's just what I'll do.

I HAVE ENROLLED IN A PHOTOGRAPHY COURSE!

I say this with an exclamation mark because Mum and Bridgit are thrilled.

I tell Bridgit about the class, but not about the floating two weeks ago. I want her to think I'm getting better. *I* want to think I'm getting better. Also, I actually want to get better.

"Wonderful news!" says Bridgit on her brown chair.

"That's great, Biz!" Mum says in the kitchen.

They both clap their hands when I tell them. If I took a photograph of their excited faces and put them side by side, they could be twins.

I send an email to Grace, like I do every few days or so, because I can't help myself. I am not a learning robot. Not even close.

"Grace,

I've enrolled in a photography course!

Grace! Pal! Good news: I'm coming back to life!"

Of course Grace does not reply. I could make a nest of all the emails I've sent her. I could curl up in them and sleep for days.

But no matter! Let's ignore the Grace-shaped hole in every single one of my days, along with the Dad-shaped hole so immense it could swallow galaxies!

We do not look at holes!

I have enrolled in a photography course! Clap! Clap! Clap!

Isn't everything just wonderful?

The course runs for six weeks on Friday nights. It's run by the local WEA, which I think stands for When Everything Alters (you try and make something of your life).

On the first night, Mum packs me snacks. She asks me a dozen times if I have everything before we go. She drives me to class. She'll pick me up—"No, it's no trouble, sweetheart, I'll be here at nine!"

I don't blame Mum for getting emotional. It has been a long time since I went to school. She thought she had a dropout on her hands. That, or a dead girl. Which was not her preferred state for me.

Nor me. Not my preferred state for me.

Not even a little? ask the thoughts.

No.

I'm turning over a new leaf. No more thoughts. No more obsessing over death, over Dad, over Grace, over the universe and death and Dad and death. No more lying in bed and not moving. No more floating.

No more useless Biz.

I am Elizabeth Martin Grey. Call me Elizabeth.

"HELLO, EVERYONE! MY NAME IS CAROL, AND I'M VERY HAPPY to be teaching this class!"

It's six p.m. and here we are.

I'm in a room filled with grandmas and retirees and they've all brought notebooks and their SLRs. The cameras look new but they are not—they're film cameras, so they are ancient. The old people have kept theirs really clean and shiny, which is an old-person thing. Much respect.

The WEA said you needed to bring your own camera. When I was registering, I saw this as a clear sign I shouldn't take the class, but Mum said, "Hey, *we* have a camera somewhere!" She rummaged through some of Dad's boxes in the garage and found his SLR—the one, it turns out, he lugged everywhere before he died.

Mum turned it over in her hands. "Look at this old thing!" she said. She smiled. "Your dad never stopped clicking, Biz. I'd be minding my own business, nursing you, or reading, or having a little think, and there your dad would be, pointing this at my face!" Mum smiled again, all wobbly love and memory, and handed the camera to me. "Isn't it heavy?"

It is heavy. The lens is dusty. The case looks like weevils might have used it for a home till the leather lost its nutritional benefits. There are no automatic buttons. It's like I've brought a dinosaur bone to class. But it's a somehow-still-working dinosaur bone that once belonged to Dad, so the old fella sitting across from me can take his judgey looks somewhere else, thank you very much.

Carol, our teacher, is excited in this twitchy way, like perhaps she's never taught a class before or was a bird in another life. Carol has gray hair and slightly iffy eyes. She can't seem to focus on us—her eyes slide over our bodies like we are made of mercury. That, or her eyes are made of mercury. Either way, something is slipping.

She stands at the front of the room holding a camera.

"This," she says, "is an SLR. Which stands for Single Lens Reflex." She lifts the camera up like it's Simba from *The Lion King*. She pauses in case we want to write this down. Some old people do, quills scritching. "You may not have used one of these before. So I'm going to walk you through the functions and some common terms."

She starts rattling them off:

Lens.

Shutter speed.

Aperture.

F-stop.

ISO.

Focal point.

Depth of field.

Carol talks on and on and on and on and on and on and on and on.

It's exhausting. I absorb nothing and after half an hour, I've taken no notes.

What is Carol even saying? I look around and everyone is scribbling, wizened fingers flying. They nod and listen and the light comes on in their eyes.

I'm lightless. I don't understand anything and it's like my sadness has drained my brain and now I can't learn.

What was I thinking, doing this class? Carol is speaking a foreign language. It's a conspiracy. (They probably all met before the first class and said, "All right. There's this sad girl coming. Let's mess with her head." Then they all tittered behind their hands and chewed their gum and one of the old men made a farting sound with his lips on the palm of his hand and everyone laughed till their dentures fell out.

Arseholes.)

A very old lady sits beside me. She has white hair and long, thin fingers. She wears a single gold ring on her left hand. Perched on her nose are half glasses, the kind that librarians peer over in the movies.

She keeps putting up her hand and answering all of Carol's questions—it makes the other ladies purse their lips. It seems she knows everything there is to know about photography. I can't help wondering what she's doing here.

"But I hardly know a thing!" she says when someone tells her: "Goodness, you seem to know everything there is to know about photography." She laughs really lightly, like she's still young and surprised to find herself inside an old lady's body.

I don't laugh. I am in an old lady's body too; I grow old, I grow old, trousers and brain and sight are rolled. My brain is shriveling where I sit. I'm melting, I'm a puddle, I'm gone.

The old woman catches my eye. Maybe I look like I'm going to cry. Any minute I'll run out of here weeping, another failed human like all the rest. Watery, unkempt, unbound.

She reaches over. She touches my hand lightly.

"Hi," she says. She smiles. "I'm Sylvia."

Somehow the world stops spinning. I look at Sylvia. I focus on the feeling of her fingers on mine.

IT'S FRIDAY, JUST BEFORE THE SECOND PHOTOGRAPHY CLASS, and Sylvia has been teaching me the ways of the camera.

This week we have gone into town, to the lighthouse, and to the harbor. I've seen the sun properly for the first time in weeks. We have walked. We have taken photographs of seagulls and boats and people late for appointments and people looking at their phones. Sylvia has shown me how to adjust my focus, how to set my aperture and shutter speed. I have held Dad's camera up to the world and clicked.

And now, I'm sitting in her living room, at her house for tea.

I would not normally go to the houses of strangers, but Sylvia is eighty-three. She has five children, eleven grandchildren, and three great-grandchildren. She has kind eyes. I doubt she's going to murder me today.

Sylvia has laid out two mugs and an enormous teapot covered with a koala tea cozy. Chocolate biscuits tower on a green plate.

I perch on her lounge in a room stuffed with photographs

and cushions and Australiana figurines—possums, frilled-neck lizards, kangaroos boxing. The walls are lined with photographs of Sylvia smiling. She's standing/sitting/laughing with women, men, children; she's holding a baby; she's holding flowers; her hair is dark and her eyes are bright.

It's been a long time since I was in an old person's house. Last time was Grandpa and Nana's house when I was little. I stood in their kitchen while Grandpa wept. He was supposed to take care of me after Dad died, while Mum and Nana got things sorted, but he couldn't stop crying. He tried to make me toast and burned it. He offered me a banana, spotted black. In the end, I sat on the couch with some crackers I'd found in a cupboard and waited for Mum to come back.

After Dad's funeral, Grandpa kept on crying, even though Dad wasn't his son.

"I wanted so much more for you," he sobbed into his hands, and I didn't know if he meant me, or Mum, or Dad. Nana told him to shush, then put her lips back into a cat bum scrinch.

Mum kept her arms folded. I could see her fingers pinching her skin through her cardigan; I could see the steep line of her mouth. They all talked after I went to bed in the spare room. Through closed doors, I could hear the rise of Mum's voice, like Mum was an elastic band someone was stretching as she spoke. And then we left my grandparents and the house Dad died in and the jungle all around and the hills like boobs. We drifted south and kept drifting, like birds who weren't migrating so much as aimlessly flying around.

So Sylvia is kind of new for me.

"Have a biscuit, Elizabeth!" Sylvia says, shoving the plate in my direction. The stack of biscuits wobbles.

"Um," I say.

"They're vegan, dear. I found them at Woolies. Isn't that wonderful? And the tea is vegan. Oolong is vegan! I checked!" Sylvia beams at me.

I can't help but smile. I told her about the vegan thing sometime this week, down by the harbor. She was fascinated. "So, no chicken? No milk? What about muffins?"

I said, "That's right. No animals of any kind," and, "I can have milk. Just not cow or goat or sheep milk," and, "I love muffins. They're easy to make vegan. You just replace the eggs and dairy."

"Well, isn't that lovely?" said Sylvia. She slapped her knees. "Isn't that something?"

That day by the water, Sylvia showed me how to read the light meter. She showed me how to focus on the boats as they shunted in and out. How to zoom in on the boats' parts, on the prow, on the mast, on the person at the wheel, their face turned towards the open ocean.

She told me about her husband who was dead, and I told her my father was dead too. She looked at me, tilted her head and considered.

"That's very sad, dear."

"It is sad, but it was a long time ago and I don't think about it much," I said. (*That's right, new and untouchable Biz. Keep it up.*)

"I think about Ronald all the time. The dead don't leave us," said Sylvia.

She was watching a yellow fishing boat come in after a day out. The boat was probably filled with carcasses. I turned my mind away from the boat, the boat driver, the snuffed-out fish.

"The dead leave us all the time, Sylvia," I said. But I didn't say it out loud. I spoke the words inside myself, and I folded the corners of the words and tucked them under my ribs.

In Sylvia's house, after I've politely eaten four chocolate biscuits and drunk two and a half cups of tea, she shows me her collection of trinkets.

"I call this one Graham," she says, pointing to a porcelain wombat.

The wombat sits on a flat plastic base with words painted gold: *Welcome to Gundagai!*

"Graham," I repeat, and Sylvia smiles.

"My first boyfriend," she says, nudging my elbow. "He was a wonderful kisser. But then he dropped me for Mary, who he married. They had ten children. Thank goodness that wasn't me; I couldn't have taken the noise."

She points to a platypus in a snow globe, bobbing through plastic reeds.

"James," she says.

I look at her, waiting.

"Second boyfriend," she says. "He wanted to be an artist."

"Did he become an artist?"

"Sad story," says Sylvia. "Died in a motorcycle accident in Ecuador. Twenty-two years old." Her eyes well up.

"I'm sorry."

"It's all right. He wasn't long for this world, Elizabeth. He had that look in his eye."

The platypus gazes solemnly at me. I hope James had a good life before he died. *Did you have a good life, James?* I ask the platypus. The platypus can't say.

We go through the animals, most of whom are named after suitors: dead loves, boys she let go, boys who broke her heart. Sylvia has had a lot of lovers. Who knew old people were so busy? Then we stand at the photographs. She points from frame to frame.

"My brother," she says. "My sister. My mother, bless her soul. My children. And ah! This was my eightieth! A lovely day."

Sylvia points to a photo in the center of the wall—there's a sea of faces on white steps outside a cottage, a banner above saying HAPPY 80TH!, babies in arms and children running, and just out of focus, leaning in the background on a veranda post with his arms crossed: Jasper.

Jasper? What the hell?

I must have gasped, because Sylvia turns to me and says, "Are you all right, dear?" And she touches me on the arm with the same look my psychologist gets when I talk too much and forget to breathe.

"Uh," I say, because now the world is shrinking into itself and of course—this is Wollongong—what did you expect, everyone knows everyone, and yet, how? And again I think, *It's because I'm a story,* and again I think, *It's because none of this is real,* and I sway where I stand.

Sylvia decides I need to sit. She fetches me a bowl of nuts because she thinks I haven't had enough protein—she's so sorry, what was she thinking filling me with sugar? The nuts rattle in the bowl.

"They're roasted, dear," she says, as though I care.

"Uh," I say, again.

And she says, "Take your time."

Which no one ever says to me.

We sit quietly while I think of a way to explain that I am a story, that Jasper is on her wall but has disappeared, and that Jasper saved my life but in fact I nearly killed him in the sea.

Sylvia leans back on her chair. When I don't speak for a good few minutes, she pours herself a cup of tea and sips it. After I haven't spoken for more minutes, she smiles at me and pats my hand. Then she picks up the newspaper and starts doing the crossword puzzle—and somehow, the silence feels so good I want to live here always, because Sylvia doesn't seem to mind if I never speak again.

At some point, Sylvia stands up. She goes into the kitchen and makes me some noodles. She tells me about the first time Ronald kissed her. "Sparks!" she says, and she tells me about traveling through Europe when she and Ronald were sixty— "All those mopeds! Those ruins! I couldn't stop taking photographs!" and an orange cat sidles in and rubs itself against my leg. "That's Zelda," Sylvia says. "She likes you!" Then a clock in her hallway dings and Sylvia says, "Oh! Look at the time!" and it's five o'clock and time to go. We get up, without me explaining anything, and we take the train to class.

CAROL MIGHT BE THE PHOTOGRAPHY TEACHER, BUT LET'S not kid ourselves: Sylvia teaches me photography.

By class three, Sylvia has shown me how to develop my film. How to swoosh the developing solution around inside the plastic canister and pull out the negatives, little flat babies. I clip them into a drying cupboard. I trim them and take them to the developing room, where enlargers hulk against the wall and trays of chemicals wait in line. The room smells hospital clean. The light is womb red.

I learn how to print a test strip, then a contact sheet. I learn to clip the negative into the enlarger, turn on the light and lay the idea of the image on the base below. I learn how to switch off the light, pull the photograph paper out from its thick, black, plastic bag and lay it on the enlarger base. I learn how long to expose the paper to light. How to lay the promise of the paper into chemical trays, move it around for the allotted time, and watch a story come to life under the tongs in my hands. I pull the paper from the trays, wash it, clip it to the line, where it hangs, newborn, from a peg.

MY FIRST PRINT:

Here is the dog. Tail waggy, tongue lolling, bright eyes, head turned my direction, ears turned towards the birds on the field.

Bump doesn't understand why I keep stopping. Why I point that box everywhere. Don't I know about the rabbits? Which require chasing? And the birds, which also require chasing? And all the lovely dead things?

The dog rolled in a dead thing once. I washed him; it was awful. Bump loves dead things more than he loves anything. Don't I understand love?

My second print:

Here is a man at the wheel of his boat.

He is pulling into the open ocean through the harbor's arms. He's hungover because last night his wife said she wanted another kid. He doesn't want one; already there are too many kids and not enough money. And all he could do was drink because he couldn't think of an answer that would make her happy.

He feels like shit now.

My third print:

Here is a boat. It goes out to sea and back. It sits on the water and hears the mumble of the fish and the bottomless call of the whales.

The boat has been a boat for as long as it can remember. Other boats say they were trees once. But this boat knows only boat.

And the rise and fall of waves.

And the rain. And the slap and pull of water.

And the weathering hulk of the boat's insides, reaching for a deep it hopes to meet one day.

My photographs drip and whisper from the line.

All around the room: the muted bustle of people standing at enlargers, pulling paper from black bags, tongs clacking the sides of the plastic trays, and the hushed opening and closing of pegs.

No one in class seems to hear the voices. No one has turned to gawk; no one has started screaming.

The photos are talking to me, and I don't know why. I don't mind not knowing—the universe is filled with incomprehensible things. We exist inside a multitude of singularities. I accepted this a long time ago.

This would make Bridgit the psychologist happy. She keeps saying acceptance is key. Bridgit has been using an approach called Acceptance and Commitment Therapy with me. It's all very mindful. I am supposed to not fight my grief, my hollow bones, my loss of Dad. I'm supposed to notice all my thoughts and feelings, *Om*, let them pass through, *Om*, instead of pushing them away.

So okay, fine.

Here I am. Here are voices, ribboning out from rectangles of paper.

Om.

Hi. I am listening. Welcome.

Om.

The photos keep whispering in my bag, on the car ride home. Voices rustle in their sleeves; the sound is like long grass, like kicking through it, wind thrumming through it, the dog rolling it flat.

Mum doesn't hear anything either. She's driving us home, telling me about her boss at work and singing snatches of songs from the radio. She doesn't hear the dog's bark, the man swearing as he steers, the *slick-slick* of a boat slipping through water.

So I guess the stories are just mine?

WHEN I WAS NINE, I CAUGHT THE FLU. I HAD A FEVER OF 102. I threw up, then slept and slept and slept. I dreamed I was rolling down a hill. The hill wouldn't stop and I couldn't stop and I needed to pee, but I kept rolling and the grass pulled at my arms and legs and went over me until I was in a tunnel of green.

I couldn't breathe—I couldn't see—I couldn't stop moving— and then I heard Dad's voice.

"Biz."

And there was Dad on the end of the bed, in his board shorts and palm tree T-shirt. He was all wispy; he kept blinking in and out. He said, "Breathe, Biz, okay? One, two, three. Just breathe."

Then Mum came in and she sat on the edge of the bed. She said, "Shh, shh, sweetie," and put a cloth on my forehead.

I pushed it off.

I said, "I want Dad," and Mum's face turned a funny crumple in the dark.

"I want him too, Biz," she said, her voice full of fuzz.

"No, I want *Dad*. See? Here he is."

And there was Dad, floating, all hopeful on the end of the bed, looking at Mum. But when she turned, I guess she saw only air.

"Shhh. Dad's not here. He's in heaven, sweetie."

"No! He's here! Dad, tell her."

Dad opened his mouth.

Out he went like a light.

And I cried and cried and the fever swept up and over me like a wave and I peed in my bed where I lay.

It was awful. I was all staggery and had to lie on the floor while Mum remade the bed.

I said, "Sorry, Mum, I'm sorry."

She said, "It's okay."

"It's not," I said. And of course we meant two different things.

Two days later, I was mostly better. I kept looking at Mum when she came in with toast, when she checked my temperature, when she brought me lemonade. Should I ask her again about Dad? Should I tell her?

Mum sat on the edge of my bed, telling me some story about the last time she was as sick as me. Dad hovered, cross-legged and silent, over my desk. I looked from one to the other, one to the other, and understood. Dad was all and only mine.

Somewhere, sometime, Mum must have let him go.

"I WENT TO SCHOOL WITH HIM," I SAY, POINTING TO SYLVIA'S photograph with Jasper in it.

It's our fourth Friday and we have a routine now, Sylvia and I. We take photographs three mornings a week, and every Friday she has me over for a vegan meal before class. The noodles were just the beginning. "I can do better than that!" she said. Now Sylvia plies me with tofu mini quiches and Thai stir-fry, and I'm eating better than I ever have.

So, I've gotten almost comfortable. Today I've relaxed and breathed and dined on lentil dhal. I've washed dishes, listened to the story of Sylvia plus Ronald for exactly an hour and then stood by Sylvia's photographs, and I've been able to say, "That guy. Yeah. We went to school," super casually, like he isn't Jasper who pulled me out of the ocean and never spoke to me again.

"Oh? Jasper? Really?" says Sylvia, delighted.

"Yeah. He goes to my old school."

"Oh, sweetie, he hasn't been to school in ages," says Sylvia.

"No?"

"That's right. He had to have an operation."

"For his leg?"

"His leg?" Sylvia frowns.

"The one that's, um?" What do I say if she doesn't know what I mean? Am I imagining the leg? Maybe I invented it, like I invented myself and my being here, in this living room, sipping tea and having a third banana muffin, though it tastes wonderful—can you be invented and eat muffins? Is that a thing?

"Oh, yes, that's right, his leg!" says Sylvia, her face clearing, and I have to remember that Sylvia is old. There's a lot to process, loaded as she is with memories of being every age up to eighty-three.

"Yeah, his leg," I say. "So he had an operation on it?"

"He did. Now, what exactly did they do? Something with the bone? The knee? I'm not sure, dear. But he's been away from school for months, the poor thing. How lovely that you know him!"

"I don't know him well," I begin, but Sylvia is off and running.

"We'll have to have him over for tea!"

"Oh. No—"

"He's not vegan," says Sylvia. "But I'm sure he'll be okay eating your food!"

"Um. We don't need to have him over for tea."

"We don't?"

"Well, I mean, you don't. I mean. We weren't friends."

"You weren't? Why ever not?"

"Oh! Nothing against him. It was me. I—" And I can see from her face that it's time to let my history out.

It takes a while to explain. I start by telling Sylvia about the waves. I tell her about Jasper appearing, *poof*. Then I tell her about everything that happened afterwards. About everyone giving up on me, about losing Grace, and me turning to dust in my bed.

I get quieter and quieter in the small room—orange cat on my lap, Sylvia gazing at me, tea going cold, a wall of faces in frames.

Just before I finish, I tell her about Dad leaving.

Then it's completely, completely quiet.

Sylvia sighs. It's long and sad, like when Bump heaves out his breath, head on paws, watching me with his eyes, wishing for something better to happen.

Sylvia reaches out and holds my hand.

And we sit together for ages before the old clock in the hall dings and it is time for class.

MY FOURTH PRINT:

Here is a little boy, digging in the sand at the harbor beach. He's tunneling to China! He has his bucket, his shovel. His face is set, determined. He's been going for over two hours. His mum just called out, "Come and have lunch, Jack!" But Jack will not.

I'm digging till I'm there. I'll go all night! I'm strong!

The photo hangs from its peg. I could have helped Jack out. I could have told him if he made it through the earth's molten core, he would actually pop out in the ocean, adrift in an unfathomable sea. I could have shown him on Google Maps.

It's good to know all the facts; then you can decide. "Is that what you want, Jack?" I could have said. "Do you want to keep digging?"

o ° o ° o

My fifth print:

Here is Sylvia, smiling at me from a bench in the Botanic Gardens.

Sylvia sat on this bench sixty-three years ago, with her second boyfriend, James. He'd just told her he was leaving for Ecuador. She'd just found out she was pregnant. She didn't tell him—he was so excited to leave, she just . . . couldn't.

He held her hand and said, "Come with me, Sylvia."

She shook her head and smiled. "I think I'll stay," she said.

And afterwards, after their baby wasn't born, and after she had time to stand by windows and think of him, and after his mother had called with the news of his death, Sylvia thought of what it would have been like to ride those mountain passes with him, on that bike. The things they would have seen: the green valleys, the blue, swallowing sky. How he would have spoken to her and she would have plucked his words from the wind and filled her lungs with them.

Sylvia stands two feet away from me, focused on her print of the lighthouse.

I stare at her. Can't she hear her own story speaking?

Sylvia looks up, catches me staring. She smiles. It's the same smile as the one in the photo, the same smile she offered me on the train to class, after I told her about Dad.

Just a few hours ago, she patted my hand. She said, "I'm sure your father will come back, sweetheart. It's a beautiful thing, Elizabeth, isn't it? To love this much?"

A WEEK LATER AND I'M HOME ALONE. THIS IS A NEW DEVEL-
opment. Mum is out with her salsa class friends and the twins
are at a sleepover. Which must mean I'm considered well
enough to be left alone at night, when Mum's worries are loudest. What a success I am!

Mum took up her salsa class when I took up my photography class. She saw a flyer at Coles, and asked, "Hey, do you
mind if I go to this?"

I heard the sound in her voice, the careful *Hey, whatever;
I don't mind one way or the other*, but of course it mattered. Of
course she minded. I've been a weight for months. I've had
to be monitored, fed, have my barnacles scraped. If it's been
exhausting to be me, imagine how everyone else has felt,
watching me wither. Probably terrible.

Mum does her class on a Wednesday night and I look after
Billie and Dart. Mum loves it. She comes back and talks about
her classmates—bald, divorced Ken with his shaky hands,
Susan the manicurist who sings as she dances, and Maxine,

who steps on everyone's feet but never stops smiling with her big false teeth.

And now it's Saturday and Mum's really letting her hair down. She has gone out for drinks and dancing, wearing a dress she couldn't stop tugging at before she left.

"Do I look okay?" she'd said. "Does this fit? Do I look like I'm trying too hard? Do I look like a cougar? Should I even go?"

"You look gorgeous, Mum," I said. I handed over her favorite earrings, gave her a kiss, and headed her to the door. I waved her down the drive to her friend's car, and you could see Mum shucking off her mum-self as she went off to play.

It must have felt fantastic.

The twins are at a friend's house; they were so excited when I took them over, they bounced the whole way, pillows under their arms.

"We're going to have marshmallows!" Dart said.

"*Hot chocolate* and marshmallows!" said Billie.

"And we're going for a midnight swim!"

"And we're going to watch a movie! I think it's horror!"

"Not horror, silly. I think it's M-rated, though!"

"And we're going to have marshmallows!"

"And we're going to swim!"

"Did you pack our swimmers, Biz?"

"Did you pack our towels, the ones with the hoods?"

Bounce! Bounce! Bounce!

So it's just me at home. My photographs from class are spread out on my bed, murmuring.

Tonight's stories: The man selling used books at the local markets is stealing from the register at work—a twenty here, a fifty there; his fingers itch with want and guilt. The girl scribbling in a notebook by the water is writing to someone she wishes she still loved. The woman walking her dog wants to be an actor but is studying optometry. She can't remember why she chose this course—at night she dreams she's on stage; she's about to go on; she's kissing a young woman in the wings.

My darkroom photos are never quiet. I keep them in my desk drawer. If I leave the drawer open when I go to bed, I can fall asleep to their muffled whispers, and it almost feels like Dad's here.

It gets me to thinking.

I pad down the hall in my bed socks and go to the photograph albums on the living room bookshelf. I pull out the first album on the left—floral, gold-edged. On the front it says, *BIZ: Year Zero.*

I look through every single photograph.

I'm in Mum's arms. I'm in Dad's arms. I'm rolling on the floor. I'm squatting beside a table, pulling myself up. Mum's in the background, mouth open, as though she's saying, "Look at this girl go!" But I can't hear her.

I'm in a park. Dad's holding my tiny fingers as I stand. He's squinting into the camera. His mouth is open too, and maybe he's saying, "Isn't our life glorious?" But I don't know.

I lean forward, listen. I go through the next album and the next—I'm one year old, two. I am three. I am four. We have a puppy! I am five, six, seven—

None of the pictures will speak to me.

Of course they won't—*so stupid, Biz, they never have*—how ridiculous to even try.

I go back to my desk and grab my computer. I take it to the printer in the corner of the living room. I print out the first three images I see when I open my photos: Grace at the beach, Grace and me smiling from her hammock, Grace, her hair sleek after a swim.

The printer whirrs and clicks. Three pictures slide out. Grace is grainy because our ink is almost gone.

What does she have to say?

Grace?

What do you have to say?

Nothing nothing nothing nothing nothing nothing nothing.

And now I am a girl in a stone body, sitting with Dad, Mum, Grace—their faces open and smiling, mouths ready for talking or kissing or singing—and all I feel is alone.

I'm in this echo of a house with only a sleeping dog and creaking walls for company, and once I had Dad alive and then I had Dad dead, and once I had friends and school and I was busy, and now life is beating on without me, everyone bouncing and dancing and talking and kissing and drinking, and all I am is alone.

IT'S FRIDAY, THE LAST PHOTOGRAPHY CLASS. HOW DID WE get here so fast?

You'd think everyone would be upset—black armbands on and someone playing a dirge on a tuba—but no. All the old people are happy because, *Yay! Next is digital photography!*

Carol is buzzing too; she's emboldened by everyone's enthusiasm over the past six weeks. So clever we have been! So quick with the learning of tricks! Old dogs, shmold dogs!

Carol has decided to teach us a final skill. She writes two words on the whiteboard:

BURNING-IN!

DODGING!

Carol even has a handout. The woman is on a roll today.

Burning-in and Dodging
from Black-and-White Photography *by Henry*
Horenstein.

Burning-in is a technique used to darken a specific area

of a print by selectively adding exposure. Dodging is a technique to lighten a specific area of a print by selectively holding back exposure. Most prints require some burning-in and/or dodging for best results. Burning-in and dodging are critical fine-tuning steps—often making the difference between an adequate print and an excellent one. With some prints, you only have to burn-in or dodge one area to produce a satisfactory print. But be patient: It's not uncommon to have to burn-in and dodge multiple areas.

Well. That's some good advice, Henry.

Be patient, Henry says. It's not uncommon to have to burn and dodge. You're not lesser for having the need; just remember this. You might have to burn some days, dodge other days. It's a constant adjustment, isn't it, to survive? But it's critical to know how to do it, says Henry. If you learn to burn and dodge, you're moving towards excellence, instead of simple adequacy. A noble goal.

We've taken all the notes we can, so we go to the darkroom.

Enlarger on, I play with the light. I look at the picture beaming down from the negative. It's Mum with the dog, taken a few days ago. She's on the back veranda with her wine, looking out at the yard. I asked her to go outside even though she didn't want to.

"That yard gives me hives, Biz," she said.

I said, "But I need to take someone's portrait," and so she went.

Mum grimaced at the long grass and brambles as I clicked. "We really should move into a flat," she said.

"But Bump," I said.

Mum sighed.

She looked pained that day and she complained about the cold, but under the enlarger, you can see her hands in Bump's fur. You can see the dog leaning against her leg. You can see her hand moving over the dog, patting him. Her hand is blurred, because the light outside was dimming and the shutter speed was slow. But you can see, even in the blur of dusk, that if Mum really had to pick—dog or flat—I'm sure she'd pick the dog.

I pull out the photograph paper. I expose it to the light. I move a cardboard square over Mum, so only the dog and the background get darker. I move the cardboard back and forth.

"That's right, Elizabeth! Keep it moving," says Carol, hovering by my shoulder. "Keep it in motion, blend the exposure in."

And it feels like a dance: dog and trees growing darker, Mum staying light; yes, let's keep in motion, let's stay moving; let's.

In the developing tray, the dog appears first. And the trees, then Mum, emerging from the shadows.

I put them in the stop bath. Mum and dog and trees and shadows pause. They sit together on the paper.

Bump is dark, his black fur thick and luxurious. The trees are gray and twisted. Mum is pale—I've made her ghostlike, a specter on a veranda.

I wash the print. I hang it on a peg, and then I have to lean on a wall because Mum's memory hits me so hard it's difficult to breathe.

BUMP WAS A PUPPY ONCE, A TINY RESCUE MUTT WITH MESSY fur and floppy ears. Dad brought him home when I was almost five. I don't remember the first moment I saw him. But Mum does.

I saw the puppy and screamed. My whole body shook with excitement. Dad stepped back, surprised. He stumbled and dropped the dog.

Dad was very tall and our floor in that house was wood.

The puppy, so small back then, hit the floor and yelped. He tried to run. His back leg dragged behind him. Shrill as a child, he cried and looked up at us, terrified. Mum and Dad had to scoop us both up—shaking girl, screaming dog—and drive to the vet. We'd had the dog for all of half an hour.

"What happened?" asked the vet.

"I dropped him," said Dad.

The vet tched with her tongue.

She came back with an X-ray.

"He has a fracture," the vet said.

Dad sagged where he stood.

Mum reached for his hand, but Dad wouldn't take it.

All this time I sat in the seat and my eyes were wide wide wide.

I looked at Mum. "Dad broke the puppy," I said.

Dad turned so suddenly even the vet was surprised.

"I did," he said, "I broke him," and he left the vet's room in a rush. The door hit the wall with a bang.

And when we went out to find him, the dog finally quiet, his leg in a cast, Dad was gone. The car was there, but no Dad.

He didn't come back for three days.

Mum rang his phone but it rang out.

She rang his phone, but it rang out.

The puppy ran and clunked into all the furniture with his cast. I chased after him, laughing.

Dad texted after the first night. "I can't do this," he wrote.

"What can't you do, Stephen?" wrote Mum.

"This. I'm no good at this."

"Where are you?"

No reply.

"Where are you?"

No reply.

The puppy ran. I ran after the puppy. The puppy clanged into the chair leg. I laughed and laughed. I said, "Bumpy! Let's call him Bumpy!" The puppy shat on the floor. I shouted, "Bumpy pooed on the floor, Mum!"

Mum rang Dad's phone, but it rang out. She rang his phone and it rang out.

"Where's Dad?" I said. I chased after the puppy. The puppy hid under the bed. "Where's Bumpy?" I said.

Mum rang Dad's phone. Dad answered on the third day.

"Laura, I'm so sorry."

"Where are you, Stephen?"

"Fischer's Gap. There's a waterfall. It's really beautiful."

Mum stood at the kitchen counter. Her legs were ice, her chest ice.

Dad described the view, the height, the trees below.

The puppy yipped into the room. I ran in, laughing, banging up against Mum's legs, and she couldn't hear Dad.

"Shit! Biz! *Stop* it!" she said. She looked down at me. "Just *stop!*" And her voice was ice.

I started to cry.

And Dad was crying too.

"Please, Stephen," Mum said. She had to sit down.

"I don't know what to do."

"Please, Stephen."

"I can't move, Laura. I can't breathe. Everything breaks." Dad's breathing got ragged.

"Stephen. Please. Please."

Please, Mum thought then, *please don't leave me. Please don't leave and please don't scare me by not being here and please don't stand at edges and call me from them and please be the way you were when I met you, before you became a father and every day began to terrify you.*

And in that moment she wished hard to go back, to the time before. To the time when they were happy and they weren't parents and Dad wasn't broken.

To the time before me.

∘ ° ∘ °

In the photograph, Mum's hands move through the dog's fur, but she's not here in the yard. She's back there.

You can see in her hand—in Bump's fur, in the blur there— her memory as she moves.

AT THE END OF CLASS, CAROL WALKS WITH ME TO THE DOOR.

Everyone else has gone out waving and smiling, saying, "See you next term, Carol!" Everyone is super excited about the next course, all ready to hop glibly off the old train and onto the new.

"Will I see you at digital photography after the break, Elizabeth?" says Carol.

Digital photography? It's like Carol is speaking Latin. I've just crept out of the dark. I've just listened to Mum basically wish me dead.

Who even is this woman standing here? What even is this room?

"Uh. I don't have a camera."

"Oh!" says Carol. "Can you buy one secondhand, or borrow one? It would be lovely to have you continue."

"Maybe. I'll see," I say.

But the truth is this:

A) I do not have the money for a digital SLR. What a funny idea. Isn't Carol funny?

B) I do not have a friend to lend me a digital SLR. Sylvia is my only friend and she doesn't have a cupboard full of cameras.

C) To be blunt, Carol:

I don't want to move forward. I don't want to do digital photography. Those photos won't talk to me. All I want is to be back in the darkroom, to crawl inside and stay. I want the red hush, the clean smell of chemicals. I want to lie inside the black-and-white mess of history. I want to not come out until I know everything.

IT'S SUNDAY NIGHT AND I AM HELPING MUM COOK. SHE hates making dinner, probably more than anything in the world, including picking up dog shit and brushing the twins' hair.

"If I had it my way—" she starts.

She's said this so many times I finish the sentence for her.

"—we'd all just take food pills," I say.

"Exactly!" says Mum.

Tonight we're trying something new: the dhal Sylvia made for me two weeks ago. We have to follow a recipe. I had to buy actual ingredients. Chili and cumin and coriander. Curry paste. Lentils. Sweet potato. They lie on the kitchen counter, strangers.

Mum says, "So this will taste good?"

"If Sylvia comes and makes it, sure," I say, and smile.

Mum looks at me. Normally I see that look and know exactly what she's thinking. But today I'm not so sure. Ever since Friday, I've been tiptoeing around her, feeling like glass.

Mum keeps shape-shifting every time I look at her: one minute Hopeful, Look-on-the-Bright-Side Mum, the next, Other Mum with all her secret wishes. *Do you really know her, Biz?*

"What's wrong?" she's said all weekend.

"Nothing," I've said. But we both know I'm lying. So she waits for me to tell her and I wait for her to figure it out.

Mum is playing music on her phone: classical music, all squeaky flutes and tinny violins.

"How do you listen to this stuff, Mum? It's so boring."

"It makes me feel calm. Cooking makes me stressed. So maybe this evens things out."

"I'm sorry cooking makes you so stressed."

"It's okay," she says. "Lots of things make me stressed."

"They do?" I turn to her, surprised. I mean, I know they do, but Mum doesn't ever talk about it.

"Of course. Work stresses me, cooking stresses me, money stresses me. Men stress me."

"And I stress you," I say.

"No!"

"Come on."

"Well." She picks up a pot, plonks it onto the stove. "I *have* been a bit worried."

"Okay."

"But now you're better," Mum says, and smiles.

I am?

"And I'm so proud of you, Biz." Mum hugs me. "You've worked so hard to get here."

I have?

"So let's celebrate. Let's go out."

"We're not making the dhal?"

Mum looks down at the bag of lentils, unopened. "Biz, I don't want to make the dhal. Just looking at this recipe gives me the heebie-jeebies." She gives me puppy-dog eyes. "Please, sweetie; don't make me make this food."

I sigh. I can't help but smile. "*Fine*, Mum."

She grins, grabs her handbag. "Kids!" she calls. "We're going out!"

Billie and Dart whoop.

We go out for Thai again, and Mum listens to the twins talk over each other and Mum tells us how happy she is to be here, out with us, and I half listen, half laugh, half talk, and at the same time I work Mum's words over in my head.

"You're better," and "I'm so proud."

Am I better? Can you be better when you're still sad—long patches of sad swooping in at night when there aren't any sounds to cover it? Are you better when you still feel blank, fog rising inside you, great empty spaces like those moors people walk on in British films? Are you better when, as you're going through the motions—talking, laughing, listening, walking the dog, helping Mum with dinner—at the same time there's this lost feeling walking beside you, so you can touch it, like a tongue on a tooth?

Here's the shape of it. Here's the gap. Here's the space where something good was. Here's the want.

IT'S THURSDAY NIGHT, AND I'M OUT OF THE HOUSE, SITTING on a bench in an outdoor corner of the mall.

The space is alive with food trucks and music, lanterns strung through trees, bean bags on rugs and couples on bean bags, children red-cheeked and running in the cold. The mall smells of fried things and chatter. It is enough to warm the cockles of your heart. I reach into the brightness and try to rub some on myself, but I can't seem to make it stick.

It's been two weeks since the last photography class. (*Dear Father, it's been two weeks since my last confession. I've lost my darkroom; I've been lonely; I've been sad. How many Hail Marys will fix that?*)

I have pushed myself out into the world because logic and Bridgit say if I keep myself busy and in the moment, I'll get happy. So look: I'm out and about! Present and accounted for! Communing with the people! Soon there'll be no sadness here!

Right?

○ ° ○ ° ○

Grace and I used to come here on Thursdays. Eat Street Markets were our thing. We'd eat vegan burgers when we could afford them, which was mostly never. We'd walk; we'd people-watch. We'd decide everyone's secrets.

"He's just asked her to marry him," Grace would say, about the man in the AC/DC hoodie, next to the girl in the strapless dress.

"And she's said yes, but actually, she's in love with the girl at work," I'd say.

"But that girl doesn't love her; she has a terrible, hopeless crush on a YouTuber."

"Greatest tragedy of all time!"

Grace and I would hold hands sometimes as we walked and Grace would beam light over all the people and their tiny lives. And if I had known she was going to abandon me, I'd have taken a picture of us, walking under the lanterns, our hands laced, and I would have wallpapered it onto my skin for warmth.

An hour ago, I told Mum I was meeting friends downtown.

She said, "Who?"

I said, "Zac and Celia. From debating last year?"

"Oh," said Mum. She looked confused for a second. Had I never told Mum about Zac and Celia? Those mythical creatures? Who don't exist?

But Mum was so glad I was going out, she didn't ask any more questions. She gave me money and waved me off. "Have a great time, Biz!"

Tonight she's shape-shifted back to Glass-Half-Full Mum—

she's so happy I'm better, but would anyone else agree? I can't ask Dad, clearly. Grace wouldn't reply. I'd ask the twins and they'd tell me to *shush!* because their cartoon was on. I'd ask Sylvia but she'd say yes, pat my hand, and offer me a muffin. Ah, Sylvia.

I'd ask Bridgit, but I'm scared of what she might say.

Elizabeth, I'm sorry to tell you, but you're still a basket case. You're still forgetting to take your meds; you haven't returned to school; you still haven't discovered your life's purpose. I suspect we'll be working together until you're ninety. And I'll still be wearing these fucking excellent scarves while you'll still be forgetting to wash.

I sit in the stir and whirl of the markets, and can feel myself slipping. *Why are you here, Biz?* I want to go home, crawl back to my bed, where nothing and Netflix wait. *No one is coming to meet you, silly.* I can feel those sweet, blank days calling, and the thoughts—which have been quiet for a minute, for a blessed minute while I did my class—are back.

Hey, Biz! Hey! We're talking to you!

Isn't that bench cold? Don't you get hemorrhoids when you sit on cold benches? Hemorrhoids! Hahaha!

Why did you bother coming? That was stupid!

Why do you keep trying, Biz? Why do you even exist? Wouldn't it be easier to just not?

Why don't you just leave?

Biz?

Biz!

Look at us when we're speaking to you!

I open my eyes.

When the thoughts get shouty, clever, sensible Bridgit has said to slow my breathing. "Then, focus on three things you can see, Elizabeth. Three things you can hear. Three things you can feel."

So I

slow

down

my

breathing,

and, focus.

I see an orange food truck. I see a tree inside a wire box. I see a huge white dog.

I hear the strum of a guitar. I hear the laughter of a woman with a purple hat. I hear the *chat-chat* of a couple going past.

I feel wind on my ears. The softness of my jacket sleeve. My feet in my boots.

And I smell churros.

I come to ground.

Here I am, Elizabeth Martin Grey. Here, now, see?

I walk over to the food truck and buy a churro.

The pastry crunches, sugar hits my tongue—it's been a while, and lord, it's good. It tastes like being five years old, like Saturday morning cartoons and sitting on laps, laughing.

The twisting panic lifts for a second—two seconds, ten—

Another gust of wind. Smell of fish, frying. A busker begins singing "Blackbird." And Evie walks past with Tim and Miff and Stu and Rob and Sal. Evie's holding hands with Tim.

Huh.

Long time no see, arseholes.

Their heads turn like all those carnival faces at the sight of me.

Miff opens her mouth to say hello—I could drop a ball in—but just before the words come out, she catches herself and says nothing. Off they go.

Well, fuck you too!

The churro has gone cold in my hands. The food trucks smell rank. The benches have bird shit all over them.

What did we tell you, Biz?

There's no place for you here.

I stand in biting wind, watching my Ex-Posse walk away. I could run after them and scream every ugly word I know. I could shove at their backs and make a ruckus. I could kick them, rip their hair . . . and then I'd get arrested and lose my caution and go to child prison.

I throw away the churro. I stalk out of the mall, stand at the bus stop. I pull out my phone to write to Grace:

You did this, Grace. You left me to this. Fuck you! It's your fault! Your fault! Your fault!

But I can't do it.

I look up Jasper online instead.

There he is: a single update on Facebook since I last checked his page (which was when? A week ago?). He has a new cover photo. He's standing on a clifftop, looking out. He looks like a beat poet—scruffy, mournful, and, I'm sorry to say, gorgeous.

I send him a message: "Hi. I have photos. You'll want to see them. Add me, motherfucker."

I press SEND, although at the last minute I change "Add me, motherfucker," to "I know your grandmother. She's cooler than you. Regards, Elizabeth Grey."

WELL, HOW ABOUT THAT? TODAY I'M SEVENTEEN.

The twins don't wait to see if I'm awake; they shove open the door and pile onto my bed, planting kisses, birthday cards in their fists. Dart's card is covered in glitter and pink hearts. Billie has drawn a picture of me, grinning, my mouth ogre-sized, my hair on end. Both cards are filled with sloppy, shameless love:

Hapy Birthday, Biz!

Your the best!

Here is a gold medal for being grate!

Hey! You are 17! I love you!

I pad to the bathroom and do my first wee as a seventeen-year-old. Afterwards, I peer at myself in the mirror. Who invented getting older? I am ancient. Fossilized. Wizened. I can see myself aging before my eyes. Old, older, oldest. I see myself at a hundred: gray haired, rheumy eyed, etched with wrinkles.

Dart knocks on the bathroom door. "Come *on*, Biz! Stop taking so loooong!"

I blink. Seventeen again.

I get dressed, head to the kitchen. The twins zigzag down the hall, saying, "Mum! Mum! Biz is awake! She's coming!"

Pancakes wait on the table—a huge stack—maple syrup beside them in a jug. Mum has set the table: four mats for us, four of the good plates, flowers in a jam jar, picked from the front yard. There's also a present beside my plate, a box wrapped in dark blue paper. But I can't open it until after we've finished the pancakes, because, Mum says, "These took a year to make, Biz. You should eat them while they're hot."

The twins wolf down their food, then sit, twitchy and excited, watching me eat. They keep reaching over and picking up the box and Mum keeps telling them to put it down.

"But we don't know what it is," complains Billie.

"We need to know!" says Dart.

"Patience is a virtue," I say, and maybe it's true? I am not even slightly curious about what's in the box. Maybe I'm turning petrified, like the wood you find under earth, buried so long it's turned into rock.

There's a lot of huffing and sighing by the twins and a lot of quiet sipping of tea by Mum, and then I finish my food, and it's time.

I take off the wrapping so slowly the twins nearly lose their minds.

"Just rip it!" says Billie.

"*Oh my God*, Biz!" says Dart.

I ease the tape off a corner, glacially. Except glaciers are now receding at the rate of knots, so I should probably get to it.

It's a digital SLR camera.

I stare at Mum. "No way."

"Yes way," she says.

"But how did you afford it?"

I know how much these cost. I also know how much I've cost in psychologist visits and doctor visits and medication and time off work. With all that money, Mum could have bought a car, a holiday, a new child.

"Grandpa and Nana helped. And Aunt Helen." Mum smiles. "And now you can take that digital photography class!"

I don't know what to say.

It's been almost three weeks since class ended. I don't want to take that digital photography class. I want what I had: the room, the light, the hush, the dark, the whispers.

Plus, I love Dad's camera. I love the heavy feel of it in my hands, all its buttons and doors, moving the film along after I take a picture, lever under my thumb. I love that Dad held this camera before me, that he put it up to his eye. How we saw through the same window, looking for stories.

"Don't you like it, Biz?" asks Billie, little frown on her face, which will one day be wrinkles; one day she will be old.

I open my mouth, close it. I still don't know what to say.

"She doesn't like it," says Dart, and he shoves his plate across the table.

"Don't you like it, Biz?" says Mum. She reaches over and touches my hand.

And they all look so worried: three squinty mice, twitchy noses, trembly whiskers.

"We can return it, Biz," says Mum, looking at me, looking at the camera, her own face fallen.

"No," I say. My chest hurts. I'm such an ungrateful bitch. "No." I plaster on a smile. "It's really amazing. I'm going to use it so much. It's so helpful. And now I can go to the class."

Mum smiles. I have made her happy. Look how easy it is, to be normal. To say thank you, to want to move on with your life! That was then, this is now. The future is yours, Biz!

Which is when the twins tell me to actually look at my present, this wonderful, marvelous machine—

"Can you turn it on?"

"Take a photo!"

"Can I touch it?"

"No, I want to!"

The camera is pretty high-tech. I could probably reconstruct it and turn it into a flying car. It has a manual the size of a textbook. It has a website. It probably has its own YouTube channel.

I turn it over in my hands.

"Take a photo, Biz!" says Dart.

"Yeah, of us!" says Billie, and she jumps from the chair and strikes a pose.

But it's time for them to go to school. "Oh!" says Mum. "How did it get so late?!"

The twins pull on their uniforms and complain about their socks (*too tight! too itchy!*). Mum assembles a limp salad for lunch and tries to find her car keys. Sylvia calls—I haven't spoken to her since class ended. She's rung me and I haven't replied, but today I see her name on my screen and in a rush of birthday goodwill, finally answer.

"Elizabeth!" she says. "Happy birthday!"

"Thank you." How did she know?

"You told me weeks ago, darling. I never forget these things!"

I tell Sylvia about the camera. She's thrilled. "Oh! Elizabeth!

That's wonderful! We'll have to have a good look at it, won't we? Would you like to come over for lunch on Sunday? I haven't seen you in ages! I have a treat for you, dear!"

A treat? How do I deserve one of those?

I agree to come for lunch. We hang up. The nest is emptying. The twins are almost ready and Mum's at the door.

Mum pauses. "Do you actually like the camera, Biz?"

"Of course I do, Mum." I smile.

"Really?" On her face is worry and want and more worry.

I walk to the door and give her a hug.

"Yes. I like it, Mum; I love it. Thank you so much. Sorry I wasn't clear."

"You'll have to email Grandpa and Nana and Helen to say thanks," says Mum.

"Yeah, sure!" Of course I'll write to Grandpa and Nana, who I haven't seen in years! And Aunt Helen, who feeds the twins bacon! I'd love to, dearest mother!

Mum kisses me.

"Happy birthday, beautiful girl," she says, and gets a bit teary.

"Thanks, Mum," I say, not getting teary.

Mum heads off and Billie and Dart hover at the door.

"Biz, take a photo of us," says Billie.

"Please, Biz! Just one! Please!" says Dart.

"Nope," I say.

Their faces darken.

"We won't leave until you do!"

"Yeah! And if we're late, we might get detention!"

"And it will be your fault!"

Billie stamps her foot.

Seriously?

"I'll tell Mum you were little buggers," I say.

"No you won't!" Billie says. She grabs my hand. "Not on your birthday!"

"Just take a photo!" Dart says, "Pleeeeeeaaase!"

And they stand on the front path, school bags on their backs, arms linked. They turn their silly faces on, thumbs up.

Fine. I grab the camera, turn the switch. The machine comes to life. I take a photo, hope for the best.

"Where am I?" Billie asks, pulling at my hand to see the camera screen.

"Careful!" says Dart.

I press the play option on the menu screen and there they are: Billie and Dart, two angel people with tiny memories. If they even bother to remember this day, it will be filled with how great the camera was, the two of them on it, bright faces filling the whole screen, immortalized.

The first photo! On Biz's new camera! Them! Them! Them!

This is all they'll know—not me. Not me holding the camera, or the look on my face as I stared down at the screen.

WHEN THE TWINS WERE ALMOST DUE, MUM SAID I COULD be at the birth.

I was ten years old. I felt so important. I thought: *How many kids get to see a baby born? How many get to see two?*

Here's my chance to shine, I thought. *I'll offer Mum treats as she pushes. I will hold her hand. I will tell her how to breathe. Maybe I'll have to pull the twins out if they get stuck. Maybe I'll have to crawl in with a headlamp and coax them out like kittens.*

The boyfriend thought Mum was mad. "She's just a kid," he said, but then Mum said, "I want her there. She will be there," and crossed her arms over her huge belly, so the boyfriend put his hands up and said, "Whatever, Laura." And I was in.

Dad said Mum lost a lot of blood when I was born.

He said she needed lots of stitches, inside and out, because I came bolting out of Mum like one of those racehorses, poor things, whipped into a frenzy the second the gate opened.

I sat at my desk and gawped at Dad.

"You were in such a rush, Biz," Dad said. "It's a miracle we made it to the hospital. It's a miracle they caught you, you were so slippery."

After Mum asked me to be at the birth, Dad had come in every night that week to talk about me being born—me being a baby, me sleeping and not sleeping, me squeaking and shitting and squalling.

But this night it was all blood, blood, blood.

"It just kept coming, Biz. She went completely white," Dad said. "As white as that book," he said, gesturing to my notebook, the one I was trying to draw aliens in. "Mum could have died. She could have died, Biz."

I hadn't thought of Mum dying. I had never thought of Mum dying. Mum was my fixed, true thing.

Would Mum die?

Next day, I went on Mum's computer while she was in the shower and searched for *mums dying when they have babies*. And then I was terrified.

I watched Mum as she stood at the kitchen counter making peanut butter and apple sandwiches for us. The boyfriend had gone to work. Mum was enormous and had this sheen—like all she was at this point was sweat and skin and baby.

"Will you be okay, Mum? Two babies is a lot of babies to push out."

Mum laughed. "I'll be in good hands, Biz. My midwife is amazing. Plus lots of doctors and nurses will be there."

"But Mum, you might die."

Mum stared at me. "Where'd you get that idea?"

I waved my hands in the air. I blinked hard. I would not cry; I would not cry.

Mum bent down so we were eye to eye.

"You think I'd leave you? Never."

"People leave, Mum. It happens."

And we stood for a second in silence, because suddenly we had slipped into the cave of Dad, the space he'd left us in.

"It's not going to happen to us, Biz. I won't let it." And Mum got this look on her face, the one she got whenever we talked about things that were not about Dad but really were about Dad. It was a mix of her stubbed toe look and her electricity bill look.

Mum said, "I'm not going to die giving birth to these twins. It won't happen. Plus. You'll be there. You're my lucky pin."

I had never been anyone's lucky anything before, so that was nice. And just like that, the moment passed. We hugged. We walked out of the Dad cave and into a sunny green field of talking about the twins' names again, and had I made my cards to them for their zero-th birthday? And we tucked our sandwiches into our lunchboxes and skipped off to work and school, rainbows papering the sky.

Dad was back the next night.

"Do you think she'll be okay?" He hovered somewhere over my desk. This time I was trying to write a book report for school.

"Do you think she will be in pain?" Dad shook his head. "Of course she'll be in pain. She'll be in terrible pain."

I looked up at Dad.

"Mum says she'll be fine, Dad. Really. Plus. I'll be there," I said. I felt so pleased saying that. I wanted to say more. I wanted to tell him about being a lucky pin, but—

Blip! He was gone.

I stared into the empty space above my desk. Sometimes it made me really, really angry that he did that.

Dad floated opposite me at the birth. I was at Mum's head, the boyfriend at Mum's other end—the end Mum said I shouldn't be at because I'd be more helpful "up top."

It was pretty full on. Mum's face got red. Mum swore a lot. Mum held my hand super hard. I kept having to switch hands.

When it came time to push the first baby out, the boyfriend got pale and had to sit with his head between his legs. Mum screamed. The boyfriend moaned. The midwife was all, *You can do this, Laura, one more push,* and into the midwife's hands popped Dart, a shriveled grape with squinched eyes and his hands in little fists. Up to Mum he came, still with his umbilical cord on, and he lay on Mum's chest while she cried.

I might have cried a bit too. Dad just bawled. At one point I had to say "Shh!" to Dad because he was so loud, and he gave me this baleful look and blipped out.

Dart got his cord cut and had a feed from Mum, and then, wrapped like a burrito, he was put into the boyfriend's arms. Dart blinked up at the boyfriend like a grizzled old man, like Dart already knew the boyfriend wouldn't be around for long.

And then we had a bit of a wait. Dad came back and paced by the window and then it was pushing time again. I totally had this. I gave Mum ice chips and I helped her breathe, and when Billie came out, wow, wasn't she the loudest baby that ever came out of a human? Mum cried again, and we were now two squinch-eyed, grape babies the richer.

And Mum didn't die. And Dad sagged beside the window in relief. And the boyfriend went outside for a smoke (yuck). And Mum fed Billie and Dart, one on each boob. And I sat next to her and grinned because I'd been a very excellent pin.

Hadn't I?

Later, I stood and looked at the two sleepers, my brother and sister. They were so small. Fragile, like Christmas baubles: thin-skinned, bald, tiny glass babies.

And I thought, *I'm going to make you so happy.*

They looked like anything could break them.

I wouldn't let it happen. I said (quietly, because Mum was asleep too): "I'll never leave you. I promise."

And it felt, in that moment, exactly like the truth.

TWO DAYS AFTER MY BIRTHDAY, I'M AT SYLVIA'S HOUSE. IT'S windy outside, warm and salty. The air feels sun-crusted. I'm in my thrift shop overalls and three-dollar flip-flops, flowers in hand, because I haven't seen Sylvia in weeks and I feel bad. Flowers fix everything, right?

Sylvia's cottage sits at the edge of the sea in the northern suburbs. Sylvia moved here with Ronald when the houses were tiny boxes, cottages built for mine workers, when the sea wasn't a prize. Sylvia raised five kids in this house. It's small, just two and a half bedrooms—a little white cottage with a tin roof and roses on the lawn. It's beautiful, gauzy and unreal.

Sylvia greets me at the door like I'm a rock star. "Elizabeth! Oh! You're here! You sweet girl, you brought me flowers! You shouldn't have!" She kisses my cheek. Her lips feel like paper butterflies.

"I'm sorry I haven't been in touch. It's just—"

Sylvia puts up a hand. "I don't need reasons." Then she peers at my face. "Unless you've been unwell? Have you been unwell, Elizabeth?"

"No. Um. Yes?" I say.

Sylvia takes me in, my fidgety hands, my fidgety face, my fidgety heart in its cage.

"Hmmm," she says. "But now you are here. So you must be a little bit okay."

"Yeah," I say. I lean into Sylvia's hope, her ancient positivity. I guess I am a little bit okay? I'm here, after all.

"That's wonderful." Sylvia beams. She claps her hands. "Oh, sweetie. I have such a surprise for you!"

I'm taken straight out to the backyard. But first, Sylvia blindfolds me. She uses one of Ronald's old ties—it smells of cupboards and laundry detergent and a hint of Sylvia's perfume. She giggles as she ties it on.

"I've never been blindfolded before," I tell her.

"I've only been blindfolded once," says Sylvia. "It was Ronald's idea. Maybe I shouldn't say any more."

That's probably for the best, Sylvia.

I inch forward down her path, arms reaching out. We circle the clothesline. "Mind the tea towels!" says Sylvia as a cloth flaps my face. She pulls me on, and perhaps she's going to drop me off the embankment at the back of her house—it's steep, sharp rocks at the bottom—perhaps this is Sylvia's moment to become a killer? But we stop at a door instead.

I put my hands up and feel rough wood, a doorframe, round handle.

"You going to lock me up in your shed, Sylvia?"

Sylvia laughs. Her laugh feels just like her kiss. God, I've missed her.

"Open the door!" she says.

I turn the handle and step in. I hear a click as the door closes, then a rustle, the pull of a curtain, the sound of Sylvia's breath going in. I'm hit first by the closeness of Sylvia, then the silence. The dark is heavy on my skin. Just a moment before, the sun was bright, bright.

Sylvia says, "Are you ready?"

Am I ever?

"Sure," I say.

"Ta-da!" She pulls away the blindfold. I open my eyes.

It's a darkroom. Sylvia's gone and made a darkroom in her laundry shed.

Sylvia tugs a string and a light comes on.

Countertops run along two walls. Four trays sit on the counters, empty. On a shelf: bottles of chemicals, a ream of photograph paper. Thin string runs along the walls, pinned with wooden pegs. On hooks above each tray: a set of tongs. All that's missing is an enlarger.

Sylvia points to the countertop nearest the sink. "That's where the enlarger's going to go, when I find one that isn't broken or too pricey! My son's teaching me to bid on eBay! So exciting!"

I turn around. There is just enough room in here for the two of us, possibly a third, if we like them. A stool stands in a corner. Above the sink: windows painted black. On a shelf beside the sink: a lamp, which Sylvia switches on. The red bulb glows, smiling.

Oh my God.

"Oh my God. Sylvia." I can't believe it. I keep turning. The room doesn't change or leave. It's a darkroom. A *darkroom*.

"I decided to do it a while ago," says Sylvia. "I wanted to tell you, but then I thought, *I'll surprise her,* and so we've been working for a while. Soon we can make our pictures, dear. Isn't it lovely? Isn't it wonderful?"

I look at Sylvia, her hands clapping, her dancing eyes, the bounce in her just the same as Billie and Dart, and in a rush, I love her. It comes with a pang: bright, like a stab.

I reach over and squeeze her. She is tiny and beautiful, this bird woman.

"How did you do it, Sylvia?"

"My daughter Samantha helped—she put in that extraction fan, do you see?" Sylvia points to a wall, where behold, a fan waits, ready to go. "Won't do to die of fumes, will it? My youngest, Jenny, she set up the curtain, and sealed up the gaps. Her boys did all the painting. Conor and Jasper. That's right, you know Jasper! And, oh, I forgot!" Sylvia claps her hands again. "He's coming for lunch!"

"He is?" My voice squawks.

Oh, Sylvia.

"Yes! You said you know him, so I told him about you, and then I said, 'Why don't you come for lunch on Sunday?' and he said, 'Okay.' Isn't that lovely?"

Sylvia, tiny bird of little memory, must have forgotten the part in my long story where I told her Jasper had decided I didn't exist and wasn't my friend. And she doesn't know I messaged him a week ago, and he hasn't replied.

I have to sit on the stool in the corner to think. It's too much input. I'm in a darkroom. I'm going to get to print out my photographs. Jasper is coming. What is that pain in my ribs?

Sylvia doesn't notice, because she is too excited and too old. She keeps talking.

"I've such a feast for us today, dear. Do you like falafel? I made falafel! Ronald never liked food with a lot of flavors; isn't that sad? I took a cooking class after he died—but you know that—I told you! I'm repeating myself! Let's go and eat, dear. I've made hummus! And the shops had some baba ganoush, which sounds funny when I say it, but oh, it's delicious!"

Sylvia turns off the lights and opens the door. She steps into the real world again, still talking. She's lit up with color, in her lilac scarf, her hair rinsed light blue, her yellow skirt printed with green lizards. I have to stand and follow her because she's not stopping or waiting for me, and she's saying, "Jasper should be here any minute! He said he likes Turkish food; he said he'll bring the bread. He said he doesn't mind eating vegan, isn't that good, dear? And I have made a cake, Elizabeth. A vegan cake! Oh, sweetie, I'm so excited. It feels like *my* birthday!"

We go up the path, one ancient, twittering bird followed by a galumphing albatross—my gut panging, filled to nearly bursting with love and worry, filled with—I'm surprised to find—*feeling*.

What am I supposed to do with it all?

HERE'S HOW IT GOES:

Jasper comes to the door. He has pita bread. Sylvia lets him in.

Jasper says, "Hello, Gran."

"Hello, dear!" Sylvia kisses him. Does her kiss feel like paper butterflies?

He steps into the living room, where I am.

"Hey," he says to me.

Jasper is walking with a tiny limp, hardly a limp, more of a lag; would you call it a lag? Just a small shiver between time and time. He is wearing a thick leather jacket and dark padded pants. He has a motorbike helmet in his right hand.

"Did you ride your bike here, Jasper?" asks Sylvia.

"Yes," he says.

"You know I don't like you riding that thing."

"I am really careful, Gran," he says, and smiles. Have I ever seen him smile?

"Yes, but still. I hear terrible stories."

Jasper is taller; is he taller? Maybe I am smaller. I am hunched, I think, trying to shrink into the fireplace, maybe hide in one of those snow globes of Sylvia's. I am a Tasmanian devil, I am a fern, I am the water in the globe.

He looks at me.

"Hey," he says again.

Did I not say hi? I can't remember. If I said it, do I say hi again? If I didn't say it, why didn't I say hi?

I say, "Uh."

Sylvia reaches up and tugs off his jacket. "It's too warm inside to be wearing that, darling."

Jasper lets her fuss over him and smiles again. That's two smiles on a boy I've never seen smile before. Unless you count the time at school a thousand years ago, when I was caught, phone in hand, in another time, another life. So, technically the boy has produced three smiles I can account for.

"Happy birthday," he says across the coffee table.

"Thank you," I say.

"I got your message," he says.

Ah.

Sylvia says, "That's lovely! You two are in touch with each other. How nice! It can be lonely when you're not at school, isn't that right, Elizabeth?"

I say, "It's not so bad."

"I haven't minded," Jasper says, shrugging. "People can be dicks."

Sylvia laughs. "Not that I've noticed, dear!"

Is Jasper talking about himself? Is he the dick? I could argue that he has been a dick; the evidence is before us:

His speech on the steps before I broke my ankle.

The no talking to me after I nearly died.

The lack of a reply to my message.

Or have people been dicks to him? People are undependable. And also people really truly are dicks; most are dicks to the bone. People should do the world a favor and die out. At least, all the dicks should die out. At least, everyone but Mum and the twins and Sylvia should go. I really should go. He should go. Should he go?

I blink. Sylvia has been talking, but stopped to look at me. Jasper is looking at me. Both of them are waiting for me to come back from where I've floated, from this impossible, enormous height.

My brain goes blank. What had they said? What do I say?

"Thanks?"

Both of them start grinning.

Oh my God. *Thanks?*

Sylvia and Jasper start laughing.

"You're welcome," says Jasper.

"Oh, Elizabeth, where'd you go?" says Sylvia.

"She does that," says Jasper, like he's known me for a lifetime.

"Yes! She does!" says Sylvia. "It's very sweet. She has a lot to think about."

"Indeed," says Jasper, and they both nod, like I'm a specimen in a box, mid-dissection.

"Sorry," I say. I know I've gone red, and then the knowing makes me go redder.

"It's no problem, sweetie!" says Sylvia. "We love you no matter what."

Jasper puts up his hand—as if to say, Whoa, love?—and it's

so fast and automatic I can't help but die a little. He lowers his hand as quickly as it went up, but I saw it.

Jasper holds up the pita bread next. "Gran, shall we have some food? I'm starving." He doesn't look at me, and I don't look at him.

"Ah! Yes! The food!" says Sylvia. She marches us into the kitchen, where a feast is laid out—gleaming, resplendent, enough to feed her enormous family and my little family and perhaps all of Wollongong if Sylvia were Jesus.

We eat and eat, and as we eat, I find out Jasper stopped going to school just before I went into the dunes with Tim, and Grace and I had our violent outburst and nearly killed all of Suryan's family, and Grace fled Wollongong in disgrace, and I had my mental breakdown. But he's heard all about it. "Oh yeah, I think I heard about it from someone," he says vaguely, not saying who.

"It's been a terrible time for Elizabeth," says Sylvia, touching Jasper's hand. "On top of losing her father—"

Jasper glances over at me.

"Sylvia," I say, and Sylvia puts her hand over her mouth.

"Oh! I suppose that's between us," she says, and touches my hand, so now she's touching both of our hands like we're in a séance. *Dear tormented spirits of Biz, please don't show yourselves now, please for the love of all that is holy.*

I pour more tea—it's proper Turkish apple tea, in a proper Turkish teapot with proper Turkish glass cups—and change the subject.

"So your leg is good now?" I say to Jasper politely.

"Yes, it is," he says back, "mostly good."

"That's good," I say.

"It is good."

"Good."

We look at each other.

"I've had to do a lot of physio," Jasper adds. "Still can't climb Everest though."

"Oh, that's disappointing," I say.

"Probably next year."

"Something to work towards."

"Always nice to have a goal."

Sylvia smiles. "You children are always so inspiring. I am constantly in awe of all the things you achieve. Just the other day I heard about a girl who sailed around the world! By herself! Only fourteen!"

"That was years ago, Gran," says Jasper.

Sylvia's face falls a little.

"Maybe someone else did it again?" I say, trying to help.

"Yes, maybe. Perhaps this girl was thirteen?" says Sylvia, frowning.

"Ah, so a different girl!" says Jasper. "Well, then. Very inspiring."

"A six-year-old is doing it next, and she doesn't even have hands," I say.

Jasper grins.

I can't help but grin back.

Sylvia laughs.

What a party!

And this boy. When did he start smiling? At me? When did he start talking to me and me to him? Is this a reset?

Maybe it is.

AFTER LUNCH, SYLVIA SITS ME DOWN ON HER COUCH. A wrapped box sits on the coffee table. The day is already so full my mind is going fuzzy. You know when the input has been so big, the computer starts to fizz and pop? That's how I'm feeling, like my stimulus intake meter has gone into the red.

This is more conversation, more newness, more smiling, more Jasper than I've experienced in months. I can feel the blankness swell and turn slowly in my brain, pushing for space. I just have to keep it together enough to not embarrass myself. *Just put one word in front of the other, Biz; that's all you have to do.*

I stare at the box.

"Open it, Elizabeth!" says Sylvia. "I think you'll love it."

Jasper watches me. Can he see how my body is inching out of itself? We've been talking like almost normal people for over an hour. I'm not a "normal people." I'm not a—

"Elizabeth! Open it!" says Sylvia.

The box. I pick it up, hold it in my hands.

It's heavy. I picture a snow globe inside, perhaps a frilled-neck lizard. Yeah, it's a lizard in this box, I'm sure—its frill out, squatting on a gold-painted rock, a picture of Uluru pasted to the back. I'm so certain of what I'll find that when I open the box and see the Polaroid camera, I turn it over, looking for the sunset, listening for the hiss of the lizard, completely confused.

Sylvia can't contain herself. "It's an original! And it still works! Not one of those plastic ones; oh, I can't bear those! I had it all fixed up for you, Elizabeth. Isn't it lovely?"

It is. It's incredible.

How do I contain how this feels?

I now have a DSLR, a Polaroid camera, and access to a darkroom.

Cup runneth over.

It's like the universe has stepped forward and said, "Here, Biz, you can have everything you want."

Except for one thing.

I start shaking. I can't control it; my body begins to tremble. And all of a sudden I slip into a different Biz—scree sliding out from under me, falling, falling.

Sylvia frowns and Jasper too, and maybe he's thinking, *Here we go again, Biz being Biz,* because isn't that what I did on the beach, started trembling so violently that he had to wrap his arms around me, and try to stop the shaking? How did I forget that part? And that's how everyone found us, so of course that's how it all started, everything a great tumble from there.

I shake more, can't stop it, because that was the moment—that was the door I walked through and everything changed—one of the thousands of doors I've gone through since Dad died, since Dad got sad, since I was born.

I can't contain this. I want now and I want then. I want this camera, this Sylvia, this boy smiling, this hope rising, all of it, and at the exact same time—time laid over time—I want what was. I want life before Dad left, before Grace left. Life before Grace's fire went out, before I put it out. Life before the waves. Life before Dad died. Life before I was born.

I want to put everything together differently, start over. I want to find all the broken pieces and lay them down and find Dad whole, me whole, life at a different door. I start crying. And it's humiliating, mortifying. I'm holding the best present I've ever been given and Jasper looks like someone's punched him and Sylvia is completely baffled, and here I am, floating above myself, watching as I shake all over and wish myself gone.

What a party.

A PANIC ATTACK. THAT'S WHAT BRIDGIT CALLS IT. SHE'S fitted me in on Monday, a day after my meltdown, and we're discussing what new thing might be broken in me.

"Or maybe it was just an excess of feeling," she says, which is ironic because I haven't felt in so long—it must have been like a cork popping.

We sit on her brown chairs. Afternoon sun plants a triangle of light over the top of my foot.

She says, "It's okay, Elizabeth; this is not uncommon. Nothing to be ashamed of. I can help you. Now, the trembling, how long has that been happening?"

"I don't know."

"Think about it. Let's just step slowly. When was the first time?"

I remember it happening after the waves, with Jasper.

I remember it happening—worse, longer—after Tim in the dunes. I went and shook in bed and my teeth chattered and my limbs seized. I crawled into the shower and crouched and shuddered. The water hit my back and at some point, the water went cold.

And then—

my mind leaps back in time like a cat, and lands, four-pawed, on the night after Dad died, the first night in bed.

The dark was smothery. The air felt like soup. The shaking came and Mum held me, and then she shook too, and there was nothing we could do to stop it. I remember I could feel Mum's heart, ricocheting inside her body—*ratatatat*—my heart thumping back—our skin frozen, the sky falling and—

I look around.

Everything is blurry. I'm looking at Bridgit from the wrong end of a telescope. I've gone too close to the sun.

Bridgit's leaning towards me. "That's interesting, Elizabeth. And if we step a little more into that day, what else—"

No.

She shifts forward. "It might be helpful to—"

No. No.

Bridgit sits back. She eyes me, measures me gently.

"Okay, Elizabeth," she says. "How about I give you some new breathing exercises to do?"

I nod.

"Shall we try them now?"

We breathe in.

We breathe out.

In, out, around. Count to four. Hold for four.

In. Out. Around.

I feel my body, here in the chair. I feel my hands in my lap.

I'm back.

And our time is up.

Bridgit smiles. She recommends a meditation app. "It's excellent. I use it myself," she says, writing it down. She'll also send me links to articles, so I can understand myself better. "All will be well, Elizabeth," she says as I leave. "It will be okay."

Yes. Of course it will be. I'll read the articles and totally figure myself out. I can send those to Sylvia and Jasper so they can understand me too.

Here: Look at these charts, these graphs, these lovely informational tools! Here is Biz: Isn't she a harmless and fascinating creature?

"I'M OKAY," I TELL SYLVIA WHEN SHE CALLS, THE NIGHT after I see Bridgit.

"Are you really, dear? I was so worried? About what happened?"

Everything's a question. Sylvia's rattled. She's almost never rattled.

"I guess it was a panic attack—" I begin.

"Oh no? I made you have an attack? I'm so sorry? Oh, how terrible?"

I can't help but laugh, which must seem weird to Sylvia. A day ago I was a mess, now I'm laughing? I must be the strangest person she knows.

"No. It's okay. Really. I'm okay. Lots of people have them. My psychologist said it was just a bit of overload. I had a lovely time. Thank you so much, Sylvia."

I can hear Sylvia processing. Her thoughts are a buzz of whirrs and clicks, things trying to go into place, which is hard when you're as old as her and you're talking about processing me.

"So you're okay?"

"Yes. I've been cleared by my psychologist. Fit to travel. All is well."

"Oh, I'm so relieved!"

We agree she doesn't need to worry. We agree that I'll come over again soon. We agree I'm not broken at all.

It's good to settle her, even though I'm only a little settled myself. What is it they say on planes: Put on the other person's oxygen mask before your own, so they don't die of worry?

Yes, that's exactly what they say.

WEDNESDAY 1:30 A.M., TWO AND A BIT DAYS AFTER THE party, I get a notification.

PING!

Jasper Alessio wants to be your friend on Facebook.

Three minutes after I press ACCEPT, a message comes in.

PING!

JASPER: Hey.

BIZ: Hi.

JASPER: Are you okay?

BIZ: Yeah. I am.

JASPER: Oh good. *Smiley face emoji.*

BIZ: Sorry for worrying you. Sorry about the lunch.

(And sorry for the taxi ride home and the crying all the way in the car, and thank you for patting my hand and saying to the taxi driver, "Her cat died.")

JASPER: That's okay. I just wanted to be sure you were all right.

BIZ: My psychologist says it was a panic attack. I don't know why. The camera was an excellent gift.

JASPER: I thought it might be that. I've heard about panic attacks. I did some research.

BIZ: You researched me?

JASPER: Not you. Just what it could have been. I thought, Well it's not Parkinson's.

BIZ: Definitely not Parkinson's. *Smiley face emoji.*

JASPER: A relief! *Smiley face emoji.*

BIZ: I really liked the camera.

JASPER: Good.

BIZ: I loved it. I love it.

JASPER: Gran told me she was getting it. From what she's told me, it sounded like a good present for you.

BIZ: It's amazing.

JASPER: Good.

BIZ: Yeah.

Then I stare at the screen.

Time tick-tocks.

I start typing as he starts typing:

BIZ: Why didn't you talk to me at school? After that night at the beach?

JASPER: Well, I'd better go. Lots of homework. Glad you're okay. *Smiley face.*

Our messages go through microseconds apart, so I'm guessing one goes PING! in his house and one goes PING! in mine at almost exactly the same time.

(A beat. Two beats. Too many beats.)

BIZ: Jasper?

JASPER: I'm really sorry about that.

BIZ: That's okay. But why?

JASPER: Interesting story . . . I thought you hated me.

BIZ: Sorry?

JASPER: After you walked away at the beach. I thought you were pissed off with me.

BIZ: I walked away?

JASPER: You stood up and walked off without talking to me or looking at me. You went back to the fire with that girl, what's her name?

BIZ: Evie.

JASPER: Yeah. You went over to her and didn't look at me for the whole rest of the night. And then at school, you wouldn't look at me, and when I went near you at school, you were always looking down at your phone, so I thought, Okay. I get the hint. So then I thought maybe my first hunch was right, and you might actually be a bitch. Again, sorry about that. Then Gran told me you weren't a bitch and you actually thought I hated you. Which sucked. So I came to Gran's party. So you could see I didn't hate you. And don't.

How is this possible? I remember Jasper getting up, at the beach. But was I already up? Was I walking away from him? And sure, I looked at my phone outside class as I waited for him to come out and speak to me. But he was always looking down at the floor or at *his* phone when I looked up at him. So, what the hell?

Truth and truth split in two and walk side by side.

I want to take a photo of it, to see which one is real—him hating me or me hating him.

If I took a photo what would I see?

Perhaps this:

Me and Jasper. We're back at that night on the beach. We're both soaked. Me with my clothes torn, him with sand in his hair.

Evie has come over with a bunch of others. She stands over us, making stupid jokes. The slick boys look us over and decide our story. Everyone laughs. Jasper says nothing. Why doesn't he speak? Does he want them to think that's what happened?

His arm has fallen from my back, where it was because I was shaking and he was rubbing my back, saying, "It's okay, Biz. You're okay." And then the others came and his arm fell and we were two sodden lumps looking stupid on the sand. Unbearable.

I spring up; I bound over to Evie and grab her arm, and I guess Jasper stands too, and the boys pat him on the back and he's the hero of this, and I'm at the whole other end of hero. Evie keeps making kissing sounds into the air and I want to thump her, thump everyone, thump them into the dunes or out to sea. I sit by the fire, knees on my chest, and stare hard at the flames. I stare at the fire until I *am* the fire.

Fuck Jasper, I think. Fuck them all. I rage silently until I'm dry and then I walk home.

And then I play "Wait For Jasper to Talk to Me." I play so hard, I forget to talk to *him*.

So that's how it was.

Perhaps.

Was that how it was?

We have no proof, so we can't pin it. All truth does is float, travel in these impossible, unpredictable zigs and zags, out to space and back. You can't find truth if you haven't captured it. You can't be sure, if you don't take a photograph and hold what happened in your hand.

PING!

JASPER: Biz?

BIZ: I'm sorry.

JASPER: You don't have to be. It's kind of funny, if you think about it. Don't you think?

BIZ: I guess?

JASPER: Like, neither of us actually hating each other? Neither of us talking. It could be a film. Two young teens: he from the wrong side of the tracks, she driving to the beach in her Porsche. He with his perfect hair and she . . . also having hair. They connect! But then! Alas! A misunderstanding! It can't possibly untangle! But then something happens! A climactic event! And, voilà. Resolution.

BIZ: Haha. A for effort.

JASPER: Thank you very much.

BIZ: Come to think of it, I could do with a Porsche.

JASPER: Can't you just see it, Biz? We could be a story.

BIZ: (Ah, Jasper. Couldn't we just?)

FOUR DAYS AFTER SYLVIA'S PARTY, I STAND ON THE BRIDGE that goes around the cliff up north. The bridge is like a snake— it ribbons around the sheer rock and swoops out over the sea.

The bridge opened ten years ago. Rocks used to fall on the old cliff road, so all the cranky drivers wrote to Council and said, "We would rather not be pulverized to death!" and Council listened and built the bridge. This is what is known as teamwork.

They really went above and beyond with this bridge. It's basically gorgeous.

I've come here with the dog and Mum and the twins. The twins love scootering over the sweeping bends, feeling like they're flying. Bump loves to try and keep up with them. Mum loves to walk here; she says it's like being at the edge of the world. Once, after a few wines, she told me she liked to lean against the railing and listen to the sea sing. And I said, "The sea sings to you, Mum?" and smiled, and she nudged me with her shoulder and said, "Let me have a little poetry, Biz," and we laughed.

The afternoon is big and blue, the waves sparkly. The twins have raced ahead on their scooters. Mum and the dog have speed-walked after the twins while I've stopped to stand at the curve that sits farthest over the sea.

The cliff rises up behind me. The sea beats underneath. I look out and all there is is ocean and sky.

Mum's right—it's exactly like the edge of the world.

I pull out Sylvia's Polaroid camera, and take a photo—my first.

Out from the camera, making a little *zip* sound, shunts the square. I flap the photo, and in time I peel the paper off to see what's inside.

Here is the bridge. Here is the railing, here are the tips of my feet tucked under the railing, and here is the sea below, churning white and fluorescent blue.

Your mum stood here, says the bridge. *Right at this spot.*

What's that? What?

Words rise out of the square, rustlerustling.

Seriously? I stare down at the photo.

She was alone, the bridge says. *It was raining. She was crying. She stood here for a long time. It was cold. She walked over me. And then she left.*

I gape at the photo, at the camera in my hands.

She comes here a lot, Biz. Didn't you know?

Yes. No. Shit.

I didn't know Mum came here to cry. I thought she came to listen to the sea sing.

I see a lot of unhappy people, the bridge continues. *I see sad-happy people walking and stopping, walking and stopping. Are you happy or sad, Biz?*

Am I? I don't know what to tell it.

Mum was unhappy here and that makes my heart hurt. I can picture the gray of her, the lowering sky of her. I feel the ache of her, all the way up through my feet. And of course Mum cries here, because when does she get to otherwise? She's always trying to be Glass-Half-Full everywhere else.

And that makes me sad.

But then a photograph is talking to me after all these weeks and that's wonderful, isn't it? Oh my God, yes. It feels like zinging and the edge of delight and holy shit, maybe I've got stories again? And that has to mean something like happiness.

And a bridge is asking me how I'm feeling . . .

so that's updown and basically crazy, right?

Absolutely.

So I'm happy/sad/updown/crazy as always, and every other feeling there is, if ever I'm anything at all because I'm mostly blank, mostly rubbed out actually, which is what I tell the bridge, and it says,

Well, okay.

I take a bunch of photos then: of the cliff beside the bridge, a silver convertible going over the bridge, two women walking past holding hands, and the clouds above the bridge.

I flap them all to life—

and words crash in.

I have been here for millennia!

He hasn't told his wife yet about us; will he ever tell his wife?

I love her, I love her, I love her.

I don't know if I love her anymore; let's hold hands until the silence fills somehow.

We fill we empty we scud we race we fill we empty here we are!
I will fall. When will I fall? I will crumble into the sea.
Fast! Fast over fast over fast fast fast!
Are you happy or sad, Biz? We can't tell!
Oh my God. So much noise.

The moral of this tale is: Be careful what you wish for. I shove the photos into my backpack. The voices keep yelling. It's like they're actually wrestling inside the bag.

I look down the wide bridge path, and I can see the twins' neon helmets like tiny UFOs streaking towards me. I see the dark dot of Mum's hair tracking through space. I need them here, now. I need their rumpled laughter and Mum's face after a walk: open, bright.

I walk towards them, and—

Isn't it lovely that we're back?! muffle-shout the photos.

Stay and chat, Biz!

We have so much to tell you!

Biz! Hey! Stop! Hey! Hey!

I walk fast, faster, and here's Mum and the twins and Bump—four flying bodies—and Billie stops her scooter and says, "I win!" and Dart stops beside her and says, "You started before me!" then Billie says, "No, I didn't!" and Dart says, "Yes you did!" and Mum laugh-shushes them and Bump barks and thank God, I fall into their light.

SATURDAY, 12:54 A.M.

PING!

JASPER: Hey.

BIZ: Hey.

JASPER: What are you doing?

BIZ: I'm drawing a possum.

(It's true. Billie got an assignment to draw a native Australian animal. She had a meltdown about it at dinner. I said, "It's not that hard!" and she said, "Bet you can't do it," and I said, "Bet I can." So here I am. It looks like a potato.)

JASPER: For real?

BIZ: It's not very good. (I send him a photo from my phone.)

JASPER: That's really bad.

BIZ: I'm not born for art.

JASPER: Me neither.

BIZ: A shame. One of us could have been someone.

JASPER: So true.

BIZ: What are you born for, then?

JASPER: Not dance. Or cabbage. Or social media.

BIZ: All excellent decisions. *Smiley face*.

JASPER: I know!

BIZ: But hang on—you're here. Online. I found you.

JASPER: The relatives require Facebook. Big family. But that's it.

BIZ: So you're invisible. A covert operative.

JASPER: Exactly.

BIZ: Bummer—I totally pictured you doing a Swan Lake tribute, and posting it on YouTube.

JASPER: It will never happen.

BIZ: Haha. *Laughing face*.

JASPER: Actually, I am a little bit born for machines.

BIZ: Machines . . . Like Transformers? *Smiley face*.

JASPER: Haha. Bikes. Cars. Anything really. I like figuring them out. I'm thinking about industrial engineering for uni. Though maths really stresses me out. What about you?

BIZ: I don't know. Doubt I'll be going to university. No HSC.

JASPER: I'm doing distance ed. It's really boring. Aren't you doing it?

BIZ: No. I'm a proper dropout.

JASPER: Ah. So, petty crime and reality TV in your future, then. *Smiley face*.

BIZ: Most likely. Or maybe I'll sail around the world. *Yacht emoji*. *Water drop emoji*.

JASPER: That doesn't sound so bad.

BIZ: True.

JASPER: Lots of time to fish. *Fish emoji*.

BIZ: Or not. *Leaf emoji*.

JASPER: Oh, yeah.

BIZ: Sometimes I think it would be good to go somewhere new . . . and not have anyone know me.

JASPER: Yeah. I go for rides on my bike, and sometimes I think, What if I just didn't stop?

BIZ: Yeah.

(Sometimes I think, *What if I leave my body one day and keep going? What if I let go of the earth and nothing brings me back? If I left, would I find Dad?*)

JASPER: I could take you on the bike sometime. If you like.

BIZ: (Or . . . I could stay.) That would be fun.

JASPER: *Smiley face.*

BIZ: Sylvia would hate it, though.

JASPER: *Sad face.* I know.

BIZ: I guess we could tell her after the fact? That is, if we survive.

JASPER: That sounds like a good idea. And I intend for us to survive, just for the record.

BIZ: Right back at you. *Thumbs up emoji.*

(*Normal girl emoji. You've got this, Biz, emoji. All the emojis for intending to survive.*

Smiley face.)

STARE INTO A FIRE FOR MORE THAN A MINUTE AND IT'S clear we humans are ridiculous for thinking we're solid. We are built from nothing, collapsible in an instant. We're elements arranged, empty atoms ricocheting, atoms coming and going. We think we're these tangible things, but really we're just ghosts walking, dust waiting. Our insides are made of flickered, fickle light.

When I was seven, I threw my doll on the fire. I watched her face melt. I watched her hands liquefy. I watched inky smoke lift from her eyes.

By the time Mum rushed in, pulled me away from the fireplace, the doll was a blob on top of the logs. I'd watched her disappear and I understood. Two months before, we'd burned Dad into ash. And even though Mum said over and over that Dad was in heaven, I understood there was no magic space for Dad to go. I had seen how fire worked.

o ° o ° o

It is ten days after my birthday party and we've made a fire on the beach, Jasper and I. He rummaged through scrub on the hill and came down dragging a branch under each arm. I sifted through bushes and found kindling. We laid the bones of the fire down: scrumpled paper, twigs, snapped branches, bigger branches. A pyramid ready to burn.

Jasper stepped back and said, "Now, that's a fine structure."

"Award winning." I nodded.

"Prime real estate."

"Eleven out of ten."

We lit the paper; we watched the fire move, tentatively at first, then snapping, popping. It licked and crackled.

I thought, *I'll take a photograph*. And then I thought, *Maybe I won't. Maybe later. Maybe not.*

We came here by bike. My first motorbike ride. Jasper rode to my place to pick me up. The twins were asleep. In the living room, Mum looked Jasper up and down.

"So, where exactly are you two going?"

"The beach, Mum."

"Can't you walk there?"

"Jasper isn't supposed to walk that far."

Mum stared at Jasper. "But you can ride that motorbike? Is it safe?"

"I've been cleared by my physio. It's safe, Mrs. Grey."

Normally when she's called "Mrs.," Mum says, "Oh no, call me Laura," but this time she didn't.

"Which beach?"

Jasper and I looked at each other. Neither of us had said,

but I knew I didn't want to go to the beach near here, where everyone went and probably was, right that minute. I beamed this into his brain and he looked at me and sent his message back to my brain: *Message received.*

"North. Coalcliff," I said.

"That's over twenty minutes away. Why so far?"

"Mum. It's nice to go somewhere new."

I squeezed her then because she never used to ask where I was going, or which beach I was going to. And maybe she blamed herself for thinking everything was fine when it wasn't. I squeezed her to say, *Mum. Don't. It's okay.*

Mum gusted out a sigh and said, "Okay. But please be careful, Jasper. You must ride that bike like a saint."

Jasper nodded. "I'll ride it like Jesus himself, Mrs. Grey."

Mum's eyebrows went up. Her mouth twitched. "Glad we're on the same page."

We swooped north, first along the freeway—my arms gripping Jasper's waist, the moon rising over the freeway walls—then onto the curving road that snugged the sea. I turned my head and watched the ocean appear in snatches, moon-glinted and metallic.

The bike thrummed under me, Jasper's back pressed against my chest, houses and trees and fences moving past, solid, solid. And for a moment, everything felt real. Here I was. On a bike with this boy, passing a house with walls and people inside them. Passing a car before it turned onto the street, the driver going to the movies maybe, or a lover's house.

Here is a curve; lean into it, Biz. Feel.

We've crossed the cliff bridge, turned off the highway, parked the bike by all the sleeping houses, and picked our way down the overgrown path in the dark.

Now we are tucked between the hill and the creek that runs down to the sea.

The sand is chilly, so we've laid our riding jackets down for rugs. We watch the fire turn over and into itself.

Jasper has brought snacks. I've brought drinks. We sit on the sand and eat seaweed crackers and half-priced hummus. We drink hot chocolate from an old thermos I dug out of the defunct camping box in the garage.

The air is filled with the ruffle of waves, the tinkling of the creek, the fire crackling, and the two of us crunching and sipping.

We don't really talk; we watch the fire. Eat, drink, listen.

It's like being in a conch shell.

And I say that, "It's like being in a conch shell," before I run it through my brain to see if it makes sense enough to say.

Jasper turns to me. "I was just thinking that."

"Really?"

"No." He grins.

I want to explain, but the thoughts are too many; how do I describe how this feels?

"I was thinking it was nice," he says.

"I meant the sound. And the warmth," I say.

"I thought it was just . . . uncomplicated."

And that might be the first time anyone has seen time spent with me that way.

We stare into the fire. It makes shapes for us to see.

Part of me detaches. Steps into the fire. Lifts with the flames. Looks down at the boy and the girl. They seem happy.

Are you happy, Biz?

Am I?

Am I—who am I and *am* I, even?

All of us can be altered in a blink. Fire reduces you to nothing. Dad's body in an urn on the bookshelf. Water erodes rocks. Cliffs crumble. *You are not real, Biz—*

It's true. Perhaps I am actually the fire? Or the sea? Perhaps I am every leaping molecule.

The fire pops, showering sparks.

"Whoa!" says Jasper.

He reaches across my body instinctively.

A wave crashes.

And I flip back in—a slow somersault into my body.

My belly is warm. My mouth is full of sweet and salt. My skin is here, my body, my bones.

Take it for now; take it in, Biz. Hold it, this trembling, borrowed time.

IF I WAS STILL FRIENDS WITH GRACE, SHE'D ASK, "DID HE kiss you, Biz?"

"No," I would say back.

"What? He didn't even try?"

"It wasn't like that."

"What was it like, then?"

"Like a conch shell," I *wouldn't* say.

She'd say, "Do you like him?"

"Yeah, sure, I like him."

"I mean, do you *like* like him?"

"I don't know, Grace."

Grace would try to understand. Grace wouldn't understand. "How do you not know, Biz?" she'd say. "How hard is it to know?"

I'd have to try and explain. *Grace, all I know is, I want to sit beside Jasper in front of a fire.*

How do you put that feeling into words?

It's not like that, Grace.

What is it like, then?

I don't know. If I could pin the feeling down I'd tell you.

I write Grace an email.

"What would you say if I told you—"

I tell her about the fire. About ash and conch shells and the rearrangements that happen when you're putting the parts of yourself back together. About the feel of sitting on sand by a fire with someone, about sitting inside something good for a second and feeling that spread into and through you, filling in your lines.

I stare at the screen.

How many of these have I sent? Do I even want to count?

Will Grace read it? Will she ever write back?

I don't know. I don't know.

Where are you, Grace?

Grace?

Fuck.

I delete almost every word I've written.

I leave only:

"What would you say, if I told you—"

I press SEND and push Grace out into the echo of space.

IT'S TUESDAY MORNING AND WE'RE BY THE SEA AGAIN, Jasper and I.

Jasper has met me at the beach; I've brought Bump and the dog is snuffling the seaweed, checking for mermaids and crabs. The day is made of gray—clouds muscling over a brisk sky, the ocean all froth and spray, the wind making a mash of our hair. We're in our jackets, walking, leaning into the wind. I've asked Jasper a question—how come he's such a strong swimmer— and he's thinking about it, his face creased like a painter, like he's taking a moment before deciding how much green to add, how much blue.

Jasper says, "I used to swim, like, competitively. I did races. Got medals and things." He shrugs. "And I learned to surf when I was eight. My uncle taught me."

"You surf?"

"Not anymore." Jasper smiles. "It's no longer in my repertoire."

"Because of your leg?" I say.

"Yeah."

"Sorry."

"It's okay. I'm used to it. Maybe one day I'll go back out."

"Maybe you'll get really good."

"Maybe I'll turn pro."

"Exactly."

"Maybe after I do that rhythmic gymnastics thing," he says.

"Good to have goals."

"So true."

Jasper squints out at the ocean.

I squint at him.

Does Jasper miss the water? Does it pull at him? How badly does he miss it? Should I ask? Do I know him well enough? *What do you miss, Jasper? How much do you miss it and in what increments? How large are your lost puzzle pieces? Do you want to find them?*

I want to unpeel Jasper, suddenly. I want to take off his jacket and shirt, sneak a look under his skin, see the cogs and wires, the tick and beat of him.

The want comes quickly, then scuttles off. Do I want to see Jasper naked? No, that's not what I mean.

I mean, I mean—

It's too hard to catch; the thought flashes, the wind snatches it, it goes. We walk like quiet birds on the hard sand between the dunes and the sea.

And at the end of the beach, we climb up the dunes, and stand by the hunched trees. I let Bump off the leash—he goes to talk to the rabbits, or at least scare them shitless.

We don't talk—the sea rises, crashes, pushes up the shore. It's crawling up towards us, the tide turned high. The wind has gone feral. It rattles the sand under our feet. It flings the grass flat. Seagulls do loop-the-loops in the screaming sky. I watch the water, look out farther, farther, and if I look hard enough, maybe I'll see past the cargo ships sitting like wobbly chess pieces on the grand back of the ocean, past the islands teetering at the edge of the earth, across to rumpled mountains and cities and past the future and past the sun, all the way round the earth and back to us on the pummeled sand, the gulls wailing, the two of us standing side by side and not touching.

And suddenly Jasper's saying a poem.

He's what?

He's saying—

what?

He starts talking over the whoosh of wind, the roar of the surf and I can barely hear him so I lean forward and just like that, he's shouting it.

Buffalo Bill's
defunct!

he says and—

wind grabs, flings it and

Who used to ride a watersmooth-silver stallion!
And break onetwothreefourfive pigeonsjustlikethat!

Jasper's grinning, his arms raised, and—

Jesus
he was a handsome man!

Jasper's fully screaming and Bump's leaping off a dune edge,
and the wind's gone crazy—

and what i want to know is!

Jasper's face is wide open—

how do you like your blue-eyed boy
Mister Death?

Jasper's laughing. He knows poetry. And it's amazing.
His words soar over the wind and water,
out, farther,
higher, faster.
Of course Jasper knows poetry, this boy who won't write
essays in English class and wants to pull apart cars. *What did*
you expect, Biz, someone mappable? He's a mystery and not a
mystery, like the two sides of a coin or a heart or the sea.

Bump's thrilled; he jumps off the dunes, chasing each word
as it flies.

Later—after I clap and Jasper bows and says, "Thank you very
much," and we go to a café and drink hot chocolates,

and after I ask Jasper who the poet was and he says, "e.e.
cummings. A legend,"

and I ask why he knows poems and did he learn them specifically to shout them at the sea?

and he grins and says, "I had a lot of time in bed with a
busted leg. YouTube can get really boring,"

and after he asks me about my favorite book and I talk for *way* too long about Gatsby—

I walk home to my blue house with poetry inside me like a pulse, the dog trotting ahead, sand-clumped and damp, and think:

I could have taken a photo.

As we stood on the dunes, I could have pulled out Sylvia's Polaroid camera from my backpack and clicked. I could have peeled back the paper, and listened.

All I would have heard was laughter, both of us.

Updown, rambling, running like water.

I could have fallen asleep to that sound.

THE DAYS TURN SIMPLE. WALK THE DOG, WITH OR WITHOUT Jasper. Visit Sylvia, who says she hasn't found a good deal on an enlarger yet but is loving the digital photography class, which just started, and maybe I'll change my mind and still come, and how am I going; do I want another muffin?

Go home on the bus and watch the world flickflick past.

Take photos with the Polaroid camera, one at a time. Some of them shout, some of them don't.

Sit with the dog in the yard after sunset, rub his ears. Eat some kind of dinner. Listen to the twins talking, talking, talking. Tell Mum maybe I'll take the next digital photography class, and, yes, I've been using the camera, and I'm teaching myself with YouTube actually, and thanks so much, Mum, the camera is great.

Message Jasper at night.

It's turned into a routine: I brush my teeth, pull on my pajamas, get into bed, prop the computer up on a pillow on my lap.

Sometime after midnight, I send Jasper a message or a message comes in.

So far, I've told Jasper almost everything that happened between seeing him in the waves and seeing him again at Sylvia's party.

Jasper has told me about everything that happened since the night in the waves, how he left school for surgery a week before my night in the dunes, how he heard—and how, well he didn't know me then, so he didn't text—

I have said, "That's okay," more than once.

Jasper has told me about his legs. About breaking his legs against a tree when he was eleven, when his dad lost control of their car.

JASPER: He overtook this guy on a total blind turn. He honked and screamed as we passed and then this van came towards us and Dad swerved, and bam.

BIZ: Whoa.

JASPER: Dad and I got really banged up, but Conor, my brother, he was okay, just a sprained wrist. I was mashed. I've had heaps of operations. Mum and Dad split up after the accident. We moved here to be closer to Gran. Dad's still in Canberra. We don't talk much.

BIZ: Wow.

JASPER: Yeah.

BIZ: I'm so sorry, Jasper.

JASPER: It's okay.

JASPER (a moment later): It's okay and it's not, you know? Like, I'm alive. And I've read tons of books now, so I'm probably incredibly intelligent. *Smiley face.* But sometimes it's shitty, not being able to do everything I want. And getting looked at. Everyone looks, even when they're trying not to look. It's always like, "What's up with that guy's leg? What's the deal with that guy?"

BIZ: Yeah. (*That's right, Biz. . .The exact thing you thought.*)

JASPER: I bet you did it when you first saw me.

BIZ: (*Um?*)

JASPER: Right?

BIZ: Sorry.

JASPER: It's okay. You probably came up with a theory or two.

BIZ: Yeah . . .

JASPER: And? Was it skydiving? Tripping on a shoelace? *Smiley face.*

BIZ: Well . . . okay. First option: tractor tragedy. Second option: you hooning your stolen motorbike into a defenseless grandma.

JASPER: Hahaha! Fantastic. *Crying laughing emoji.*

BIZ: I'm sorry, Jasper.

JASPER: It's all right. Really.

Is it, though? I think of Jasper tilting through the school corridors, carrying his history. All those glances, the unspoken everythings. I think of all of us, passing each other like turtles, heaving our pasts on our backs.

I have told Jasper about Dad being dead.

And Jasper has said, simply: "I'm so sorry, Biz."

I haven't tried to say, "It's okay."

I haven't told Jasper how Dad died.

I haven't told him about the years with Dad—Dad by the bed, by the window, by the sea.

I am not ready. When I imagine telling Jasper everything, I feel myself sliding out of myself.

(*I'm a normal girl, Jasper! Really. Look at me, messaging and walking on beaches and pretending not to miss my dad so much I burn.*)

I haven't told Jasper about Dad turning hazy and disappearing. Or about floating out of my body, or the blankness that slides in.

I haven't said how slippery things can seem.

I have sent Jasper some pictures of my darkroom photos, seeing as he has pestered me and pestered me: "You sent me a message specifically, Biz! Don't forget, Biz, your message—that first message you sent. *Smiley face, smiley face, smiley face.*"

(I have tried, many times, to forget that message. I have tried not to die of embarrassment every time Jasper mentions the first message I sent.)

Jasper has liked the photos, thumbs-upped and gold-starred them.

"They're brilliant!" he's said. He's printed out the one of Sylvia and put it on his wall. I haven't asked Jasper if it talks.

I've also told Jasper about my medication and about seeing Bridgit. I have said something about brains and puzzle pieces and he's said, "Puzzles can take ages. At least, the good ones do."

"True," I've said.

Smiley face.

Jasper has told me how much he likes it here.

JASPER: I know our nation's capital is the center of all civilization, Biz, but Canberra has a serious lack of ocean.

BIZ: And a very serious case of the terribly colds.

I told Jasper then about our class excursion there last winter. We traveled three hours south to see politicians bicker like seagulls at Parliament House, and freeze our bums off outside the War Memorial.

JASPER: Just imagine. I was there, somewhere in the frozen tundra . . . Probably on my way to steal that motorbike.

BIZ: Maybe we passed you on the bus, just before you ran over that poor old lady.

JASPER: If only you'd known! You could have leaped off the bus and said, "Stop! Don't do it, Jasper! Rethink everything!"

BIZ: If only I had!

JASPER: I'd be a new man!

I have told Jasper all the towns I've lived in, and Jasper has told me his. Ratio of my towns to Jasper's—10 : 1.

Jasper has said, "Why all the moving?"

"A rolling stone gathers no moss," I've replied.

And he's said, "Ah, that explains why you've literally got no moss on you. Except for that tuft in the back. You might need to get that seen to."

I have told Jasper that Mum thinks I'm better.

And Jasper has asked:

"Do you feel better?"

And I've said, "Sometimes."

Which is possibly, almost, don't-look-too-closely-or-it-might-go-away, true.

"IS JASPER YOUR BOYFRIEND, BIZ?" BILLIE ASKS.

The twins and I are in the living room, eating spaghetti and peas. Mum's out dancing. We're watching a singing show on TV. Dart fed Bump something he shouldn't, so the dog's farting beside the couch. It's another Wednesday night.

I gawp at Billie, a forkful of food halfway to my mouth. *Sorry?* Dart turns to me and grins.

"Yeah, is he, Biz?" he says.

"Yeah! Has he kissed you?" says Billie, bouncing in her seat.

"Yeah!" says Dart. "Has he?"

Jasper came over for dinner last Sunday. He asked me over to his place first but I couldn't say yes—the thoughts wouldn't let me. *His mum will measure you with her eyes, Biz. What has she heard? And his brother Conor—what does he know? What will they think?* So I said, "Come over to mine," even though I knew it would be a serious step down, food-wise, and Jasper would have to eat something gray, something boiled, something green.

Jasper was very polite. He ate the whole dinner without gagging. Mum drank three wines and said to call her Laura. The twins were totally quiet—no one had been here since Grace, so this was a huge deal. Their eyes bugged out. They didn't talk over each other. They didn't punch each other under the table.

But now they're two beans bouncing on a couch, wanting to know all about my love life. Fantastic.

I stare at Billie. "He's not my boyfriend, and no, he hasn't," I tell them. "And anyway, it's none of your business."

"Do you love him, Biz?" Dart says. And he wraps his arms around himself and starts making kissing sounds into the air.

Jesus. I turn up the volume on the TV. The person on the singing show has his eyes closed. He's so moved by his own voice he sways. Everyone in the audience loves this song. Billie has heard it on the radio—she starts to sing along.

Dart thumps her. "That's not how it goes, silly."

"Does too!"

"Does not!"

The dog farts again. It stinks.

"Ew! Yuck!" says Billie.

She runs out of the room. Comes back a second later with a towel wrapped around her face, with only a tiny gap left open for her eyes.

Dart laughs, three high, bright notes. He runs out of the room. Comes back with a towel for me and him. We watch the rest of the show with towels around our heads, which is excellent, because the twins can't ask me questions. I wouldn't have the answers for them if I tried.

SATURDAY 12:53 A.M.

PING!

JASPER: Want to go for a ride next week?

BIZ: Where to?

JASPER: South.

BIZ: Okay.

1:15 a.m.

PING!

JASPER: I forgot to say, you should bring your swimmers, if you want.

BIZ: (Are we going in the sea? Aren't you worried about the water because of that time? Don't we already have too much water inside us? Aren't we all sinking?)

Okay. Sure.

JASPER: Smiley face emoji. Emoji of a wave.

o ° o ° o

We head off on Tuesday morning; it's cloudless, warm, a sunshine day. Mum has fussed over me since breakfast—"Make sure you hold on! Make sure he doesn't speed! Make sure you tell him if he's going too fast!"—so when Jasper arrives at 8:30, she's worn out. She sees me off from the front veranda as the twins bounce beside her, saying, "Why can't we go on a motorbike too, Mum? Mum?"

"Bye!" I call from the back of the bike.

Mum says, "I love you!"

The twins tug at her hands and say, "Why can't we go on a bike, Mum? Mum? Mum?"

Mum mouths at me: "Help."

Jasper kicks the bike into being. The twins, wild with want, run alongside us all the way to the end of the street. They slump into each other's arms when we turn. If they were wolves, they'd sit on their haunches and howl.

We ride the road south and it unzips the escarpment from the sea. We pass small towns: houses, shops, trees, kids on pushbikes, people walking into and out of clothes shops and bakeries. We go over gray-blue rivers, over kayaks, boys with fishing poles, a heron on a rail. We go through farmland and bushland. We go through a bigger town: warehouses and supermarkets and fast food. We go on the wide, wide freeway with semi-trailers stampeding past and we sit with our little bums on our little seat, perilous. I squeeze Jasper's sides and he turns his head a little, as if to say, *It's okay, Biz. We're safe.*

We ease left, onto a thin road that winds past grizzled gums and messy underscrub, past a wire-and-post fence with stuffed animals tied to it. I point them out to Jasper. He nods and gives me a thumbs-up, like he's seen them before. Which he must have, because he's bringing me here, to someplace that maybe means something to him. And maybe he's had someone else on a bike pointing out the animals, or maybe he's pointed the animals out to them. Either way, the stuffed toys are only new to me. When we leave them behind, I feel a little pull, like they're mine, like I tied them to the fence so someone could see them and maybe be a little bit charmed.

We get to a town, and it's tiny. We pass beach cottages in cream, yellow, and teal green; we pass the entrance to a caravan park, a shop tucked in behind some trees, and more houses in cream, blue, green, cream. Jasper turns left, drives a minute or two, and slips into a car park with a toilet block and a single roof-racked car. We are surrounded by trees again. I can feel the ocean nearby; it hums.

Jasper flicks off the engine. He pulls off his helmet and grins like a maniac, like nothing in the world is wrong, like life is actually one amazing thing after another. It makes my insides thunk.

"We're here!" he says.

"Where?" I say, pulling off my helmet.

"Cunjurong Point," he says.

He unclips the pannier at the back of the bike. "Come on," he says, and even though I have to pee, even though I've needed to go for ages, I follow him, moth to sun.

The sand squeaks as we walk down the narrow path between the gums and out to the beach. The sea opens like a hand.

It's turquoise, clear, a gift.

I make a sound, I can't help it. It's beautiful.

"It's great, isn't it?" says Jasper, and he gestures with his arm to take it in and offer it at the same time—the blue out to the horizon, the white sand, the island just off shore, so close you might bite it.

I don't know what to say. I feel all the beauty and Jasper's joy start to pull my feet off the ground. But I don't want to float today. I want to be here. I lean down and take my shoes and socks off, just to get my toes into something, substance to substance, something real pressing against something real.

The sand feels like a touch. It feels like my mother's hand on my skin, cool against warm. It feels like talking at night. It feels like stories and it feels like being seen.

I shuck off my jacket. I drop it to the sand. I unzip my pants and Jasper's eyes widen, because suddenly, I guess I'm stripping.

Off go my pants. Off goes my shirt. In thirty seconds, I'm down to my undies and bra, and it feels amazing. I want sun on skin and sand and water. I want to *feel*. Now.

And Jasper's pulling off his shoes and socks and jacket and shirt and jeans too, neither of us speaking, and he peels off his clothes until the two of us are standing on the squeak of sand in our underwear, and we both start to laugh.

I run to the water, Jasper following as fast as his mending legs can take him. I run in, legs pumping, turn for Jasper to catch up, and when he does and when we reach the see-through curl of the first big wave, we both dive—under water, into water, becoming water.

And the water is laughing; the water is saying, "Hey! You! Here!" and it's not slapping me or turning me inside out. I feel every speck of it on my arms and legs and belly, my face, my mouth, open, drinking.

We burst up from the water like those videos of whales breaching. We lift up from the sea and spin, sun glinting off our skin.

AFTERWARDS, DO WE CARE THAT WE'RE NEARLY NAKED? No—I don't know why, but we're not embarrassed. We don't laugh awkwardly. We don't cover our bodies. We don't even have bodies; we're just two people who needed the sea. Afterwards, we walk up to the pannier, pull out our towels, and dry off like we planned to be nearly naked all along. I pull on some shorts and my shirt, and he pulls on shorts and his shirt, and we are happy—if you took a photograph of us, you'd see it is true—and maybe that's a miracle for the both of us.

I pull out Sylvia's Polaroid camera.

"Smile!" I say.

I take a selfie of us, two people making silly faces with the sea at our backs, thumbs up, tongues sticking out, fine sand dusting our chins and cheeks. We're both grinning. Have we said more than two words in the last half hour? No, I don't think we know words.

The picture zips out of the camera. I flap it into life.

Peel the paper back.

Here's Jasper. Here's me.

Here's us, laughing. You can hear us; you can hear the updown sound of us.

Here we are! Here we are!

And in the distance, there's Dad in the water near the island. On his board, sitting on a rising swell, waiting for a wave.

DAD SAYS:

It's a perfect day, the best day! Great left break, fantastic two-meter swell, great long runs! Don't ever want to leave, but I do, because Laura's waiting in the caravan park and that woman does me in. Five years together and still, she's all I think about.

Her belly, the round of her, the sweetness. I can't believe we made someone; I can't believe I'm going to be a dad! It's like I'm God. We're God.

Here's a wave—maybe I'll take it in, go see Laura, maybe we'll walk, maybe watch the sunset. Ah, sunsets! Who made all those colors? I'm a color, she's a color, we've made a color. I can't believe it, the luck; blessed, I guess, is what I am.

BIZ: Dad? (I message silently into the Dad-shaped whisper on the water.)

DAD: *Yeah, Biz?* (Dad's voice in my ear, close but faint.)

BIZ: You were happy here?

DAD: *Oh, mate. Blissful.*
BIZ: Dad?
DAD: *Yeah?*
BIZ: Where are you?
DAD: *On a wave, sweetheart. Not far.*
BIZ: So you're close?
DAD: *Yeah, Biz.*

Dad.

Ohmygod.

So this is how I'll find you.

III

III

WHEN JASPER AND I GET HOME FROM CUNJURONG POINT, it's after dark.

Mum grabs me and hugs me and I can tell she's happy I'm off the bike.

"Was the ride okay, Biz?"

"Yeah, Mum, it was good."

"Was Jasper a good driver?"

"Very safe, Mum."

"Did you tell him not to speed?"

"I didn't have to, Mum."

We go over the bike ride in detail. The twins drape themselves over me like squid and ask, "How fast did you go?"

And, "Did you see other motorbikes?"

And, "Did you fall off?"

And, "Did Jasper do a wheelie?"

Mum shoos them off to bed. I give them kisses and promise to let them know immediately if Jasper ever does a wheelie. Then I sit with Mum and tell her about the rest of the day.

Everything except seeing Dad surfing seventeen years ago and daydreaming about Mum and babies and sunsets.

Afterwards, she says, "It sounds wonderful, Biz."

"Have you ever been there?" I ask, even though I know the answer.

"Actually, yes! What are the chances?" Mum gets this happy/sad smile on her face. "Three months before you were born—we went on a trip south. Your dad took a lot of photos, mostly of my belly! They're in . . . the yellow album, maybe?" Mum drifts off for a second, then shakes her head. "Anyway, he surfed almost all day. I could hardly get him out of the water! I read so many books. It was lovely."

I squeeze her arm.

She squeezes back.

Things I don't tell her:

I know you went, Mum, because I saw him on the water, on his board.

I took a photo of him, and he talked about you.

I know he loved you more than he loved the water, Mum.

When I meet with Bridgit, I don't tell her about seeing Dad, or my epiphany about how I will find him.

When I meet with her, I just say how happy I was by the sea and she says, "Elizabeth! That's wonderful!"

I say, "Yeah."

I tell her about swimming with Jasper and how comfortable we were, like two merpeople moving in the water side by side, like two peas in a pod, two kindred spirits who'd found each other.

I even use those words: *kindred spirits* and *peas in a pod*, which is a winning combination. Bridgit's spellbound.

She doesn't ask, "Did Jasper kiss you? Did you kiss him?" She's a professional—not sniffing into my personal life like the twins do and Grace does, like she used to, like she always did.

Jasper and I didn't kiss; neither of us leaned in towards the other. We walked up the road to the café and ate bread rolls and fries and orange juice. "My wonderful vegan options," I said to Jasper, and he laughed and didn't get some big greasy burger. And then we wandered around the beach, just breathing it in. He pointed out where he learned to surf when he was eight, before his legs got mashed into a tree and before he stopped talking to his dad.

"Last time I was here," he said, "I'd just had my third operation. Mum and Conor helped me onto the sand, with my crutches and everything. My legs were all wobbly like I was a baby. It was pretty embarrassing because, you know, I was almost twelve.

"But the first time I came here"—Jasper gestured—"totally different. I was eight. Best day ever. It was our big family gathering and Dad wasn't there 'cause he had to work, and Mum was all relaxed and laughing and I remember thinking, *When did she last?*

"Uncle John took me out on his board, just off the beach where the waves were wrinkles. After a bit I could stand up, only for a second or two, but jeez it was great, Biz. It felt like flying, like I was a superhero."

We walked and I listened to Jasper talk. The island turned new colors in the distance. The sand squeaked under our feet.

And then low tide came and a stretch of land opened up between the island and us.

"Come on," said Jasper, and we went past the warnings about rips and the possibility of death and walked between the two waters like Moses. We scrambled around the island, picking up seashells and chucking them into the blue.

I pulled out the Polaroid camera and snapped photo after photo. In one, Dad wasn't there, only the rumble of the rocks and the squawk of seagulls, and in another, Dad was surfing off the side of the island, easing down a churning wall of water, the waves crashing and cackling.

Best day ever! said Dad, his voice a bright thrill in my ear.

I tell Bridgit that Jasper and I rode home as dusk rose and made the light purple and it felt like floating but also not like floating, because between my arms was Jasper's body, solid, and under me was the bike, and the white lines on the road were like dashes, pulling us forward.

I didn't tell Bridgit that, as we flew, I saw how I'd get Dad back.

I'd go to all the places he was happy.

I'd take photos and pin him to paper.

I'd put him together, piece by piece, and return him to me.

When Jasper dropped me home, I stood on my driveway and said, "Want to go on a road trip?"

"Yeah."

"Like, a long one? Like more than one?"

And he said, "Yep," and didn't ask why. He just looked at me and I looked at him, and then he hugged me for the first time.

° ° ° °

I tell Bridgit all the brightest bits of the day, none of the secrets. I give her the highlight reel, I guess, the one that has me better, so much better she can feel she's done her job well—the best of all the psychologists in the world.

At the end of our session, Bridgit says, "Do you want to meet again in two weeks? Or do you want to leave it open, just make an appointment when you need one?" And in this way she says, "Gold star, Elizabeth! You win—you're well."

She isn't wrong. I totally am.

I am on the hunt for Dad. You can't do that if you're sick.

WE DECIDE TO GO TO SYDNEY FIRST.

The morning we leave, Mum says "Be careful" so many times, she sounds like a glitch in the system, a glitch made of fear and fret.

"I will be, Laura," says Jasper. "I've been riding motorbikes since I was seven."

"But you've only been riding with Biz since last month," says Mum, and I can see she regrets the whole "Call me Laura" thing. Her arms cross and her face sets. I know that look.

Just before she changes her mind and tells me not to go, I say, "He's a good rider, Mum. He's done classes."

"A lot of classes," says Jasper. "My mum wouldn't let me ride if I hadn't."

The twins are practically foaming, jumping off the couch, trying to get Jasper to notice them. He gives them a grin and it's like Jesus has come down the chimney with a sack of presents. Billie and Dart flop over each other and make faces and then Dart pinches Billie and Billie shoves Dart, and Mum has to step in.

"Fine, go. Have a good time," says Mum, but you can tell it isn't fine and she doesn't want us to leave. She'd rather I stay in my bubble. Maybe. Certainly not ride a death machine on two freeways in one week.

I don't want Mum to worry, but I want to go more than I don't want her to worry, which makes the ratio of my want to her worry approximately 5,000 : 1.

Jasper and I ride the bike north up the Pass. We rise and rise—the sea a plate of blue in the distance and the houses like dots. We buzz along the freeway through the Royal National Park, and Jasper keeps calm when we're in front of a semi-trailer and behind a semi-trailer. I try to shut my mind off and not think about being hit by a semi or what it would be like after being hit by a semi, or what it would be like to be found after being hit, or whether there'd be enough of me left to donate my organs, or what the ratio would be between me being missed and me being forgotten.

I turn my head. I watch the bush flick past. I think of being a tree and I think of roots. I think of papery bark. I think of leaves. I think of being a leaf and how uncomplicated that would be.

And then we're in the outskirts of the city, moving through traffic, and Jasper's stopping and starting and stopping and starting. At one point, a car changes lanes without warning. Jasper has to brake suddenly and I slam hard into his back.

Jasper shakes his head, and I can hear him swearing through his helmet.

It's fraught, that's what this is. Why did we ride? Why didn't we take public transport just like Mum suggested—*think of the environment, Biz*—it doesn't matter how long it takes, this is crazy. I wrap my arms tightly around Jasper and at some point he stops at a light, flips up the front of his helmet, and says, "Biz, I can't breathe."

"Sorry," I say, but my helmet doesn't flip up, so Jasper probably can't hear me.

The light goes green and we weave through the churn and grind of trucks, utes, cars, semis, other motorbikes—the riders glance at us—they know we're infants about to be squished by something much, much bigger.

I'll probably die today, I think, and then I think, *Well, I'll die* one *day,* and my chest pinches and sets. So then I have to concentrate hard on the taxi beside us, and I name everyone inside: Malcom, the driver, who lives alone in a grotty studio with a cocker spaniel. Simone in the back seat, hair silver white and lacquered, sitting next to her assistant, June, who's looking at her phone; she just got a text from her lover who wants to go out for sushi tonight, which makes June feel less insecure about her small breasts and the gap in her front teeth.

Then I name the people inside the gray car on my left, the green car behind the taxi, and the white van behind the green car. We move forward, and the city turns into something manageable—a breathing, electric pulse I can hold in my hand.

We're at Mum and Dad's old flat by midday.

THE SUN GRINDS ONTO THE TAR; THE BUILDING SQUATS ON the cliff, and the sea sharpens its blue against the rocks.

The building is like the pictures I've seen in the album at home and not like the pictures in the album at home. When I was born, the flats were a red-brick block. Now the whole building is polished gray, rendered. It looks like it's dressed up for a party.

Our flat was the corner one, right next to the building entrance, with these big, sky-grabbing windows. Mum and Dad got the place two years before I was born—their first, "Hey, it's just the two of us, and wow, this place doesn't have mold and isn't falling down or leaking or beside a highway!" home. They were thrilled.

Mum told me about the flat when I was thirteen. "We couldn't believe we got the place, Biz. Dad shaved for the interview. I put on lipstick! We both bought new clothes. Dad looked great. That man sure knew how to wear a suit—"

Then Mum got that look on her face, the one she always

gets whenever she walks too far into a memory of Dad—sort of sad, sort of hopelessly in love, sort of happy, sort of lost. I patted her hand. I made her tea. At some point, she pulled down the photo album of my first year and opened it.

In one photo, I'm on Mum's lap; she's on a chair in the living room of the flat, smiling up at the camera. I've got my mouth open—yawning or crying, it's hard to tell.

In another photo, Dad stands by the front windows, looking out. He is a sideways silhouette, and I'm in his arms. You can't see Dad's face or mine, just the shape of us against the light.

In another photo, we're all outside the flat, and someone has taken a picture of us as a family. The red bricks glare in the background and the hot pavement bakes under Mum's and Dad's feet. In this photo I am definitely crying. Dad's face looks like someone poked it with pins.

"Hey, this place is kind of amazing," says Jasper, and I'm back. The sea sprawls, silver-blue, below the cliff. The view goes all the way to the edge of the earth.

"Yeah," I say. "I don't remember it."

"I can't believe they ever left."

"They were itchy," I said.

"Your parents?"

"My parents' feet," I say.

Jasper laughs.

I semi-smile. But I'm distracted. I want to take a photo and find Dad.

I pull out the camera and take a picture of the flat—the corner windows, where Dad stood with me, seventeen years ago.

I flap it. Peel off the paper.

And there he is! Dad!

Pressing his hands to the glass. Staring out at the sea. Eyes glazed, unfocused.

Dad?

Dad?

I'm not getting through to him. He's not moving, not seeing, not holding—

Worst of all, he's silent.

Dad?

I walk up the ramp towards the entrance. I stand under the windows and try to press my hand to the spot where, in the Polaroid, Dad is pressing his. But the ramp is too low. The flat is too high. The spot is too far and I can't reach.

Dad?

"Do you want to go inside?"

I look at Jasper.

He thinks I want in. He's here on the ramp, alternating between trying to peer into the flat and glancing at me.

Jasper says, "Do you want to try and visit? Maybe someone's home? Want to knock on the door?"

I say, "No. That would be weird."

"People do it all the time."

"It's okay," I say, "I don't want to." I don't know what I'd find in there. Would I just end up with square after square of silent Dad? I'm not ready for what that might feel like.

I go back down the ramp. Jasper follows and we walk to the clifftop.

We stand on the path, five or so steps away from the sea. I could run and jump and in a second, I'd be in all that water.

And the sea would say, "What took you so long, Biz?"

Jasper says, "Now this is an excellent view. Ten out of ten." He touches my arm. "Can't believe your mum and dad got to live here, Biz."

I nod.

"Can't believe you got to look at this view from just out of the womb."

I step back into the cul-de-sac, and take a photograph of Jasper, the path, the edge, the water.

I flap the photo. Peel off the paper. There's Jasper, his hand shielding his eyes, squint-smiling—there's the path, edge, water—and there, beside Jasper, is a smudge. It's Dad. He's moving, running away from the flat, down towards the tiny cove at the base of the cliff.

DAD: *She's due in a week, holy shit, I'm going to be a father!*

Dad's voice is like static. I have to bend forward to hear him, my nose nearly touching the picture.

DAD: *Quick run! And then I'll go to work—or should I stay? Just in case? Maybe—I'll ask Laura. Should I even go for a run? Yeah, I should. A quick run!*

Dad's a blur. It's like when he disappeared months ago, turning to fog. He's running out of my sight; there's happiness here, but it was just before I was born—

Jasper gives up on me talking. "I'll head down to the beach, Biz, while you reminisce. Okay? Okay." He wanders down the path, headed for the cove in the curve below the cliff. He walks in the same direction as running Dad, shadow Dad, Dad-of-the-past, Biz-less Dad.

You came out and they nearly dropped you, says Dad from the other photo in my hand. The one at the window, Dad's palms on the glass.

I lift the photo, look at him while he stares at the sea.

BIZ: No, they didn't, Dad.

DAD: *I was that scared. You could have died.*

BIZ: But they didn't. I'm alive. I'm here.

DAD: *Your body was so tiny, Biz. You were so small and slippery, and there was so much blood—*

I can hear his rising panic, then the wind catches it. Dad's voice turns into a fading whistle and goes out.

Dad?

. . .

. . .

I can feel the quick prick of tears behind my eyes. A white tightness in my throat.

What did I expect?

This isn't where I'll find him.

It's too close to me.

I'll have to get as far from myself as possible, and then he'll be here. And then I'll fix the breaks. I'll show him; I'll glue his pieces. It will be okay.

Will it be okay?

The ocean rolls over itself. Wind spins around my legs, gusts my face. I can see Jasper in the cove through some trees. He's a dot, waiting.

I wander down the path. I can hear magpies *oodling* in a tree. Slats of sun slide over me. I can feel the cracked cement where Dad ran and some of my steps must be touching the same places as his feet—the laws of probability say so. I'm alone; I'm not alone; my feet walk over the ghosts of Dad's footprints. I am a ghost of the future walking over the ghosts of the past. I step on each crack and the cracks open wide, wider—

I step on sand. It scrunches. I'm at the cove.

And Jasper's at the water's edge, skipping stones.

"I've made a pile for you, Biz." He gestures to a stack of flat rocks, ready.

"Thanks," I say. He hands me a smooth rock. Round. Warm.

We skim stones over the green water. We hear the smack of waves against moored boats and Jasper says, "Shall we steal a sailboat, Biz?"

"Sure," I say. Why not? Let's sail to where Dad was happy on every surf break before I existed.

We wander over to an upside-down rowboat. It's sitting on the beach, just asking to be taken out to one of those hooded sailboats in the bay.

But when we flip it over, there are no oars. So I guess we won't find Dad by sea today.

WHEN WE GET BACK FROM SYDNEY, I SEND AN EMAIL TO
Grace.

I say, "Grace. Guess what: I think I've found a way to get my
dad back."

She doesn't reply.

You'd think that was a pretty intriguing message. You'd
think she'd write, "Holy shit, Biz? Your dead dad? You're going
to get him back? How? How in God's name?"

But no, Grace is stubborn. Or she's comatose. Or she's
decided I never existed.

I write again the next day. I say, "Grace, I'm going to go to
Dad's old places to find him—Temora and Hobart and Broome
and Maleny and if I think of other places I'll go there next. He
grew up in Temora, did you know? It's totally near Wagga. So I
can come and see you, Grace. In person. In the flesh. Two mus-
keteers, back together!"

She doesn't write back.

I write again: "Grace? Please."

Nothing. God. Why do I keep trying?

WHEN I TELL MUM WE'RE GOING TO RIDE JASPER'S BIKE TO Dad's birthplace—far away in the outback, a trillion miles from the sea—Mum puts her foot down.

"No. Not happening," she says. "Not a chance."

Mum strangles a sponge over the sink. I've caught her in the middle of trying to clean out the fridge. Too late, I realize this is terrible timing on my part. But I want to go to Temora more than I care about my timing or the set of Mum's shoulders, so I can't seem to stop myself.

"Why not? Give me one good reason, Mum."

"Too far," she says. "Too far for two people who are very young, one of whom is my daughter, to head out in the middle of nowhere on a motorbike, with barely any mobile signal. And if you crash, then you might not be seen for hours, and how am I supposed to know if you're safe? So, no! Just no! No way. Absolutely not."

Mum takes in a breath—she seems to have turned a whole other color—who knew she had this much *no* in her?

"And," she continues, "what's this all about? What about digital photography class? What about your new camera? It's still in its box, Biz! I *saw*! When were you going to tell me? When are you going to use it? And what about going back to school? What about getting a job?"

I open my mouth to answer, but how do you answer seven completely different questions at the same time?

1. *It's about Dad, Mum. I need to find him. He's everywhere but here.*

2. *I don't want to do the digital photography class—Dad's not in those photos, don't you understand?*

3. *I didn't ask for the camera. That was your idea.*

4. *I wasn't going to tell you. You liked the lie so much better, Mum.*

5. *I'm never going to use the camera. Someday? Maybe.*

6. *School? Are you fucking kidding?*

7. *A job. I haven't got time. I have to find Dad.*

I stare at Mum with my mouth open and I guess I look like I've suffered a blow to the head, because Mum sighs.

"Biz," she says, "do you want to get better or not?"

Which is an out-of-nowhere question. Did Mum not recently say I *was* in fact better? Have I not been getting my wayward life back on track? Look at me—up and about, doing things in the world. What the hell?

"Oh," I say, "so you've changed your mind, Mum? In your humble and oh-so-expert opinion I am not healed enough for you?" I know my sarcasm is off the charts, but I wasn't ready for this.

"Shit, Biz. This isn't a holiday! You're heading off to God knows everywhere with that kid, a kid I just met, I might add. And who is paying for your food and clothes and meds while you're out on that bike? Me. I don't have all the money in the world, you know. You're not supposed to just be lounging around. You're supposed to be studying, or doing *something*. You're not supposed—"

"What? What exactly am I 'supposed' to do, Mum? Not fall apart? Not want to die? Too late. Dad made sure of that. And you too, for not getting help for him when he was fucking screaming for it—"

Mum looks like she's been kicked. Like someone has literally kicked the breath out of her.

She raises her hand—*quickquick*—like she's going to hit me—even though she never has—not once in all my life—and I flinch, step back, and Mum starts to cry.

I want to say I'm sorry. I want to say, "Oh my God," and I want to reverse time. But it's too late because time only ever goes forward. Time is an arsehole that way. You can't undo anything, ever.

Mum lowers her hand. She takes in the world's most ragged breath, grabs her keys, and walks out of the house. She gets into the car and drives away.

She leaves just as the twins come running in from the backyard: Billie with a scrape on her elbow from tree climbing, and Dart shouting about a tick buried in his leg. I have to try not to shake all over. I have to put on my Sister Smile and fix them both, and not freak out because I think this is the first real argument Mum and I have ever had.

SYLVIA, WHO I HAVEN'T SEEN IN AGES BECAUSE I'VE BEEN off to "God knows everywhere with that boy on his bike," hears an abbreviated version of the fight—just the parts where I am not to blame. Basically, the parts where Mum said no to a motorbike trip to the middle of nowhere and certainly not the parts where I said certain things and was almost slapped for the first time in my life.

Sylvia agrees with Mum about the motorbike ride, mostly because of dear James; do I remember poor, lost James?

Yes, I tell her, of course I remember James.

Then Sylvia offers me her car.

"I haven't used my old Renault since I was sixty," she says. "But it's a good worker—I'm sure it would get you out to the countryside!"

She digs around in a kitchen drawer and pulls out a troll doll, a pink ruler, some fifty-cent pieces, and finally, two keys tied together with plastic twine. She takes me behind the house. She creaks open the peeling door of the garage. Inside, a rusted-out husk of a car hulks on four concrete blocks. The engine is missing.

"Oh," I say.

"Oh," says Sylvia.

"Well. I mean, it's got a lot of promise," I say.

"I think my son John may have let his children work on her one winter. Now, when was that? '98? Tom's in the Philippines now and Marianne has her PhD, so it must have been before that—"

Sylvia mutters to herself as she peers into the car's bonnet.

"It's okay, Sylvia," I say.

But is it? How am I going to get out of here, and all the way out there?

Mum and I have barely spoken all week. She's pointedly left printouts of different educational webpages on the kitchen table—there's a senior college giving kids a chance to finish their HSC, lucky things, plus all these online uni courses and TAFE courses in art, design, music, photography, hairdressing, and butchering—which is just cruel, thank you, Mother.

"Maybe she just needs a little fix-up," says Sylvia, staring into the hole where an engine once was.

"Sylvia, I think this car has gone to car heaven," I say.

Sylvia gazes the length of the Renault. The car looks like a kid sucked the color off it, then whacked it on a sidewalk for three years.

"You might be right, dear," she says, a little wistfully. She sighs. "Ronald and I made love for the first time in this car."

"Is that right?" Pictures of Sylvia and Ronald fumbling around in the back of the car vault into my head. I give them a kick.

"Yes, I think we conceived Samantha in the back seat!"

"On your first time?"

"Yes! Isn't that exciting? It was our honeymoon. We went down to Eden, and Ronald had never—" Sylvia smiles. "And, well, we couldn't wait for the hotel to have our room ready. It was delicious. That man smelled so good, Elizabeth; I can't even tell you."

I don't know how to tell Sylvia that her memories might be too R-rated for me.

I change the subject:

"I don't think I'm getting to Temora in this thing, Sylvia."

Sylvia pats the car, her memories far away . . . then looks at me.

"I think you're right, Elizabeth. I suppose it's the bus for you."

THE BANK SAYS I HAVE EXACTLY THIRTY-TWO DOLLARS. That is not remotely enough to get me to the outback or Tasmania, or across a continent to Broome. *Why'd you have to go so many places, Dad?*

I haven't earned money in a long time. I've never had a regular job. I've done odd jobs in the various towns we've lived in, but nothing lucrative—just some babysitting here, dog-walking there, some baby-walking and dog-sitting here and there. Every year there's Nana and Grandpa's Christmas money—a crisp twenty-dollar note in a Hallmark card. And one time I found ten dollars on a pavement while walking to the beach.

This particular thirty-two-dollar stash is left over from summer last year. Grace and I did some painting for her parents— they wanted to use professionals but Grace convinced them she and I could do a better job for less. We painted three walls of the spare room a faint aquamarine. Grace's mum had this whole idea for the room—pale walls, steel furniture, and accessories that "popped." The theme seemed to be a mash-up of Art

Deco and Bad Acid Trip. The bedspread was bright orange; the bed was a chrome four-poster. We wallpapered one of the walls in fizzy gray semicircles, which made you dizzy if you tried to follow the lines with your eyes.

"Who's going to stay in here, Grace?"

"You mean, who'll be able to without vomiting?" said Grace, smoothing down a strip of paper, rubbing over and over a bubble that I would have left, but Grace's mother was a stickler.

"Yeah. Is there a relative your mother hates? Is this an elaborate revenge plot?"

"Are you clairvoyant, Biz?"

"Not today, I just had lunch."

Grace grinned.

"My stepdad's mum is coming for a visit," she said. "She and Mum have some issues, let's say. She'll be staying in here."

"Ah. I feel sorry for her."

"Don't. She said Mum was a lesbian last time she visited."

"Is your mum a lesbian?"

Grace gave me a look.

"Bi, then?" I said.

"It's not the lesbian part Mum minded. The woman meant it as an insult. And Mum doesn't like homophobes." Grace paused. "Or racists."

"Well, then, why don't we leave the bubbles under the paper, Grace? Let's really make this room sing."

Grace laughed and the sound of it made my body warm, like I was in a bath, like every day would always be sunny—puppies frolicking and daisies blooming.

We left exactly one bubble under that paper. What rebels we were.

o ° o ° o

It's clear I need a whole lot more than thirty-two dollars to fund my mission. I need money for one train ride, two buses, another train, another train, a ferry, a bus, a bus, a ferry, a plane, another plane, a train, and another train. Plus I have to pay for accommodation, food, and any unforeseen expenses. I could try to foresee the expenses, but I think the list would get long and peculiar.

How is this going to work?

I could sell one of the twins. I could hock Mum's car. I could sell Mum's jewelry, but even though I am a dropout/disappointment/monster who makes Mum cry, I would never.

I look through my stuff. I rummage in drawers, go through boxes and things on the floor. I find clothes no one would want to wear, my dental plate from after I had braces, two clay brooches painted gold and silver the twins made in school, my phone, Dad's SLR, Sylvia's Polaroid camera, and one boxed DSLR, unused since the day I got it.

There we have it.

FOR SALE: ONE CAMERA

As new DSLR. Canon (blah etc. blah).

Asking $1,100.

Pick-up only. Wollongong area.

Seller—Zib17

THE DSLR GOES FOUR DAYS LATER TO A GIRL WHO HAS BEEN having a tough time. Her mum wants her to have something—anything—good to think about.

The girl has been bullied. She's changed schools, but life is still hard. There's this nice art teacher at the new school; she teaches an after-school photography class and says this girl has a knack. And even though I don't have the art teacher in front of me to check she's not some dickhead, I sell the camera to the mum and the girl because how is this not fated? How is this not my story but sweeter—one where the girl is actually grateful for the mum's help, is excited to do photography after school, whose photos don't speak to her, and whose dad is not dead?

It's meant to be.

I get one thousand dollars for the camera. The girl's mum hands over a wad of cash. I immediately want to shove it into my sock like in the movies.

The girl gives me a hug when she leaves. As she walks away,

the Polaroid of her—the picture I took through the window as they pulled up in their car—says from my back pocket: *What a great moment this is! I feel better already. Is that what hope is? Maybe I'll become a photographer. Maybe I'll travel. Maybe I'll be famous. Maybe I'll be loved. Maybe everything will be okay.*

I feel toasty all the way to my toes.

The next evening I write an email to Grace, Missing Person:

"Grace, I'm coming to Temora, and after that, I'm coming to find you. You can't hide from me. I'll leave no stone unturned."

I press SEND. This email feels commemorative. It's the one hundredth message I've sent since Grace vanished and took a whole slab of me with her. I can't wait to scream in her face.

I then write a message to Jasper:

"Hey. I'm heading out to Temora tomorrow. Temorrow. Hahaha. *Smiley face emoji.* Want to come? The train stops at Thirroul at 6:08 a.m. I'll be in the last carriage. *Steam train emoji. Thumbs up emoji. Smiley face emoji.*"

But I don't send it, because suddenly Dark Biz slinks in.

Dark Biz sends a text straight to my brain:

Hey, stupid.

Why should Jasper care? How ridiculous you are; aren't you silly, Biz? You're making a fool of yourself. He doesn't want to come to Temora. He's just being kind. He feels sorry for you. Maybe he's just worried you'll walk into more water without him and pity is no basis for a road trip.

Plus: He's got schoolwork and he actually wants to go to uni. UNLIKE YOU.

Plus: You're a bad influence.

Plus: Mum's right. You need to focus on getting better and not drag anyone down with you while you're doing it.

Plus: All the other reasons I haven't thought of yet, but I will.

I delete my message to Jasper.

It's true—Jasper doesn't need me or my relentless strangeness. Not inviting him is for the best. Some would call this a noble sacrifice. But I feel lonely already.

I send Jasper a GIF instead. It's of a baby blowing out candles, toppling over, and planting its face in the icing. It's so very LOL, so lighthearted, breezy, and carefree, Jasper will think everything's fine for days before he realizes I've left without him.

THAT NIGHT, I MAKE MUM AND THE TWINS A LASAGNA.
Sylvia made one for me last week, when I told her I was leaving and told her not to tell anyone.

She said, "But I can't keep secrets!"

I touched Sylvia's hand and said, "Sylvia, you and I both
know that's a lie."

So she made me this incredible meal, a vegan lasagna with
salad and crusty bread and wine, just a little, and we lit candles
and toasted to my orgiastic future: Biz the runaway, moving
from place to place in search of her dead dad.

It felt hopeful, there in the candlelight, Sylvia serving lasagna with her trembly hands, her red lipstick on, her laugh.
When I left, she pressed her lips to my cheek and said, "Call
me, dear, when you get there."

I said, "Where?"

And she said, "Everywhere."

o ° o ° o

Mum is still furious with me. I'm still silent, and we've been tiptoeing around each other in this weird way, like someone has spun us new bodies out of glass and we can't move to hug each other without fear of breaking.

The night she drove off, she came home really late. I don't know where she went, but I could picture her: standing on the curved bridge, body against the railing, listening again in the dark to the sea sing.

I waited up for her; I kept my door cracked open and my lamp on, but when she got home, she went past me to her room. The next day she left for work before I got up.

We've become like those married couples who go to sleep with their backs turned, or in different rooms, or one of them in a hotel. We're the married couple that sits at the ends of the table with their newspapers up; we're the couple that sits in counseling with their arms crossed, refusing to look each other in the eye.

It's so sad.

I have always had Mum to talk to, after every terrible thing that's ever happened. Each time, she's been the one with the dustpan and brush, sweeping up my pieces.

I guess this time I broke her?

My lasagna comes out of the oven—it's the first one I've ever made. The twins go "Oooh!" and Mum gives me this tight smile that doesn't reach her eyes.

It's kind of perfect, this lasagna. And as I cut into it, it feels symbolic, like all those books we analyzed in school—the last meal, the knife cutting into the perfect top, me serving up my scrambled insides while holding my secret close. I'm a metaphor, ladling carrots and white sauce and lentils onto mismatched plates and handing them over to my unsuspecting family.

Over dinner, we talk about school: The twins had a science experiment and they had to make a volcano, and the red went everywhere and it was awesome and, "Can we make a volcano at home, Mum?"

Mum says, "Maybe Biz can help you," and with my mouth full, I promise I will.

I'll be gone tomorrow. I don't know when I'll be back. When will I see them again? I lie to all their faces and something inside me goes *crick-crick*, the glass of me turning into a filigree of broken lines.

Mum says, "Biz."

I say, "Yes?"

"Thanks for dinner; it's delicious."

I nod. My throat feels thick, my chest tight. I want to say, "Mum, I sold your beautiful gift. I've got my bag packed and I'm leaving tomorrow and I don't know when I'll be back and maybe you will be heartbroken but regardless, I am going, and I can't be your good girl or your survivor until I fix this."

I look at Mum and she holds my look for one, two, three seconds before she looks away and in that moment, I know she can't hear what I want to say.

So I just say, "You're welcome, Mum," to her hands holding the fork, to the body that birthed me a lifetime ago, to her elsewhere eyes.

I LEAVE THE HOUSE JUST BEFORE DAWN. THE SKY IS A DEEP blue with a pink tinge past the trees. I can't remember the last time I saw the sun rise. It makes my breath catch to think of it, but maybe that's because I'm terrified.

I've left a note on the table. It says:

Gone for a ride with Jasper. Back tonight. Love, Biz.

I creak the door open, close it carefully behind me. I step down the path and hear the crunch of gravel like gunshots. The dog woofs, once, twice, from the backyard, and even though we just spent a good fifteen minutes saying goodbye—Bump's face in my lap, his deep brown eyes looking soulfully into mine—I know he's feeling betrayed.

Walking! Without me! Leaving town! I can tell!

Three birds loop the sky above the gums down the street. No one else is out, except for a Siamese cat sidling across a lawn in the semi-gloom. One house has a light on. To the person inside, I think: *Are you up because you're off to work or because you've got a baby in your arms or because you're sad and can't sleep?*

In which case, I feel for you, sleepless wanderer of houses. I'd come in and say, "I relate," except I have a train to catch.

Two guys in fluorescent jackets stand on the platform, heading to some worksite somewhere, about to do something useful for society—probably mending a pothole, which, if left alone, could cause a motorist to swerve around it, overcorrect, careen into a tree, and die. These guys are lifesavers.

They look over at me—my hoodie up, backpack on. I would smile at them to say, "Good job, superheroes!" but they might misinterpret that as: *Come and take me, lads! Come and have your way with my body, right here on this platform!* so I just glance away like I'm a rock, skimming. They go back to talking to each other quietly, and one even lights a cigarette, though everyone knows train platforms are smoke-free zones. A rebel. I'd respect that but all the smoke is coming my way and now I hate the guy for dooming me to a near-certain future of emphysema and blood clots.

The hate warms me while I wait—it's chilly out here.

The train slides in. I step on just like any normal person. The train slides forward, and so it begins.

THE SEA IS METALLIC. THE BUSH IS GREEN, DENSE. THE escarpment is lit up—cliffs glossy—with the sunrise. We *clickety-clack* between the mountains and the sea, shunt around the curve of the coast, through tunnels and over ravines, through and up and over the mountain.

I've done this ride a million times and I never get tired of it—it's like the sea is scooching along beside us as we ride, and this time it's even more stunning because the sun is stepping out of the ocean like a goddess, shedding cloud clothes and strutting naked into the sky. I take a photo with the Polaroid camera and the sun says:

Here I am, bitches!

Seriously. Check me out. I am a wonder.

In the picture, the whole ocean is golden and the sun's arms are spread wide.

I can tell you admire my bad-assery, Biz! says the sun. *But it's really no big deal. I rise out of the ocean every day and you could do it too, at least, you could if you'd been born a burning nuclear mass instead of that fragile human body. Don't despair, though—you'll probably get to try this sometime, when your atoms have dispersed and re-formed over millennia! It could totally be your turn one day, and you'll get to dazzle some other being on some distant planet, over some kind of molten sea. Be patient, babe.*

I think about how the sun is right. How in a blink, I'll stop being Biz and become something other. I think about how the "me" I am will end. Any moment really. Any time.

My chest aches, hardens—

But it's okay; I know what to do. I float out of my body. I rise out of myself and leave the train.

And instantly, nothing hurts.

I flit over the ocean, across to the sun. I lay myself out inside her light. Solar rays fly out of what once were my fingertips— just the idea of fingertips now, just a memory, and it feels so completely perfect I never want it to—

"NEXT STOP, HELENSBURGH! (WAKE UP, MOTHERFUCKERS!)"

The conductor shouts over the intercom and I slap back into myself, reenter my body with a snap.

I feel the photo in my hands shaking as the sun laughs.

I'VE BEEN TRAVELING FOR FORTY MINUTES AND I'M ALREADY hungry.

I check my supplies: four vegan muffins (baked yesterday as part of my goodbye offering to the twins), a container of roasted almonds, two bread rolls, three carrots, and a small tub of hummus. This is meant to last me to Temora, maybe even beyond, because who knows what people eat in Temora? Maybe just the hearts of small ravens and the bleeding stumps of lambs. I've never been to the outback. What do they live on? What do they do with vegans?

I suddenly feel ravenous, like if I put my head into my backpack I might just inhale everything—chew through the bags and containers and swallow all the food in a couple of bites like a monster lizard.

My throat clangs. My skin itches. My bones hurt. Is this how it feels to leave everything you know and reject your mother's care and do something no one will understand? It feels like the flu.

We rumble through the writhing bush. We've left the sea behind. I look at my phone; I want to text Jasper, or Mum, or write an email to Grace, message anyone about anything, but there's no signal here in the middle of the jungle, only snakes and sharp-beaked birds and shriveled trees for company.

Do I even want to leave? Should I get off at the next station and go home? Crawl into bed before Mum finds out I've gone and stay there forever, with her bringing me tea and the doctor tut-tutting over my body like I'm no longer a human but some kind of moss?

It would be so easy.

"NEXT STOP, SUTHERLAND! DISEMBARK HERE FOR TRAINS TO BONDI JUNCTION, JANNALI, AND LIVERPOOL. (OR, IF YOUR NAME IS BIZ, GET OFF HERE TO GO THE FUCK HOME!)"

That conductor. She's like some kind of archangel, omni-sciently riding in the back carriage, sending messages to all the runaways.

Do I want to go home?

I have four minutes to decide. Pass through Sutherland and I'll be too far gone to get back before Mum wakes up.

Four minutes.

I rummage through my notebook, where I've written my entire plan. It's itemized down to the dates, costs, accommo-dation, places Dad might have gone, based on information I've gleaned from asking Mum questions and a childhood spent poring over the photo albums on the shelf.

The list is meticulous. I am good with lists. Good with bullet points and subsets. That is, I *was* good, and then the fog came. So this list must be emblematic of a fundamental change in my system, right? A "have you tried turning off the computer and turning it back on?" reboot. This must mean I'm basically, definitely better. Right?

Three minutes.

Do I get off the train? Do I turn around?

Do I stay or do I go now?

Look at you, Biz, having doubts, says the sun. *It's perfectly normal, but listen, friend: You've got your lists and that must mean something. I mean, I know I'm the sun, but it's terrifying up here sometimes. I've so much energy in me I think I might explode and where would that leave us? Seriously in the dark, hahaha. But I persevere, Biz, that's what I do, so, whatever you do, don't get off that train, or you'll regret it. And let me tell you: Regret's a bitch.*

Two minutes.

The train slows.

I shove a muffin into my mouth; it's raspberry and choc chip—Sylvia has taught me well—and chew. It takes me a minute to get down the first bite, then the second. It takes another minute to get through the third and fourth bites—as the train slides into the station and the door opens on the platform—as people leave and people stay, and people keep reading their phones like nothing out of the ordinary is happening and there isn't a girl having a crisis while making her way through a muffin with raspberry and chocolate pieces—as the train slowly pulls out of the station and the sun chants, *Yeah! Biz! Staying on the train! Yeah!* outside the right window, light spilling over our laps like wild honey.

We arrive in Central station at 7:21 a.m.

I'm on the train for Cootamundra at 7:33, after a long wee in the toilets.

The train trundles out of Platform 15 at 7:42.

I'm really, really, really going. Where's the sun?

At the window. Beaming in.

MY PHONE GOES PING! JUST AS I'M TUCKING INTO MY NEXT muffin, half an hour out of Central.

MUM: Hey. Where r u?

Shit.

Do I answer? I've already lied on paper. Can I lie twice? She wasn't supposed to text. In the perfect scenario in my head, she was supposed to nod at my note, say, "Fine," go off to work, spend the day looking inside mouths, and have a whole day before she came home and I didn't and she freaked out.

We are ahead of schedule.

Shit.

I eat the whole muffin without answering.

PING!

MUM: I didn't say it was ok to go anywhere with Jasper. Where r u? Come home now pls.

Skin pricking, sweat on brow, pins and needles in extremities. I could be having a heart attack—maybe this is the one time I'm not panicking and actually dying? Can seventeen-year-olds have heart attacks?

I don't text back.

The phone rings now, buzzing on my lap—the phone is silent because I'm in a carriage with what looks like Zen priests and novelists who might shout at me if I so much as blink.

Mum's profile pic shows up on the screen. I turn it over so she can't see me.

The phone buzzes out.

MUM (on voicemail): Biz. Is everything okay? Please answer your phone.

MUM (via text): Biz?

MUM (calling again): Biz. I'm getting worried. Please could you pick up?

This goes for about an hour. Mum's voice rises and rises on the voicemail, until it becomes this high-pitched noise only dogs can hear.

I turn off my phone. When in doubt, ignore the problem. It's worked for centuries. This is how we humans have ended up in such a shit puddle. Fires, floods, storms, plastic islands in the ocean; how else do you get here if not for shoving your head under dirt until the problem goes away or you die? I mean, and you die?

At which point, I don't know if I'm Biz anymore—I feel so pulled out of my normal self it seems ludicrous I was ever me. Only a different Biz would make the woman who birthed her, fed her, watered her, and held her after her father died, cry and swear over a phone on a Wednesday morning, when the only thing that woman should be doing is driving to work with peace in her heart and a daughter at school.

My body is not even slightly the same body I had when I was born. We alter completely, constantly—our cells die and are replaced, every day, week, decade—our organs, our skin, our bones. Which means the Biz who popped out seventeen years ago ceased to exist hundreds of times since birth. All except the lenses in my eyes and my cerebral cortex, which I guess are the lone keepers of the keys to me.

The city unspools, and there's a kind of heady freedom in realizing I've shucked myself off, and I don't have to miss the me I'm leaving behind.

I open my notebook and write that pithy realization down.

Ratio of old Biz to new:

17 : 0.0000001

17 : 0.0000002

17 : 0.0000003

Here I am. Here I am. Here I am.

I'm regenerating with every single click and clack of the wheels on the rail.

I'm reborn, I'm reborn, I'm reborn.

It's beautiful.

It's so beautiful, I barely recognize Jasper when he shows up in front of me at Moss Vale station, at 9:22. I hardly understand it's him, I'm so infinitely renewed.

"HA!" JASPER STANDS IN THE AISLE, POINTING AT ME. "FOUND you!"

How? What?

"Jasper?"

Jasper grins. "I knew I'd find you! I'm a fucking genius!"

For that he gets a frown from a crotchety across the aisle and a solid, "Excuse me!" from the crotchety in the seat behind.

Jasper puts his backpack on the shelf above, flops down on the seat beside me.

"Uh. Jasper? What are you doing here?"

"I got your message this morning. Couldn't get to Central in time. So I rode my mighty steed and met you at the pass." Jasper looks wildly pleased with himself. I haven't seen him beam like this since, well, never.

"Message?" I never sent that message.

"The one that said, 'I'm leaving. Going to Temora. Etcetera-etcetera.'" Jasper waves his hand vaguely in the direction of the message he received this morning, the one I didn't send.

"I didn't send that message."

"Beg to differ," says Jasper. He pulls out his phone, flicks Messenger on, and there, like a beacon, is the message I deleted.

I shake my head. How?

Sliding doors open, close, open, close. Somewhere, in some alternate universe, there's a Biz riding a train alone, message deleted. Somewhere, there's a Biz who got off the train and went home before her mother woke. Somewhere, there's a Biz who didn't, wasn't, hadn't, isn't.

I start to shake.

Jasper puts his hand on my leg.

"Hey. Hey. Biz, breathe."

I have closed my eyes—panic rising—but Jasper puts his arm around me. He says, "Biz, Biz. S'okay. Everything's okay."

I'm trembling. Jasper's patting my shoulders. He's saying, "It's okay. Biz. No biggie. We're just going to Temora. Just a little road trip! Train trip, I mean! This is so much better than maths."

Jasper rubs my shoulder with one hand. Taps my knee with the other. He says, "Whoa! You brought muffins! Great. I'm starving."

I feel his hands leave. I hear the sound of a container, unclicking.

I open my eyes.

Jasper's got both my muffins and is holding them up like trophies. He's grinning at me and if I took a photograph of him right now I'm certain light would beam from every opening, maybe even his belly button.

"We're going the fuck to Temora!" he says. He takes a massive bite of muffin.

All the crotcheties turn their heads, their reveries a mess.
"Shush!" they shout in unison.
"Shush!" says Jasper back, spraying crumbs, laughing.
He's so happy.
I breathe. I stop shaking.
Huh.
Here we are. Here we are. Here we are.

WE'VE GONE WEST AND WEST AND WEST AND NOW WE'RE a half hour out of Cootamundra, which is handy because I'm ravenous. Somehow we've eaten everything, including the snack Jasper brought along—a muddle of cracked corn chips in a rumpled bag, slightly stale.

I think it's the stress. Whenever I'm nervous I either eat food or gnaw my fingernails down to the nub. By lunchtime, I'm out of both.

Jasper has settled into the ride and is no longer saying "Fuck yeah!" every thirty seconds.

He's spent the last three hours staring out at the unfolding everything: the train cutting through open fields, in and out of bushland, past little towns, bigger towns, graffiti blipping past on the backs of buildings, a swirling cone of birds, the sun sailing higher, the light slapping his face. It's been three hours of Jasper saying "Hey, look at that. Hey, look at *that*."

Who knew he had the capacity for this much joy? It's like watching a man-shaped kitten playing with tinsel. He says, "It's the freedom, Biz. I haven't run away before."

But of course, he hasn't run away. When pressed an hour ago, he admitted, "Okay, I told Mum I was going with you. I told her Gran said it was urgent I accompany you so you didn't get murdered in the countryside."

"Hmm." I considered this. "Both of us could get murdered, Jasper. Murderers kill multiple people all the time."

"Well, regardless," Jasper said, "Mum agreed. She's easy that way. She said as long as I get my schoolwork done, I'm good. I can study anywhere, remember?" Jasper gestured up to his backpack. "Laptop, check! Avant-garde poetry, check! Clean underwear, check!" He grinned.

I wish it were that easy for me. When the fight with Mum happened, I told Jasper about it, messaging at one a.m. when I couldn't sleep. But I didn't—I couldn't—tell him the depth and breadth of our fight, the sting and sadness of it. I told him some of the words Mum had said, but very few of the words I had said. Isn't that convenient? All he knows is Mum drove off in her car; he doesn't know I'm the terrible person who made her do it.

So when I told him an hour ago I wasn't just playing at being a runaway but was legitimately and in fact precisely a runaway, his face was a mixture of pity and awe.

How about that? I was capable of being an actual delinquent. Was he sure he wanted to be on a train with someone like me?

"So she really doesn't know?" he said.

"She thinks we're out for the day on your bike."

"Ah. Is she okay with that?"

"Not exactly. No."

Jasper shook his head. "Huh. So I'm the co-villain in this story."

"Yeah. Sorry."

Jasper was quiet for a while after that, processing.

He'll probably get off at the next station, I thought. *He'll turn around and go home. I would. Would I? It would be the most logical option—a) do you want to go down Biz's path of delinquency or b) do you not? The answer is b. Every time, it should be b.*

But when we pulled into a station, Jasper didn't move. He looked out the window and said, "Hey! Look, Biz." There on the platform stood a blank-faced woman in a Pokémon hat checking her phone.

"Nice," I said.

"I forgot my Pokémon hat," said Jasper. He looked over at me. "What about you? Remembered or forgot?"

Palms out, I shrugged. "Forgot."

"Sad."

The train slid out of the station. "No matter, Biz," he said. "We can wear them next time." Then Jasper saw two Chihuahuas running in circles in a yard.

"Look!" he said. He turned to me. "Did you see those dogs? I could fit them in my shoes."

Then he pointed out a house with a rose-tangled fence. He pointed out an ancient 1970s station wagon. We rolled into farmland and Jasper took a photo of the horizon with his phone. And we two villains tumbled towards Cootamundra together.

COOTAMUNDRA GLIDES INTO PLACE BESIDE OUR TRAIN, right at 12:44 p.m. as scheduled. We grab our stuff, step onto the platform, and are hit by a blast of air so scorching Jasper spins around, like his body is trying to get away but can't, so it just turns like a sad chicken on a rotisserie.

"Whoa," says Jasper, blinking. "Hello, fifth circle of hell."

"I heard the outback was hot, but *Jesus*—" I say, peeling off my hoodie.

"Dude, if we were in the outback," says Jasper, yanking off his jacket, "we would have already turned crispy and died."

I stare at Jasper. "*Dude*, are we not in the outback?"

"We are in Cootamundra, Biz. The outback is not here."

"How do you know?"

"How do you *not* know?" Jasper smirks. He's annoying. Holy shit, it's hot.

"*Fine*. Doesn't matter. Fuck. My lungs are frying."

"We should seek air-conditioning."

"Agreed."

We head out to the street, and in that instant all thought of shelter is swallowed by the sky.

It's gigantic.

There's so much sky it's hard to believe it's not falling on us. There's no escarpment here—just low hills and cars and houses and us. We're baby ants squatting under an impossible blue.

I stop in the street to look up.

I would take a picture, but there's no room on any square for space like this.

I open my arms. I try to take it in, but I'm too small. I put my head back. Maybe I look like Jesus, arms out, when he was on his mountaintop telling everyone to be kind, though maybe he was secretly saying to God, "Beam me up, Dad, these humans are ridiculous."

The honk *blats* into my brain the same time as Jasper shoves me, and it turns out the sky is a trickster—trying to hold me still so a delivery van can mash me flat on a Cootamundra street.

Not cool, sky. Fuck you.

I stumble onto the pavement and Jasper says, "What was that, Biz?"

"Just looking up, Jasper," I say, but I know he knows better. Poor Jasper—he's got to watch out for murderers *and* sky? He shakes his head.

I pull out my phone, ignore the million messages from Mum, open Google, and type "vegan cootamundra." The phone has a little think. A moment later it says: *Go to the Khaya, Biz. Inside you will find tantalizing delectables and a delightfully quaint ambience.*

It offers me a map.

"Come on," I say to Jasper, and four minutes later, past a pub and a smudge-brown Centre for the Arts, we're standing in front of a building so red it looks painted with fake blood.

"Pretty," says Jasper.

Arts! Crafts! Gallery! Café! shout the awnings.

We push open the door. Step in.

Cold! shouts the café.

Whoa. It's freezing in here. It feels like we've stepped into the negative of a second ago, the arctic inverse of outside. The air conditioner clatters on the wall, going full speed.

We might get hypothermia in a minute, but on the plus side, the place smells delicious.

Tucked behind shelves of knickknacks and whatsits, a bunch of old people sit at tables with toasted sandwiches and cappuccinos and slabs of devil's food cake. They're all chit-chatty and cozy and they look up at us like we're almost friends, like maybe we remind them of their beloved grandkids, and maybe they'll invite us over for a bite of whatever it is they're having, and I have a moment—a pang—where I wish we'd done this trip with Sylvia. She'd be best friends with everyone in five minutes. Why didn't we bring Sylvia?

Jasper reads my thoughts. "Wow. Gran would love this place."

It's true; the walls are covered with art. It's a photo exhibition.

On one wall: photos of children in playgrounds, swinging from swings, sliding down slides, hanging upside down on monkey bars. On another wall: a row of smiling old faces. On the third wall: a series of ducks in close-up. Round waddly bodies. Beaks and feet. Black-and-white water.

The minute I look at the photos, they start to talk.

I can swing so high I can touch the moon! Keep pushing me! Keep pushing!

If that human comes any closer, I'll snap her nose off! I'll peck her eyes out! Oh, she's got apples, that's different. I'll have some apple. Apple, apple, apple!

I stare at the photos. Sorry? How is this possible? I didn't develop these pictures; I've had nothing to do with them.

Irrelevant! shout the photos.

The stories roar out, falling over themselves to get to me.

I'm upside down! Look, Mum! I'm a monkey! Mum! Are you looking?

I walked her to the train and kissed her. I said, "Will I see you again?" and she said, "No, I'll be married next week." It's been fifty-three years and still, I think of her.

Lord, I know every corner of this town. Every layer of the sky. Something has to change. Please.

I had four babies and five babies and one time eight and we crossed the road and I said, "Babies! Come!" And they came and a car came too and I said, "Babies!" and only seven crossed the road.

I start to shake. This doesn't make sense. This doesn't—

Jasper has found a seat for us in the center of the room. He's trying to get my attention over all the *talking! talking! talking!*

Jasper's holding up a menu. He's saying, "Biz! Vegan goodies! Look!"

I turn. All I can hear are voices.

How?

I don't under— *She said No Hey! Up! Hey! When will I? The eighth was slow I wanted Hey! Maybe next I'll leave Sky and Hey! Fast! Apple Kiss APPLE APPLE! HEY! HEY! HEY!*

The words push in. I can't breathe. I step back and bump into a chair. I tilt into one of the shelves; knickknacks fall to the floor. I have to get outside.

I stumble-run, shove the door open and all the stories tumble after me and *SHOUT!* and *SHOUT!* until the door closes and I can't hear them anymore. But I can *feel* them—on my skin, under, inside.

I lean on a pole.

I bend in half to breathe.

The door opens.

Closes.

Jasper's standing beside me.

His hands are on my back. He's rubbing my shoulders.

I gulp at the burning air.

WE EAT TAKEAWAY FOOD INSIDE THE COOTAMUNDRA station. I chew, swallow—it tastes amazing, it tastes like nothing—lunch tastes like magic and cardboard at the same time.

Fragments from the photos have leeched out of me in whispers. Bit by bit, two by two, the stories have hung their heads and shambled out of my skin, scattering as they hit the air.

We're sorry, Biz, that was probably too much, we should probably have taken proper turns, we should probably not have crawled inside you, that was probably an invasion of your personal space, we won't do it again, Biz, sorry sorry, apple.

Jasper keeps looking over at me.

"Biz?" he says finally.

"Yeah."

"Want to talk about it?"

"Uh." How do I talk about it? Dear Jasper: My dead dad has been visiting me for eight years, but now he has disappeared, and when he disappeared I had a mental breakdown, and then the photographs I took for my get-better class started talking to me and now photographs I never took are talking to me, and how is that possible, the science on this is unclear, and everything's really loud and I'm not sure I'll ever find Dad because I might be turning into a story, I might already be a story, I am a door, sliding—

I shake my head. My skin hurts. I think I might throw up.

"Should we go home?" Jasper says quietly.

I shake my head.

"You can, if you want," I say.

"And leave you to be murdered?" he says. He touches my knee.

"I'm sorry, Jasper." My voice cracks, which is mortifying.

"It's okay, Biz. Really."

"It kind of isn't. But I still have to go."

Jasper stares at me. He looks at my bent body, my half-eaten food, the way I'm holding on to the sandwich box like if I let it go I might sink to the ocean floor, even here, all the way from the sea.

"All right then." He squeezes my knee. "Let's keep going. Let's have a fucking adventure."

"Really?"

Are you sure, Jasper? I can't promise anything will go right. I have no idea what's happening.

"Yeah."

Okay then. A fucking adventure it is. Carpe diem. Tempus fugit. What doesn't kill you . . . makes you not dead yet. Right?

"I can pay for the shepherdess," I say. Specifically, the figurine I broke when I ran out—the poor shepherdess who toppled from a shelf and lost her head. Jasper had to pay.

"Nope." Jasper waves away my offer. "She's mine."

THE STATION IS COOL AND QUIET.

Jasper finishes his lunch, which is the size of a VW Beetle, and then polishes off mine. Mum keeps pinging messages at me until Jasper says, "Maybe you should just text her back? You don't want her thinking you're dead."

Do you not, Biz?

Wouldn't that be easier?

No. It would not.

"Can you do it for me?" I ask Jasper. "Please?"

Jasper frowns.

"Sorry?" he says. "You want me to text your mother who thinks you might be dead and tell her, 'Hey, this is Jasper, the guy you didn't want your daughter riding into nowhere with, out, in fact, in the middle of nowhere with her, supporting her delinquency'?"

"Yeah."

"Uh. No, Biz."

He picks up the phone and looks at the stream of messages Mum has been sending all morning. Sighs.

He hands it to me. "You really have to do it, Biz. It's cruel not to. It's totally not vegan to not contact your mum."

I hold the phone, turn it over in my hands.

Jasper hasn't done anything but tap my knees and rub my back all day as I've steadily unraveled. I guess the least I can do is tell my mother I'm not dead.

BIZ: Hi, Mum. *Smiley face emoji. Palms together emoji because a prayer would be good at this time.*

MUM: Oh my God, Biz! What's going on??

BIZ: I'm fine. Sorry for not messaging.

MUM: Where are you???

BIZ: In Cootamundra.

MUM: What??? On Jasper's bike? I can't believe it.

BIZ: We came by train.

MUM: We? Are you with him? Shit, Biz! You've had me so worried.

BIZ: Jasper decided to come (*so that I don't get murdered or get tricked by the sky*).

MUM: I've nearly lost my mind worrying. I'm so upset right now.

BIZ: (*And Jasper helped me out of the shop when the photos started talking to me.*)

MUM: It's been a terrible morning. I can't believe you left without telling me.

BIZ: I'm really sorry. (*And then I couldn't breathe, Mum. I couldn't breathe because my skin was crawling with stories. Just imagine you had bugs under your skin, Mum, just picture that, actually crawling with words I couldn't get out.*)

MUM: I've been so scared. I thought about calling the police but I didn't know where to send them.

BIZ: (*And when I could breathe again, the stories all said sorry.*) I'm sorry, Mum. I'm really sorry for worrying you.

MUM: Don't ever do it again.

BIZ: I won't. (*Can I promise that? I don't know what's going to happen, Mum. Life is unpredictable—don't you know we're living in a chaotic system? Don't you know you can't pin anything down?*)

As Mum and I chat, Jasper lies on a bench and considers the train station ceiling. I tell Mum I'm heading to Temora. She says she can't stop me, but shit, Biz, why run away; why not talk to her? Is she that kind of mother, is that how I see her? Shit, Biz.

I don't know what to say, so pretty much all that comes out is, *Sorry, Mum, sorry, sorry, sorry.* I tell her I'll come home after Temora, which is a lie. Mum says she'll see me soon, and we'll talk when I get back (which is code for: Mum will yell a lot and cry a little, or maybe the other way around).

MUM: Please be safe, Biz.

BIZ: I will. (*Will I? Is that possible? We are, all of us, going to die.*)

MUM: I love you. You have no idea.

BIZ: I love you too. *Emoji of a heart, emoji of a heart, emoji of a heart.*

The whole conversation is over in a couple of minutes.

I put down my phone and look over at Jasper. He's blurry.

The station is blurry behind him; the walls are wavy, and

the train tracks through the station door are hazy and indistinct. It's like I'm looking at everything through a shower door and the steam's between me and everything else.

I blink and Jasper comes back. Then the station comes back and it's like I've turned the focus on Dad's SLR. Here we are.

"So that wasn't so bad." Jasper sits up and slaps his knees. "Damn, I should be a psychiatrist."

"You totally should."

"I am that good."

"No question about it. You've fixed everything, that's for sure."

Jasper laughs.

I laugh.

Look at us laughing together under the Cootamundra sky!

At which point!

The bus comes to the station house!

And waits for us to get on!

Come on, Biz and Jasper! Two young'uns with the world at your feet! Come and ride the road to Temora, where Biz will begin to get her father back! It's all golden from here! Hop on! Let's go!

We get on the bus and it's half-full of old people; the world has so many old people in it, doesn't it? There's also a young guy asleep at the back. And a middle-aged man with his cap pulled low: either a celebrity or an escaped convict; he's not to be disturbed. And a twenty-ish-year-old woman, crocheting something green. She's really, really pregnant.

"What if she has her baby on the bus?" whispers Jasper, poking my arm.

"That's okay. We can deliver babies. We're smart."

"I'll watch. I'm not good with blood."

"Fine. I'll do it."

"Fine," says Jasper. He pulls out a banana from his bag.

"Where'd you get that?"

"The shop."

"When did you go to the shop?"

"When you were calling your mum."

I stare at him. I didn't call my mum. We texted while Jasper lay on a bench.

But Jasper has a banana.

He pulls a second one out of the backpack.

"I got one for you. Want it?"

Do I want a fictional banana that Jasper didn't get from the shop when I wasn't calling my mum?

"Sure."

Cootamundra crawls away from us. Bye-bye, Cootamundra. The land opens up like a big, flat flower and soon, all we have in front of us is road, road, road.

WE GET INTO TEMORA AT 3:39 P.M., GIVE OR TAKE A MINUTE or ten. Buses can't keep to the same times as trains, especially out here, because they have to swerve for falling koalas and kangaroos.

At one point between Cootamundra and Temora, I saw a kangaroo hopping across a field and then another and another!

I grabbed Jasper's arm and said, "Hey!"

He sat up, squinting. "Yeah?"

"Kangaroos!"

"Yeah, Biz. It's Australia."

Jasper's tired. I think I woke him up. I think he ate too much at lunch. He's been sleeping most of the way from Cootamundra. Maybe he's seen kangaroos a hundred times before—we're only two hours north of Canberra after all, rolling fields everywhere around that city, perfect for roo spotting—but I have not.

Once, Dad told a tourist in Sydney he used to ride his pet kangaroo to school. The guy believed him. And then of course that guy must have passed the story on to someone else, and maybe Dad became some kind of awesome Australian legend to all the people who heard about it. But Dad told me he'd heard the story when he was a kid.

"I heard that story from my uncle Charlie. He was told it by some other guy. I think that story's been around as long as white people have been telling stories like they own the place."

Dad laughed then, his voice a murmur in the dark. I was eleven. Dad was floating cross-legged over my desk under the window. I could see his profile. The wind came in through the opening; the curtains moved, but Dad's hair stayed completely still.

Temora is even hotter than Cootamundra, if that's scientifically possible. The sun—so tetchy now that she's away from the sea—hammers our faces and barbecues our tender, juicy skin. We wander down some street, looking for Dad's house. I have no idea where it is, and come to think of it, it's probably not just sitting here, waiting for us. Mum said Dad grew up on a farm.

"What kind of farm was it?" I asked Mum when I was ten.

"Sheep," Mum said. "Lots and lots of sheep."

"For eating or shearing?"

"Both, I think," said Mum, and we each made a face.

But *where* kind of farm is it? And how am I supposed to get there?

I know a lot of things about this trip: I know exactly when the next bus will leave to go back to Cootamundra and when the ferry will leave Melbourne for Tasmania, and I know the cost of a mango smoothie in Maleny, but I didn't figure out how I was going to get to Dad's childhood home without a car.

We walk around anyway, because staying still might turn us into melted-flesh puddles.

Temora isn't looking great. The yards are flat squares of dust and yellow grass. Withered trees hunch beside the pavement—they look like they're having a collective last gasp in the heat. Every house seems to be brown or gray, one brick box after another.

We pass a school—kids gone for the day—weeds gruntling up through the cracks in the playground. We pass a garage; we pass more brick houses and more brick houses. We pass a huge church: fancy, white and brown brick, pointy crosses like pimples at its tips. We are in the baking innards of Temora and there's not an interesting color or sheep to be seen.

I'm so hot, I feel like I'm disintegrating. Flies keep buzzing at our lips, our eyes. I can sense a thousand cancerous moles sprouting. Any second now I'll look like the burned end of a match.

"Maybe we should go indoors," I say.

"Yes. Yes. Yes," says Jasper, his face oozing sweat.

(Is that what I look like right now? God help us all.)

We turn right and right and we're beside a pub, two grizzled men sitting out the front downing some beer.

The men have eyebrows like white bushes. They look us up and down.

We go to step into the pub. One of the old fellas lifts a wrinkled arm.

"Can't come in here if you're not eighteen," he says, pulling on a cigarette, his eyes squint-closed in the smoke.

"No babies allowed," says the other, tipping beer down his lizard throat.

"Hahaha!" says the first, and starts coughing up a lung.

"Fine," mutters Jasper, tugging me away.

We move down the street to a fish and chip shop. We step in—heat pulses from the deep fryer, the boiling fish call out, "Run! There's no hope for us! Save yourselves!"—and we turn straight back around.

Three kids in school uniforms shove past us out the door, milkshakes in hands. Everyone's mouth is full of *Fuck* and *Shit* and, *Watch it, faggot* when they bump into Jasper.

Jasper laughs, but in a way I've never heard before. High, like he's pushing the laugh out from a tiny opening, like those balloons you let the air out of so slowly they squeal.

Out on the street, one kid turns and spits at us, actually spits. Suddenly Jasper's shoe is covered with wet froth.

"What the hell?" I shout.

Jasper puts his hand on my arm. "Leave it, Biz."

"But they're dicks," I say, glaring at the kids as they laugh and walk away.

"Yeah. But I've heard it before," says Jasper. I look at him, ready to fight the kids, ready to take down this whole beige town, but something in Jasper's face stops me. And in that instant, the indisputable fact that Jasper is gay stares back at me.

Huh.

How did I not catch that? How did the photos not tell me?

IF I WERE TALKING TO GRACE SHE'D SAY, "WELL, DUH, BIZ. That's why he hasn't been kissing you."

I'd say, "First up, I never said I wanted to be kissed. And, b), there are infinite reasons not to kiss me."

GRACE: Name one.

BIZ: Hahaha. All right: too tall, too vegan, too sad, and seriously strange.

GRACE: Okay. Well. Sure, only if that person has, like, no legs. And even then, they could find a ladder. Two (*Grace would start counting on her fingers*): You're compassionate. You don't put corpses in your mouth. Any sane person would do the same. Three: So you've got the sads. No shit, Biz, don't we all? And four: In actual fact, you are interesting, unusual, rare, remarkable, and idiosyncratic.

BIZ: Thank you, thesaurus app.

GRACE: You're welcome.

BIZ: Five: I am most likely mad.

GRACE: I've got a secret for you, Biz. *We're all mad here.*

WE GO INTO THE TEMORA TARGET, JASPER HOLDING HIS secret (why hasn't he told me?) and me holding mine (I know. I know. I know. Why haven't you told me?).

It's mercifully cool inside. I want to kiss the floor.

Jasper strides to the electric fan display at the front. "We need to get all of these, Biz. Let's strap them to our bodies, attach a battery pack, then get selfies at that pimple church."

"Sounds like a good use of our time, Jasper," I say. "Certainly more important than finding my dad's farm."

"Fine. We'll find the farm, go see the farm, return to town, triumphant. And *then* we'll take selfies at the pimple church. At night. When the sun has pissed off."

Jasper goes to the hat section next. He finds a pile of flat skater caps on sale, all neon colors. Jasper chucks a lime-green one to me. "Perfect for shade, Biz. We'll be twins," he says, pulling a pink cap over his curls.

"Won't these hats make people spit at us more, Jasper?" I look at him. The world slows, and I think of Jasper, spinning inside his own story—I'm at the beginning of it, and does he want to tell me more? (*Do you want to be visible, Jasper? Is that what you want? Is there anything you want to say?*)

"This protective headwear will shield us from the spit," Jasper says. He stares at me. "Fuck the world, Biz."

I stare into the spin of him, the blue-eyed whirl of him. I picture the years of glances and whispers, the wonderings, the questions, the weight of history, everyone just wanting to know—

And I get it.

Fuck it. Fuck it, *fuck the whole world.*

I put on the hat.

"Fuck the whole world!" I say, much too loudly for a young lady in a Target in the decent, law-abiding countryside.

Jasper grins.

I grin back.

And it's like when someone touches an electric current and you're holding their hand, so it passes to you, and suddenly there you are: seizing, pulsing, filled with light, unable to let go.

We launch out of Target like lime-green and strawberry comets. We walk to a different corner pub, where the Target cashier said we might find a cab. Five minutes ago she rang up our hats and said, "Is it still a scorcher out there?" and I said, "Yep," and she said, "Oh, I'm glad I'm in here then!" and she smiled and added, "It's never usually this hot this time of year."

And I smiled and said, "I blame climate change."

And Jasper smiled and said, "Did you know there's an island of plastic floating in the Pacific? It's the size of France."

And the cashier opened her mouth to speak but couldn't seem to think of what to say.

And then Jasper asked about taxis and she gave us directions, and we shot outside, trailing sparks.

AT THE PUB, MORE OLD MEN SUCK ON THEIR SMOKES AND pull on their beers and stare at us like we're aliens.

I want to say to them, "Not aliens. Comets, actually," but instead I walk past them to the guy leaning against a dented sedan with a TAXI sign on the roof, part of the T missing.

"Hi," I say. "Is this a taxi?"

That might seem like a stupid question but the TAXI sign is pretty decrepit. It could be from the previous owner, like those people who buy old hearses and drive them around with no dead bodies inside.

The guy laughs. "Yeah, mate. What's it look like?"

I would explain, but I don't feel like it. "Can you take us to my dad's farm?"

The man drags on his cigarette, drops it, stubs it out with his shoe.

"Sure. Which one?"

"Uh. It's a sheep farm."

The man looks at me.

"The Greys' farm," says Jasper.

"Oh?" says the man. He raises his eyebrows. "That hasn't been the Greys' farm for years."

"Who lives there now?"

"Some new fella. George."

One of the crusties says, "Yeah. George. It's George bought the place off Charlie's kid, come up from Ardlethan he did."

"Where are all the Greys now?" I say.

"Dead, mebbe?" says a crustie, his face scrunching.

"Not all of 'em," says another. "Bill went to Brissie."

"Sonya's in Warnambool."

"You Sonya's kid?" says one to me.

"Sonya didn't have kids," says another.

"Mebbe she had a kid when you were sleeping, mate!"

The old fellas laugh. They don't know me; they're trying to help, sort of. They're not helping.

I don't know Bill. I don't know Sonya. I definitely don't know George. I *do* know that Dad was expected to work the farm and when he left, his uncle Charlie said, "Good riddance." And when Dad died, we didn't hear from a single one of the Greys.

When I was ten, I asked about Dad's mum and dad. I knew almost nothing about Dad's childhood, only that Dad had lived on a sheep farm and had an uncle called Charlie who once told a kangaroo story and was glad Dad left. That was it—my whole Grey family history.

"Hey, Mum?" I said.

Mum was reading one of her historical fictions in the chair by the window. The boyfriend was out. I was on the floor, belly on the rug, drawing. The twins were asleep in their baby beds and for a second, the house was quiet enough to think.

"Yeah, Biz?" Mum peered over the top of her book.

"What happened to Dad's dad?"

"Martin?"

"Yeah."

"He died." Mum put her book facedown on her knee and looked at me.

"How did he die?" I said.

"Farm accident, I think."

"What kind of farm accident?"

Mum's shoulders went up-down. "I don't know. Your dad never told me."

I kept drawing. I put darker green into my grass, thinking about another dead dad. My thoughts skittered around the word *dead* very fast and went to a picture of Dad on the end of my bed, laughing. Maybe Dad's dad had come to talk to him like Dad talked to me.

I said, "What about my other nana? Dad's mum?"

"Dad's mum?"

"Yeah."

Mum's lips pushed together, like she didn't want to say. But Mum always answered my questions.

"Sweetie, she left when Dad was six. Dad never saw her after that. I don't know where she is."

I looked down at my drawing—a large, twisty house, dark green grass, and a yellow front path. Mum, the twins, and I stood outside with our wings on, every feather drawn. I thought, *What would that be like? To not know your mum?*

I pictured not knowing Mum. I pictured a space with her

not in it. I flipped backwards, a cartwheel through time, into my body months earlier, just before the twins were born, when Dad said Mum could have died.

I crawled over the rug and up into Mum's lap, even though I was ten and much too old for laps. I curled on top of her and turned myself into a mollusk, the kind you see in tide pools, fixed to rock.

Mum laughed and wrapped her arms around me. She rubbed my back, and after a long time or maybe only a minute, the twins cried from their beds and she had to go to them and wipe poo from their bums. I hovered at the bedroom door, even though the whole room stank, and not for the first time I tried praying to God, to make sure Mum would never leave.

THE SUN IS SLIDING DOWN TOWARDS THE HORIZON WHEN the taxi man takes us out to the farm. We take a road that seems to have lost all its bends—we drive forward then forward then forward. We pass pods of sheep. Reams of wheat. More sheep, more wheat. Twenty minutes later, we're at a gate facing a dirt road. The taxi man says, "Want to go on up? Is your mate George expecting you?" and he laughs.

"Yeah, sure. I texted him," I say, even though it's such a lame and obvious lie. Just for a second, I want the guy to think we're loved, that we've texted ahead and chatted with our old friend George and right now he's got iced drinks tinkling on the table for us, fans flicking cool air through our guest rooms, and a cat at the end of each bed. I glance across at Jasper and will him to agree, even though he's gone all quiet; he looks like he might have changed his mind about being a comet.

The taxi man's out of the car, opening the gate, and Jasper says, "Uh. Biz?"

"Yeah?" I say.

"We're really going up? To talk to some guy you've never met?"

"Yeah."

"Because?"

"Because I need to see where Dad was born. I need to see."

Jasper measures me, to see how big the need is and whether the need vs. madness ratio is sufficient enough to warrant rocking up to a strange dude's farm at sunset.

It's big, Jasper. 600,000 : 1.

There are no lights on in the house when we trundle up, and for a second I'm so scared I blink out of my body like a lamp with a faulty power point. I see the place like it's on a screen: the hulking house, the slam of sky above the house, the rusting car beside the barbed wire fence, the truck beside the rusting car, and the dog loping out from under the car, its growl already started. In a second, the scene will switch to inside the house, looking out the window at the taxi on the dirt. In another second, the camera will cut to an axe held by a hand, the blade's edge glinting in the fading light.

We grab our backpacks and slide out of the car. My feet touch the ground. *We will probably be killed tonight*, I think, followed by: *or raped, or raped then killed, or bashed then thrown in a boggy dam to die—*

I pinch the back of my hand hard to try and stop the thoughts. *Or we will be fed to that dog by the taxi man, who pretended this was George's farm or—*

Pinch, pinch, *pinch.*

Jasper bends down to the driver's window. "Do you mind waiting while we visit?" he says.

"Yeah sure, mate, got nothin' better to do." Taxi man grins and lights up a cigarette.

The dog barks, its hackles up.

It barks, and barks, and barks.

From inside the house a door slams.

"Shut the fuck up, Byron!" shouts a voice.

The dog whines. Barks again, then slouches around the corner of the house and turns into a man, because a man comes around the corner precisely where the dog just went.

The guy looks seven feet tall. He's got a filthy shirt, filthy jeans, and what looks like blood on his hands, dear God.

Jasper squeaks. I didn't know he had that sound in him.

I open my mouth to scream. But I don't have that sound in me.

"Who the fuck are you?" says the man, wiping his hands on his jeans.

"Uh," is all Jasper and I can say.

The man's eyes narrow, move across us like he's wiping *us* off on his jeans. "Why the fuck are you here?"

From inside the taxi, the driver says, "These kids wanted to visit, mate, and this one"—he thumbs over to me—"says you were expecting them."

"Oh really?" The man stares hard at me. "Well, we both know that's a fuckin' lie."

"Thought so, mate, but she still insisted on coming. Guess this place was the family farm or something, before you got it."

Why am I letting two strange men talk about me like I'm not here?

"This was my dad's place," I say, trying to sound assertive, trying to be master of my fate, et cetera.

"Who? Bill?" George looks curious, suddenly.

"No. His name was Stephen. Stephen Grey."

"Ohhh," says George, "the one who bailed. Heard about him."

"We all have, mate," says the taxi driver, and the two men laugh.

"Heard he got twisted in his head like his dad, couldn't handle farm work, poor precious."

"Is that right?" I say.

"Yeah, his cousins said he was a fuckin' pussy, couldn't hack the hard stuff, went off to Sydney to polish his nails."

Jasper's and my eyebrows go all the way UP.

"Actually, my dad's dead," I say, anger making my spine hurt. "So maybe watch your mouth."

George opens his mouth. Shuts it. Looks down at his filthy boots. Shrugs. "Sorry, girlie. Didn't mean to disrespect the dead," he says, and then he crosses himself. For real. The man's got God in him, and a soul like a sewer.

The taxi driver looks over at me. "Sorry, mate," he says, and he does look sorry, because maybe no one actually heard Dad died? Maybe they all think Dad's still somewhere in Sydney, in his silk pajamas and painted nails, being alive and a fuckin' pussy and a failure? If only.

"Yeah. Okay. Thanks," I say. I feel like I'm going to cry and that won't work here. No weakness, Biz. Be a comet. "I just wanted to see where he grew up. Take some photos. Sorry to disturb."

George says, "Okay, fine, whatever, you can take some photos, but I haven't cleaned this place in, like—"

"Ever," says the taxi driver, and both men laugh.

"I won't be long," I say.

The driver gets out. He passes a cigarette over to George, who says, "Nah, mate, I've given up," and the driver says, "Ya have? When?" and George says, "Yesterday. It's a bitch," and the driver says, "Marie asked me to give up when the kids were born," and George says, "How'd that go?" and wow, howaboutthat, they're just two mates talking about their addictions like old hens in a coop, how adorable.

I go over to the house. Jasper follows; he hasn't said a word since George showed up. I look over at him—he's a faded string bean in the dusky light. I feel bad I've brought him somewhere so ugly.

I hold up the Polaroid camera and click the house and its leaning beams and chipped paint. I go onto the veranda and click the view from the front door—long dirt road, distant sheep huddled dimly behind sagging fences. I go around the back where the dog isn't (I hope) and take a photo of the clothesline standing sentry in the gloom. I take a photo of the land sloping down, past dots of sheep to a grove of trees where maybe a creek is, and I take a photo of Jasper leaning against a fence post, probably hating me.

I don't flap any of the photos to life; I shove them into my backpack and Jasper and I walk back to the taxi. George and the driver are now having a beer together, George with a ciggie in his mouth, the driver lighting it for him. So much for resolutions.

"Um, are you drinking?" I say, even though it's bloody obvious they are.

"Yeah, won't be long, mate," says the driver.

George sucks on his cigarette, glances at me. "Want to take pictures inside?"

"No," says Jasper. His first word in about half an hour.

"Yeah," I say, and Jasper shoots me a look that could be a warning about the corpses in the freezer, but I don't listen to that look. I just walk over to the veranda steps, go up to the front door, and hear the slough and sigh of the screen door falling behind me as I step inside.

Well. Here I am.

Dad got brought back here as a baby—he got to live here with his mum and dad and dad's brother, and there's history here, I can feel it.

Dad got to toddle this corridor as a little kid, piled now with old newspapers and mud-crusted boots, and he sat in this kitchen, at this table maybe, which has a stack of plates and bowls and gunky ashtrays on top. He got to do his homework on this couch possibly, the arm of it sticky with godknowswhat and marked with rings and cigarette burns, and he watched that TV, which looks like the kind people bought before Jesus was born.

Dad got to walk down the hallway to his little bedroom with his cute bed, but when I walk between the dank walls there's a mess of towels piled by the bathroom door and a smell of something rank coming from the toilet. And it's just like a horror movie except in movies you can't smell. It's hard to breathe and there's mold in the far corner; I can see it, and holy shit, this is the grossest place I've ever seen.

Still, I step through the stifling rooms; I take photo after photo, because somewhere here—before George destroyed the place, and before Uncle Charlie married whoever my aunt was and had all the cousins who called Dad a pussy, and before

Dad's father died and his mum disappeared—maybe there was happiness in this house?

I step outside and it's fully dark. I will need to shower, for sure, when we get back.

Taxi man and George are still drinking beer, and Jasper walks quickly up to me before I get to them.

"Um. That's his third beer, Biz," he says, nodding his head towards taxi guy. I've never seen Jasper so grim.

"Shit," I say.

"No shit," he says.

"What should we do?"

"I'll drive," says Jasper. He goes over to the taxi guy, whose name we may never learn, because unlike the rest of this town, we're not on a first-name basis with every person here.

"Mate," says Jasper.

"Mate!" says the driver. "Your girlfriend all done here? Good-oh!" he says cheerily, and swigs down the last of his beer.

"Mind if I drive?" says Jasper, quietly.

George starts laughing.

The driver looks a bit stunned. "Sorry, mate?"

"It's just. You've been drinking," Jasper begins.

"Mate, that's nothing. I've driven on a case before. Didn't hit anything. No one died."

"I'm sorry, but I'm not comfortable with you driving us back."

"Not comfortable?" the driver laughs. "Fuck me!"

"Fuck him!" says George, laughing, belly rolling up and down.

"Then I guess I won't drive you back," says the driver, and he puts his ciggie into the empty beer can, throws the can on the ground, gets into the car, starts the engine, and—waving an arm out the window to George—drives away.

George just laughs and laughs and laughs and laughs.

And George's dog, who has sidled back to hang out with us, barks and barks and barks and barks.

IT'S REALLY, REALLY LATE WHEN WE GET BACK TO TOWN. WE have had to walk the whole way. Turns out Temora likes to do a complete 180 at night and freeze. Jasper is so cold and angry he's actually gone purple. We make it to the pub—the accommodation I wrote down in my travel plan a century ago—but it's closed.

I knock and knock on the glass door. Minutes pass. Stars crawl over the sky. I keep knocking. A guy comes downstairs. He cracks the door open and says, "What do you want?"

I say, "I'm sorry. I think I have a booking? For Elizabeth Grey? I'm sorry we're so late. I'm so sorry to disturb you. I am so sorry."

I am exhausted. I am sad. I haven't any grit left.

And maybe we seem like little kids then, or junkies, or runaways, or all three, because the guy takes pity on us. He lets us in and we follow him up some wooden stairs with the carpet worn through, the smell of beer and cigarettes in every step.

He unlocks a room, swings the door open. "Toilets are down that way." He thumbs to his left. "Here's ya key."

"Thank you," I say.

Jasper says nothing.

"S'all right," says the man, who might be someone's dad, or maybe he's glad he's not a dad, looking at the state of us. The man eyes Jasper and me. "Youse two look knackered. You can pay in the morning. Get some sleep," he says, and heads down the stairs. We might be the most pathetic babies he's ever seen.

I'm starving. I'm chilled through. Jasper hasn't spoken to me in three hours. It's past midnight. There's just one double bed in the small room, but it's clean, warm, and doesn't smell like rank squid, thank God.

Jasper falls onto the bed, fully dressed. "I'm going to sleep."

"I'm going to have a shower," I say. "That house was just—ugh."

God, that house. The hard dark slamming in, the way George said "Get the fuck off my property" after the taxi guy left, the way the dog turned with George and they walked into the house without looking back, and the look on Jasper's face when he realized we would be walking all the way back to town. All of it prints itself onto my skin.

"I don't want to talk about it," says Jasper. His voice is glacial. He shuts his eyes. Rolls away from me. Closes me out.

"Fine," I say. Which is what I said to myself over and over when Grace's face closed up that time, when Dad's face closed up that time, when nothing was fine, when all the doors closed.

I stand in the hollow room, and Jasper says nothing and Jasper says nothing and Jasper says nothing.

And suddenly I feel so alone it's like the universe has yawned open and sucked me in, rolling me like a moth in spider silk. I'm cocooned by nothing, and there's no path out.

I grab my bag and the towel on the chair, and head to the

toilets. The door to the bathroom creaks with nothing, and the tiles echo nothing under my feet, and the showerhead pours nothing onto my bare skin. I stand under the water and want to cry but of course there's nothing inside me to let out.

MY EYES SNAP OPEN AT SIX A.M. I'M WIRED AND FULLY awake, which is wild because I didn't get to sleep until three, and even then I'm not sure you could call those garbled moments sleep. I spent most of the night lying awake in a rigid line next to Jasper, him dead to the world beside me, my pinwheel thoughts sparking, and time sliding by, laughing its head off.

When I did sleep, I had jumbled dreams of running, chasing down buses and watching Jasper get on one without me, then turning to find myself in Dad's old room looking down at an empty paddock, and Dad standing there in his pajamas saying, "Want to swim in the creek, Biz? It's not too cold."

But when I got in, the creek was too fast and I left Dad on the bank with his eyes staring after me and I was underwater, tumbling, and in the dream I knew I was drowning, and all I had to do was let go of my body, just unhitch from it—it wouldn't take a moment, *just release, Biz, and breathe*—

and I woke up.

Jasper is so out of it he doesn't budge as I get up to pee, as I creak our door open, creak the door closed, then creak-repeat as I come back from the loo. I scuttle into bed with my Polaroids because the floor of the bathroom was cold and my feet have remembered how frozen they got last night. Jasper doesn't move at all as I shift onto my side, feet wrapped in the blanket, and peel the paper from my photos to see what they say.

Oh my God.

A PHOTOGRAPH OF A LIVING ROOM:

I am a boy. I am five and my name is Stephen Grey.

I bump off the couch and onto my bum and Mum laughs. She's wearing her dress with red flowers, the one she kisses Dad in.

Mum picks me up in her arms and says, "Stevie, want some bacon?"

I say yes because bacon is yum.

The bacon spits in the pan and hits Mum and Mum cries out and says the S-word and I say the S-word back to her. She turns and says to me, "Don't, Stephen."

Why? I like the word—how it starts soft and ends hard like you're throwing mud at the big shed wall where the tractor lives. Dad goes out on the tractor and I wait for him to come back.

Mum gives me a plate of bacon and it's getting dark. Dad isn't back.

Uncle comes in a rush rush and his hands are red and Mum says, "What's happening?"

And he says, "Martin. It's Martin."

Tractors are not good.

A photograph of a veranda:

Dad is in bed asleep. Uncle is pushing his hand under Mum's dress, which has red flowers on it. I can see through the screen door out to the veranda where Mum and Uncle lean against the rail. Uncle doesn't think I can see.

I can see.

Dad is like a jigsaw on the bed, but not finished. When they brought him back after the tractor, they forgot to put him all the way back together. So he takes lots of medicine.

Mum went outside to smoke and Uncle went with her. I snuck to the door.

Uncle says, "Leave him."

And Mum says, "I can't."

Uncle steps forward and kisses her, and I can see his tongue. And her tongue.

I push the screen door all the way open and they jump apart like when you throw a big rock in the deepwater part of the creek and the water rises up around the rock and flies.

A photograph of a clothesline:

Twilight. Four metal spokes, spread out like a stripped umbrella. Wires for clothes, strung between the spokes. A rusted handle for spinning the line.

On the line: a stained shirt, a stained cloth, mismatched socks, both stained.

The line used to be full—work clothes once, church clothes too and skirts and shorts. Life was peg and promise, but now the line is lucky to get a shirt once a month.

It remembers the time everything flew off in the storm of '74. She came out crying, saying, "It's always like this. God help me," and picking things up from the mud.

The line used to spin and spin and spin for her. She didn't see.

The rust is inside the handle now, and it can't turn.

A photograph of a kitchen:

Dad's cooking dinner. It's funny, because he's so slow.

I say, "Dad, I could drive out to the shops and get Chinese before you finish that stir-fry."

He says, "Don't be a smart-arse, Stephen. Anyway, you haven't got your license."

I might be only nine, but I know how to drive. Uncle takes me out and we do burnouts in the top paddock and Uncle puts his head back and laughs. He's happy. He wasn't for ages after Mum left, but then he met Daisy at the auctions.

Dad isn't much good for working. Sometimes he goes off his pills. He shouts and shakes and sometimes he punches things: walls, Uncle, fence posts, me. (Just the one time and then he looked at his fist and me sprawled on the floor and said, "Fuck.")

He said sorry. He hasn't done it since. That was a couple of years after Mum left. I thought if I had a smaller thing than me to punch I'd do it too.

o ° o ° o

A photograph of a bedroom (in seven parts):

1. A woman stands beside a bed, her hand on the mark on her face.

A man sits on a bed. He stares at his shoes. "I'm so sorry," he says.

The woman says, "Do it again, Martin, and I'm gone."

2. I wander in with my yo-yo—up/down it goes—and see Dad pressing Mum up against the wall beside the bed. Dad's hands are like claws on Mum's shoulders and Dad is saying jumble-words. He must be pressing hard because Mum is crying, crying, crying.

3. The man is on the bed. He's so blasted he doesn't know the boy is here. The man calls out to his wife for his meds. His wife is gone. The boy is a ghost against the wall, listening to him beg.

4. The room is made of moths and moths in mouths. The man cries out in his sleep. He can't get up. He can't move, he can't move; he is buried under a thousand splintered wings.

5. Midnight walk. I go round and round, stand at all the doors, and,

There's Uncle asleep on the bed with Daisy.

Mum's not here and Dad's not here. Where are they?

Dad's gone, Stephen.

Mum too. Where'd she go?

I don't know, she's been gone a long time, hey.

Don't talk to yourself, Stephen.

Why not?

People will think you're crazy.

6. The boy lies on the bed where the aunt and uncle sleep. The boy is touching himself when they come in and say, "What are you doing on our bed, Stephen?"

7. Cousins snicker at the door. They call me a weirdo nutcase fuckin' pussy.

Uncle and Daisy gave me this room—they say I seem to like the view. The doctors want me to feel comfortable and everyone says it might stop all the funny thoughts.

I didn't ask the thoughts to come, I say to the walls, the dark, the holes in the air, the holes. *They came when I wasn't looking.*

A photograph of the house:

I am room, I am step, I am window.

I am roof, I am wall, I am house.

I see how he and she touched each other and stopped touching each other. I see the boy at doors, listening. I hear the sound of man and woman, and woman and man, talking and kissing and shouting and hitting and crying into sinks.

I see the woman opening my front door and shutting it,

leaving down the long drive laid out like a tongue.

I see the man opening my door and shutting it.

I see him walking away from me and into water.

I am a box. I am like the box that held the man when they brought him back.

A photograph of the creek:

A man is in my water,

a man where I pool into the curve

—magpies quarreling in the trees,
a wallaby drinking upstream—
a man facedown
where my water is dark with deep
and tannin from the gums.
The boy sees him.
His mouth opens.
You could put a pebble in,
fill his mouth with pebbles,
but he runs,
falls and runs
up the hill and
into the house and
out the window and
up the tree and
onto the roof and
into the sky
and
up
into the sun.

A photograph of a roof:
    I am a boy. I stand on corrugated iron, screaming.
    I slip and fall.
    I break my arm, my wrist, my ribs on the ground.
    I howl and shake and howl and shake and howl and howl
and howl.

I AM IN A BED IN A ROOM IN A PUB
    and all
    I can hear is
    Dad.

All I can see is water, a man in
    water, a boy weeping and falling,
    rust and bleat and hit and blood.

I shake and
    all I can hear
    is my voice calling out to Dad.
    "You didn't tell me!"
    And Dad says nothing
    because he is a boy
    and he's eyes and open mouth and
    break and sky.

o ° o ° o

I feel myself
   shatter.

Weeping,
   knees up on chest, snot out of my nose.
   Jasper's awake, startled bird.
   I hunch on the bed—
   knees grabbed
   —arms hitting hitting, scratching
   down
   and
   down.

Jasper's fussing and flapping—
   what's he saying?
   Eyes wide and brown.
   I say, "Why didn't you tell me?"
   Jasper's mouth moves.
   But I can't hear him.

Jasper has no sound at all.
   His mouth moves
   but he's
   not here
   in a room on a bed, how silly
   when we are molecules.

o ° o ° o

I am atom
   against atom
   battering
   and I'm so
   sad I can't
   breathe.

Dad.
   You didn't tell me.

"I will make you so happy,"
   you said.
   "Here we are," you said. "We were so happy,"
   you said.
   "Do you remember, Biz?
   That time
   and that time and that?"
   But
   you never
   told me
   this.

Dad?

                We were so—is a lie—

Dad?

                     happy—is a lie

I am not

        you were

             not

Dad? Am I not? am I:

                    are we?

Dad?

            We are not.

Dad?

Dad?

Dad?

Dad?

Dad?

Dad?

Dad?

Dad?

Dad? Dad? Dad?

Dad? Dad? Dad? Dad? Dad? Dad? Dad? Dad? Dad? Dad?
Dad? Dad? Dad? Dad? Dad? Dad? Dad? Dad? Dad? Dad? Dad?
Dad? Dad? Dad? Dad? Dad? Dad? Dad? Dad? Dad? Dad? Dad?
Dad? Dad? Dad? Dad? Dad? Dad? Dad? Dad? Dad? Dad? Dad?
Dad? Dad? Dad? Dad? Dad? Dad? Dad? Dad? Dad? Dad? Dad?
Dad? Dad? Dad? Dad? Dad? Dad? Dad? Dad? Dad? Dad? Dad?
Dad? Dad? Dad? Dad? Dad? Dad? Dad? Dad? Dad? Dad? Dad?
Dad? Dad? Dad? Dad? Dad? Dad? Dad? Dad? Dad? Dad? Dad?

Dad? Dad? Dad? Dad? Dad? Dad? Dad? Dad? Dad? Dad? Dad?
Dad? Dad? Dad? Dad? Dad? Dad? Dad? Dad? Dad? Dad? Dad?
Dad? Dad? Dad? Dad? Dad? Dad? Dad? Dad? Dad? Dad? Dad?
Dad? Dad? Dad? Dad? Dad? Dad? Dad? Dad? Dad? Dad? Dad?
Dad? Dad? Dad? Dad? Dad? Dad? Dad? Dad? Dad? Dad? Dad?
Dad? Dad? Dad? Dad? Dad? Dad? Dad? Dad? Dad? Dad? Dad?
Dad? Dad? Dad? Dad? Dad? Dad? Dad? Dad? Dad? Dad? Dad?
Dad? Dad? Dad? Dad? Dad? Dad? Dad? Dad? Dad? Dad? Dad?
Dad? Dad? Dad? Dad? Dad? Dad? Dad? Dad? Dad? Dad? Dad?
Dad? Dad? Dad? Dad? Dad? Dad? Dad? Dad? Dad? Dad? Dad?
Dad? Dad? Dad? Dad? Dad? Dad? Dad? Dad? Dad? Dad? Dad?
Dad? Dad? Dad? Dad? Dad? Dad? Dad? Dad? Dad? Dad? Dad?
Dad? Dad? Dad? Dad? Dad? Dad? Dad? Dad? Dad? Dad?

MUM COMES TO WAGGA HOSPITAL, WHERE I HAVE BEEN
taken. She sits beside my bed in the psych ward where I must
stay.

She looks gray, diluted, dissolved.

I look at her. I want to say "Sorry," and "Sorry," but I'm really
drugged up, so it's hard to speak.

She says, "What happened?"

I want to say "Everything," and "Dad." But I'm so tired.

I close my eyes. When I open them again she's gone.

The nights are hard. I hear a lot of calling out and crying. The
doors echo when they close. The moon is a white curl against
the paper of the sky.

I think maybe I am the moon, but I check the tag on my
wrist and it keeps saying *Elizabeth Martin Grey,* and the Martin
is for my Dad's dad who drowned in a creek before I was born.

o ° o ° o

Dad's by the window; he says, "Well, here we are."

Dad's cross-legged, making ice cream.

It's the middle of the night. I can see out the window how the moon is like a spoonful of ice cream, like when you scrape your spoon against the top of the tub and it comes up in a perfect coil.

Dad says, "This will taste fantastic, Biz," and I'm five and I'm on our kitchen counter kicking my heels against the cabinets. Mum comes in.

She says, "Stephen?"

"Yes?" says Dad.

"It's two in the morning."

"Perfect ice cream weather."

"Why is Biz awake?"

"I needed her help."

"To make ice cream?"

"To eat ice cream."

Mum can't help herself; she grins,

and Dad grins

and their light is my light.

Dad floats beside the window. He's curled into the moon's curl.

"Do you remember, Biz?" he says. "When we ate the ice cream? And it went down your chin, and I let mine drip down my chin and we pretended we were vampires?"

I say nothing.

He smiles at me from across the room. He's so far.

I reach out for him.

He reaches out for me.

I say, "Fuck off, Dad. You're not real."

And Dad blips out.

Another night:

> I'm sorry, Dad. I didn't mean it. Dad, please. I'm sorry.
> Dad.
> Please.
> Dad?
> *Please.*

Another night:

> Dad hovers beside my bed.
> He says, "Of course I am real, Biz. Come find me."
> I'm so relieved.
> Thank God, Dad. Of course I will.
> I walk out of the hospital.
> I walk to Temora. I find the creek and it's deep in the corner, dark and deep. An owl watches from a bony gum.
> I say, "I'm going in," and the owl says, "About time."

The psychiatrist in our consulting room says, "Elizabeth, we want to help you understand what's happening. It sounds like times have been tough and your mind has had to get creative to cope. Which is okay, you know; the mind is an amazing thing—without it we wouldn't have cars, would we? Or music. Or toasters." The psychiatrist smiles.

We have walked to this room, through a door the psychiatrist swiped a card to unlock, then another door—*swipe*—like we were stepping into a secret. The doors clicked open, clicked closed. The psychiatrist's shoes tapped the floor.

We sit on green chairs, a coffee table between us, a fern on the table. The psychiatrist crosses his legs. He wears patterned socks. Isn't that interesting? *Isn't that funny, Dad? You and he?*

The psychiatrist coughs in his seat. "So, Elizabeth, the thing is, things that seem true right now may not be true. We want to help you make the distinction."

The psychiatrist is made of water. Does he know?

I tell him how many molecules he has and how he will become rain in time and he coughs again and says, "Let's focus on you, shall we?"

The psychiatrist murmurs beside my bed; he's talking to Mum, but I'm sleeping and not-sleeping so the conversation is like a glass I dropped.

HE: *Something something*—trauma—*something something*—

SHE: But—*something something*—will she be—

HE: *Something*—different treatment options—*something*—need to stabilize—*something*

SHE: Is she, how did she—

HE: *Something something*—Martin—*something*—did you—

SHE: I didn't—*something*—I didn't know—

Mum's voice breaks.

And their words turn into birds.

I say to the psychiatrist, "Can I leave?"

"You can leave, Elizabeth, of course, that's what we want too. We want you to go home and get good care. We just need to make sure you're stable before you go."

I say, "I am stable. I would like to leave so I can go to the creek and go under the water. There I will find Dad's dad, whose name is Martin. I will pull him out of the water and reverse time and then everything will be better and then Dad won't die."

The psychiatrist doesn't hear me. I try to explain, but all that comes out are speech bubbles, like in cartoons.

My bubbles are empty.

It is pitiful.

I want to walk off this paper. I want to walk out of this story.

Jasper sits beside the bed.

He waits for me to speak.

He holds my hand.

I don't know what to say. Except "I'm sorry."

"For what, Biz?"

"My brain is broken. I think. Sorry."

Jasper's face.

I can't read it.

"I'm really sorry," I tell him again. Is this my new word? Sorry for existing, sorry for scaring, sorry for dragging you here, sorry for breaking?

He says, "I'm sorry for telling you."

"For telling me?"

"What I heard them say."

"Who?"

"The taxi guy. George."

"What?"

"On the walk home, Biz. I was so angry. I just said it."

On the walk home? But Jasper didn't speak. He never told me anything.

Jasper, no.

You didn't tell me about Martin. You didn't tell me about the creek. You didn't say anything. You were silent the whole way to town. *Jasper.* Don't you remember?

I start to shake. The earth tilts.

Jasper says, "Biz—"

and the nurse comes and says, "What's happening?"

and Jasper says, "Nothing!" but that's not true.

Is it?

Jasper?

A doctor comes.

Jasper has to leave.

People fuss and flap around me.

I shake and shake and shake and shake and shake.

A door slides open. Closes.

Jasper visits. I tell him my brain is broken. I say I'm sorry.

Jasper says, "Do you know there are eighty-nine billion neurons in the human brain? Almost the same as the number of galaxies in the observable universe, Biz."

I look at him.

He says, "Do you know monks can increase their temperatures by seventeen degrees just by meditating?"

I know these things. How does he know these things? Did I tell him? I don't remember—

He says, "The mind is miraculous." He squeezes my hand, hard. "You've got a fucking miraculous mind, Biz."

I close my eyes. I try to turn off my miraculous mind. It needs to be quiet for one second. A millisecond, I'll take anything. Please stop so I can rest.

"Also, I got you a Pokémon hat."

I open my eyes.

Jasper pulls the hat out of a bag. He puts it on the table beside my bed.

Then he holds my hand and I hold his until a nurse comes and tells him it is time to go.

Mum looks tired. I am tired. I had to go to yoga this morning. I mean, I was *encouraged* to go to yoga. I went; we downward dogged; we sat and counted our breaths. Yesterday I had to do art, which is funny because once I used to draw upside-down houses and now my brain is upside down. I would laugh. But I am really, really tired.

Mum sits with me and leans her head on her hand. When she thinks I am sleeping, she bites her nails and reads romance novels from the hospital shop.

When I am awake, she says things about the twins and about Aunt Helen and she says things about me getting better. She says she didn't know about Martin—she didn't—Dad never—and inside her words I hear:

If I had known, I would have put us in a bubble, Biz. I would have put my body in front of yours. I would have taken us all to a hut on a mountaintop and never come down.

I watch Mum as she leaks and talks. I watch her and don't say:

No point, Mum—the mountaintop would have crumbled. You can't escape your history. It's like a river that follows you, blood that moves without you thinking. The past turns corners to find you.

o ° o ° o

The psychiatrist's face is wrinkled, like someone scrunched his paper face, then unfolded him. His hair looks like he's been walking in the wind.

"You have complex issues, Elizabeth," he says from his green chair. "But you can get treatment. You will get good therapy at home. You'll feel better. It might be hard sometimes, but you will be okay," and then the psychiatrist yawns, his mouth stretched wide. He blocks it with his hand, says, "Sorry! Not much sleep."

I try to picture what "sleepless" might look like for him. Watching TV, maybe. Dancing tango till morning with dark-eyebrowed women. Eating cookies in bed with his cat, crumbs prickling the sheets.

The psychiatrist smiles. "Paperwork, actually. And maybe a little Netflix. Just a smidge."

Whoa, Biz, he's a mind reader.

No.

I was talking. I think?

When? Just then. Embarrassing. Yes.

I am in bed. This morning I had to exercise in a gym with some people. We are supposed to be up and awake in the day and in bed and asleep in the night, but at night the walls creak, doors *click-click*, and the air groans. At night I lie awake and watch the clouds make shapes with their hands.

Grace comes in and sits on the chair beside me.

She reaches for my hand and holds it.

I open my eyes as wide as they can go; I let all the light in.

Grace.

If I had my camera I would take a photo.

"Biz," she says.

Grace looks crisp and clean. She's wearing a uniform, which is ironed. I don't remember Grace ironing things before. It has been six months since I saw her. I guess that's enough time to learn how to iron.

"Grace," I croak. I clear my throat, and say, "Grace."

"Your mum rang me," she says.

"Oh?"

"And Jasper. He texted and DM'd and emailed."

I tried doing those things, Grace. I tried to reach you. All of the above: A, B, C, and D.

"I convinced Dad to bring me to see you, even though I'm supposed to be studying *all the time*." Grace rolls her eyes. "It's a fucking hard school, Biz. They barely let you sleep. It's like we're being trained to be NASA astronauts. I'm taking extension chemistry and maths. And commerce! My head's all numbers, all the time. I dream about them, cosines and factorials and quadrants." Grace laughs, then coughs. She squeezes my hand.

"Did you die?" I say.

"Um?" says Grace.

"I think you did. I think you are dead. You are not real, Grace," I say.

Grace is confused. Grace shakes her head.

Doesn't she remember? How I went into the water that time—

when the waves slapped and tripped me and Jasper came
and how the doors slid open—
and she died?

No?

Grace, pal, you were *right there.*

Poor Grace. It's all a blank. So I tell her in detail: how she was somewhere in the water too that night, with Suryan, having sex, and as Jasper pulled me from the water, a rip came and tugged Grace out of time and Suryan's arms. And then Grace —hapless, hopeless—floated out to sea like a mermaid going home. She called and called for help but no one listened, and then not much later Grace was quiet and a seagull flew down next to me and said, "Too bad. She's dead."

I look at Grace. Her dark brown eyes are wide, wide.

"And that's how you died," I say. I lift and drop my hands as if to say, *Such Is Life.*

Grace doesn't believe me.

"That's crazy, Biz," she says. She keeps shaking her head.

I say, "But that's how these doors work, Grace."

I would explain more, about doors and unpinnable matter and the unbound universe, but Grace has stood up. She's crying; she's looking for a doctor.

Oh, Grace. A doctor won't help. Doctors can't see dead people.

"Such a shame," I say. "I am truly sorry for your loss."

Grace cries harder. She leaves the room. I let her leave.

It is hard to accept. Death is a hard sell. You need years and years and years and years and years to get used to it.

Mum sits beside the bed, reading. She looks up and sees me watching her.

She smiles. "I love you, Biz," she says.

I look at her and see her pieced-together smile, the wobble of her. I see how Mum is made of molecules, how she's only just together.

"Why do you love me?" I ask.

She hiccup-laughs. "So many reasons," she says.
She sits beside my bed and lists them.

Jasper comes to say goodbye. He has to leave because his mum and dad had a "talk"—probably about why the hell he was roaming around the outback with a crazy girl—and his mum has summoned Jasper home.

"I have to go, Biz. I don't want to."

Is that true?

I can't tell. I would take a photo, but they have taken my camera away.

Jasper leans over me. He squeezes my shoulders. He gives me a kiss on the forehead and he's crying a little, and a part of me melts into him so he can carry me home.

And in that moment—reaching through the fug and gray and cottony walls—I remember lying on the bed in the pub, looking at the photo of Jasper leaning on the fence. The line of his body, the angle of him, the measured *him* of him, there with me, not leaving but staying.

And the photo whispered:

I love Biz. She's fucking hard work, but I'd walk through fire for her.

Jasper stands by the bedside, holding my hand.

(So, I guess Jasper loves me?

And I guess I love him.

And maybe Jasper's not gay? Or maybe he totally is.

You can kiss anyone you want and still be gay, Biz.)

Jasper's eyes look into mine. He's saying words.

(Or maybe he's bi? Maybe he's demi? Maybe he's pan . . . ?

Maybe, maybe, maybe. I don't know. Jasper can tell me, when he wants to. If he wants to. Does he want to?

How do you like your blue-eyed boy, Biz?

. . . and how does he like you?)

I look up at Jasper.

I'm so tired.

I close my eyes.

When I open them, Jasper's gone. Two hours later, I can still see the echo of his body, standing there.

If I were real and Grace was still mine, she might say:

"Biz? So what does that mean? Do you like him? Does this mean you're not allthewaygay? Maybe he's not allthewaygay?"

BIZ: . . .

GRACE: Do you love him? Do you think he loves you? Will you be boyfriend and girlfriend? Or bi-friend and gay-friend, hahaha? Will you marry him, will you have ten kids together? Will you never leave each other until you die? Will you forsake all others? Will you step in front of bullets for each other? Will you, Biz? Will you?

BIZ: Grace.

GRACE: Yes?

BIZ: Get the fuck out of my head.

It is morning.

Today I ask a nurse what the date is—how long have I been

here; how long have I been asleep in this castle; how many barnacles can she see?

The nurse looks at her watch, at the date on her watch. And it turns out today is the day Dad died. Ten years ago exactly.

Mum comes in. She plops her bag on the chair; she kisses me on the forehead.

"Hello, sweetheart," she says.

I say, "Ten years, Mum," and she bursts into tears.

And then all we have, all we can do, is hold each other—as we swim in the water of losing Dad, in the water of missing him, in all that water. We hold each other tightly, tightly, tightly.

It is night.

The dark is smothery. The air feels like soup.

The moon is gone. The floors squeak when the nurses walk on them. The pills make my skin paper-thin and I can't smell any flowers. When did I last smell flowers?

I hear weeping in every corner, through every wall.

Dad?

Dad?

Why did you leave me to this?

Why didn't you tell me it would be like this, so I could go before it hurt this much?

Dad comes and hovers beside my bed. He smiles at me, his face streaky.

He has been crying for some time. And floating, just like me.

Always floating, he and I, somewhere not quite here—an inch, an arm's length, a sky away.

And just like that,

I remember three things.

ONE.

I am five and we're in the big shop, looking for a bra for Mum. I'm bored. I want to look at the toys.

Dad's gone hunting for socks. I asked him, "Can I go with you? Can we look at the toys?" and he said, "Not right now," in the voice that meant maybe we'll never look at the toys.

Mum takes me into a fitting room. It's small and hot. I say, "Mum! Can we go look at the toys?"

She sighs and says, "Biz, why don't you wait on the couch," and points to the one at the entrance to the fitting rooms. I sit there for a bit, and the couch smells funny. It's itchy; it scratches the back of my legs.

So I get up and go look for the toys.

The toys are a long way away. I have to walk past cooking things and electric things and cushions. I have to sneak left and right and it's like a maze, like a real life one, not one you draw on.

A man stands at the end of an aisle between some shiny shirts and ugly sweaters. He smiles at me.

"Hello," he says.

"Hello," I say, because Mum always says to be polite when people say hello and to not just look at my feet.

"Where are you going?" he says.

"I'm looking for the toys," I say.

"Oh, I know where those are," the man says, and he puts out his hand.

I don't take it, but then he says, "Let me show you," and smiles again, so I take his hand because Mum always says "Be nice, Biz" when I forget to be nice.

We walk left and right and left and I think I see the toys over by a wall and I say, "Is that them?"

The man says, "I know where you can get really good toys. Better than those," and I think, How? and Wow!

The man smells of peppermint and his hand is cool, like it's made of plaster, like the plaster figures Dad and I made one Saturday when he wasn't working or running or sleeping.

We get to the entrance of the big shop and I say, "Is it far?"

The man says, "Not far," and, "Do you want a peppermint?"

But when I hold out my hand to take it, I hear Dad shout behind me and he sounds so loud I jump. And the man jumps next to me and he spins like a floppy puppet, because Dad's running for us and he's not being friendly at all. So the man lets go of me and he runs and I don't know who to watch—Dad coming towards me with his face purple, or the peppermint man running away, zipping around people like he's a race car.

When Dad reaches me, he grabs me and picks me up and squeezes me so tightly I can't breathe. And now Mum's here, and she's squeezing me tightly too, so I'm stuck between them, and I think they've forgotten I'm here, because they're holding on to me and each other and not letting go. They're snuffling and trembling and I can't crawl out because my feet aren't even touching the floor, so I pop out of my body. *Whoosh* I go.

I look down at the three of us. Here, the air is not hot and wet, and there's space to breathe, and I can see almost all the way to the toys. And maybe we will go there when Mum and Dad stop holding me, and maybe they'll get me a toy and maybe we'll get a milkshake after?

And that is the first time.

TWO.

I've just turned six and for three nights my fever climbs. My body is a temple of steam and terrible dreams. On the fourth day, Mum's at work, and Dad's home laying cloths over my belly, my face, my legs. He puts the thermometer under my armpit. The glass is cold. I say, "Turtle. Pumpkin, pajamas. Alice."

I get so hot, Dad freaks out. He puts me in the bath.

I scream.

Mum's on the phone. "It has to be warm, Stephen!"

"But her temp's 105!"

"She'll go into shock if the water's too cold."

The water's too cold. I go into shock.

"Shit!" says Dad.

I arch my back. I jerk. I seize. I throw up.

And then I stop breathing.

"Shit!"

I'm here and then I'm not. I glide out of my body and it's so easy, just a slip, a snick, and I'm out. I float over us. There's

Dad, soaking wet, and me soaking wet. There's the phone; a lady is saying, "One, two, three," and Dad's got his mouth over mine. He's pushing air into me.

I think, *Counting is fun.*

The bath is full and has my duck in it.

The bath is blue. The water looks blue because the bath is blue.

The dog scratches at the door. Dad doesn't notice the dog at the door because I am not breathing. I go to the door and through the door and think, *Here is Bump.* The dog looks up at me and wags his tail. Clever dog!

I like floating but Dad doesn't like it. He's crying all over me, making me wetter and I think, *Dad! Stop making me wetter,* but I feel bad because Dad's so sad.

And the lady on the phone says, "One, two, three."

I think, *I can count to a hundred and sixty-four,* and I want to tell Dad, but he's busy breathing into me and saying, "Biz! Please."

And he's praying. I can hear his thoughts. *Please please please,* he's asking God.

And the ambulance people whack up the stairs and Bump goes *Bark! Bark! Bark! Bark! Bark!*

And they've got a special thing for my breathing which PUSHES the air into me, and *thwap,* I'm flicked, slapback in my body. I cough and cough and cry hard, and Dad says, "Thank you, oh, God, thank you," and this is the first time I've ever heard him talk to our Heavenly Father.

I think, *Then God must be real.* And I look up at Dad's clear-water eyes and think, *Maybe you're God?*

And that is the second time.

THREE.

I am seven.

There is a sound in this house I do not understand.

The sound makes the walls of the house quake.

The sound is unreal and real. It hurts my teeth. Bump whines and crouches with his tail between his legs.

Where is it coming from?

I run first to the back veranda, but there's just my bike for riding, and the backyard sloping down.

I run to the front yard, where the car is parked with its dent from Dad's prang with the postal van.

I run to the laundry room, where Mum has taught me how to put on a load. Then the lounge room, where sometimes Dad sits for ages with his head in his hands.

Then faster, to the kitchen, faster, to the downstairs toilet, fast up the stairs to the landing, and the sound is louder here.

The sound tries to lift the roof off.

I run to the bathroom where I have my bath but it's empty now.

I run to my room, where my toys are all awake.

I run to Mum and Dad's room—

and the sound is here.

The sound swirls around my legs and up my body. Mum kneels at the bedside, her arms splayed over Dad, who is in the bed.

The sound is hers.

Wetness slides between my legs and slicks down

and I don't care because there's Dad, but it's not Dad,

Dad doesn't look like that—

and Mum doesn't see me—

and Dad doesn't see me

—because Dad can't—

Dad—

won't

isn't.

I turn and bolt down the stairs.

Slam out the back veranda,

down the steps,

I tear down the hill,

tumble-race down and down,

over the creek and up to the big tree and

climb,

up to the top,

through the leaves,

into the clouds,

up,

up,

all the way out of myself I climb,
and crawl into the sky.

And that is the third time.

IS THAT HOW IT WAS FOR YOU, DAD?

Before you fell off the roof?

After you saw him?

Did you slide out of yourself like me and sit in the clouds for a while?

Did you always float like me?

Dad?

Was it always beautiful where you went?

Dad?

How did you manage to come back?

Dad?

Did you always wish you hadn't?

Dad?

How did you manage to stay so long?

DAD'S ON THE END OF MY BED.

He is made of paper.

He is pixels and grain. He is a figment of white and black.

He is a measurement of light.

Dad opens his mouth. Closes it. Thinks.

He says:

"When you were born, Biz, I thought I would die. I mean, I knew I was going to; we all do. I mean. I know I did."

He blinks at me, slowly, like he's in slow motion.

"I mean," he says, "when you were born, I held you and thought, *I might die of love.* I understood, then. What it all means, you know? I thought, *I would throw myself in front of a truck for you.* I would not hesitate. I knew this, .01 seconds into holding you.

"You were tiny, Biz. You were so fragile. I held you and sang a song to you, and you slept in my arms and I was hit by this *thunderfeeling*, like I was swimming inside a storm, you know?

"What did I sing to you? Nina Simone, I think. 'Mr. Bojangles.' Yeah, that's right. I don't know why. I didn't plan it.

"I remember thinking: *I'm going to make you so happy.*

"I thought: *You're going to make me so happy.*

"I thought: *I'll breathe for you, Biz, beat for you, walk and work and live for you.*"

Dad is a shiver in the air. Dad is see-through. Dad's voice is a hum.

"I am so sorry I couldn't do it for longer, sweetheart. I am so sorry I didn't stay. I wish I could explain it—if there was a way—but maybe there isn't a way or a why. If I could, I'd show you, I wish—"

Dad leans forward. He picks up my hand, his hand/my hand; we are figments, fragments.

Dad is a measurement of love.

"Don't come find me," he says suddenly. "Please, Biz?"

He says, "Promise? You don't need to. I'm right here."

And I feel a thump in my chest. Like someone has dropped a rock onto my ribs and it's a wonder my bones don't crack.

I can feel the stone settling,

round rock into riverbed.

I am the riverbed.

We are the rock.

Dad.

Dad?

"Yes?" says the rock, says the riverbed, says my fleshbone, says my father.

Tell me a story?

"I can do that."

I lie in the dark, and listen.

THE FIRST TIME HE SAW A CITY. RISE AND GLINT OF BUILD-
ings upon buildings. Sound, steel, and sinew, walking for hours.

The first time he saw an ocean. Tumble, breath. Rise, fall.
Blue to always.

"Biz, it was beautiful. It was like waking up."

The first time he saw the sun rise over the ocean.

The first wave he caught.

Electric, electric, electric.

The first time he was dumped off the wave.

The first salt-in-mouth-kiss of a wave.

The first time he saw Mum. She split him open and laid him
out.

The first time he heard Mum laugh.

The first time he kissed her. It was honey and sunlight.

The first time they made love, his skin zinging.

The first time he flew a kite.

The first time he ran on sand. The first time he ate a
nectarine.

The first time, the first time—

the first time he saw me.

The first time he kissed the top of my head.

The first time I fell asleep in his arms.

The first time I walked towards him. Arms stretched out.

The first time I said his name.

The first time he said mine.

"Biz."

Laughter, toddle feet, sand and sun through leaves.

"Biz."

Ice cream on chins, rainbow lorikeets.

"I love you," says Dad.

He's faint now. He's talked for hours. He's laid my stone-work down. It's hard to see him; he's fading out.

Biz, he says.

I love you.

IV

SYLVIA'S DARKROOM IS ALL FINISHED WHEN I COME TO VISIT.

She's so thrilled to see me, she hugs me until I'm pretty sure a rib shifts.

I squeak.

"Sorry!" she says. She lets me go. She quivers; she's basically dancing in place.

"It's okay, Sylvia," I say. I speak slowly, like I need to practice. Like casual conversation is a language I've forgotten after all this time. It takes a while, doesn't it, to learn to walk again? That's what they say.

She walks me around the darkroom. She has the amplifier, no, the whatsit, no, the projector—the enlarger, that's the word.

The enlarger sits in its spot like a little photo-making time machine. Hanging above it are Sylvia's photos. I lean forward and touch them. There's a photo of the sea, leaping and frothy, and on the horizon a cargo ship is heading to Russia or China or coming back. I don't know—it doesn't tell me.

The new medication means I don't hear the photos

anymore. I mean, I could, if I wanted. I could keep listening, if I wanted. I could listen harder, but I am trying to let the pictures be quiet so other sounds can come in.

The medicine means I should be able to think more clearly. Or is that less clearly? I am not sure. Anyway, it's supposed to make me better. I am waiting to be better. At least, better than I have been, better than before. It's a waiting game; I am a waiter, would you like fries with that, haha.

I can still make jokes. That's a good thing. I check for what's missing and what's not. I am still tall. I am still here.

Sylvia's photos hang in a row along the wall: A dark-haired woman beside a window, Sylvia's busted car, a frangipani flower, a patterned cat on a driveway.

I can see, objectively, that the photos are lovely.

To the right of the cat is Jasper—a rectangle of him in black and white, smiling in front of the lighthouse—and my insides pang.

He hasn't come to see me yet.

That is, I haven't texted him yet and told him I am home. I keep picking up the phone, putting it down.

If I text him, what will he say?

"Sorry, I'm busy?" or,

"While you were gone, I realized you were too crazy to deal with, so from now on I will only be friends with people who don't talk to their dead dads?" or,

only silence?

I look at Sylvia. She's looking at the photo of Jasper. She smiles. "Can you believe he let me take his picture?" She moves on, chattering. "He'll be so happy you're home. I can't wait to tell him!"

I touch her arm.

"No," I say. And it comes out harder, sharper than I meant. My throat tightens.

Sylvia stops. Looks at me.

"I'll tell him," I say.

I try to smile, to reassure her. My smile must look like a two-year-old's drawing, because Sylvia sees right through it.

She takes my hand, wraps an arm around my back, walks me out of the darkroom into the afternoon sun.

"I think it's time for tea," she says.

I've been home for three days. I dropped in on Sylvia without calling. This is my biggest outing so far. I haven't been anywhere much at all.

I've gone for walks with Mum and the dog, slow strolls to the sea, the two of us talking or not talking. I've made an appointment to see Bridgit; soon I guess we'll start putting me back together, bit by bit by bit. I've been home for hugs with the twins when they get back from school. They keep running in and jumping on the bed in the mornings.

Mum says, "Dart! Billie! That's too much!"

But I say, "It's okay," because they are like puppies and I remember being a puppy.

I remember a lot of things.

I sat with the psychiatrist in Wagga after telling him all the things I remembered.

He sat with his knees facing my knees. His face was gentle, empathic, understanding. It was a good face for what I had just told him.

"Elizabeth," he said, "I am so sorry you had to experience all of that."

I looked at my knee, at the hole in my jeans. *If I picked at the thread,* I thought, *if I made the hole larger, how long would it take to unravel my jeans and sit here under a lapful of thread? Would that startle the psychiatrist? Would his eyes go wide and would he have to say, "I think you should put on some clothes, young lady"?*

Nothing would surprise him. He's trained to be unflappable, like Navy SEALs and the Queen.

But I was surprised. I was surprised it all came out—all the clag and muck of memory—pouring and piling onto Max the psychiatrist's floor.

Why'd it happen?

Maybe I'd hit a tipping point, of moments sitting in chairs looking into the eyes of people who were paid to care about me.

Perhaps it was because of the medication.

Or, perhaps Dad laid enough stone down for me to speak.

I sat in my chair, all those words out of my body. They laid themselves in front of Max, who had a sorting tray, all his notes, and his PhD.

And the two of us began to talk.

Sylvia sits on her couch and pours me another cup of tea. The cat lies on my lap, asleep. Muffins sit in a circle on a green-painted plate. I've already eaten two. They're amazing. They have soft apple and dark chocolate pieces. They taste like apple-chocolate clouds.

I've just told Sylvia about the photos. And about the hospital.

And my medicine. And the psychiatrist, and what he said and what I said and said and said.

And I've told her about Dad.

Sylvia has nodded. She has touched my hand, sighed, smiled with her eyes. She has sat closer and closer as I've talked.

She sits now, in the quiet, with me. We sip our tea.

"I visited a psychiatric ward once," she says.

I look at Sylvia.

"I went to see a friend, Desiree," says Sylvia. "She had an accident. She said one minute the world was round and next it was flat. She said she fell off the edge of it and bumped her head. She couldn't understand it. So we walked in the garden. There were bees in the lavender, hundreds of them. Round or flat—there were still bees," Sylvia says.

I nod. I pick up another muffin, take a bite, close my eyes. Lord. Somehow they're still warm.

"I also knew someone who could see auras," Sylvia continues. "I met her at a party. Her name was Tash. Oh, she was gorgeous; she had amber eyes like a cat, you know? And lovely boobs, like cushions when you hugged her. She was delightful." Sylvia smiles, remembering. "Anyway, she said I was orange. I've never really liked that color, but there it was. Tash said it was the perfect color for me."

Sylvia picks up the teapot with its tawny frogmouth tea cozy. Her hands are trembly; she's getting old, older, oldest. She's my bright bird, pouring herself oolong.

"And ghosts, well"—Sylvia waves a hand—"I mean, they're everywhere. My cousin Matthew has one in his upstairs bathroom."

I look at Sylvia.

Sylvia looks at me.

"I love you, Elizabeth," she says.

"I love you too, Sylvia," I say, swallowing.

"The world is full of strange wonders, darling. Maybe you're just lucky enough to see them."

She scooches across the tiny gap between us and hugs me.

Sylvia feels like she is made of bird bones. Her body is so light I could pick her up and put her in my pocket. I could carry Sylvia everywhere like a talisman.

When we sit back, we both wipe our eyes. "Sorry," I say.

"Tiny oceans in our eyes," says Sylvia.

"Little sailboats crossing tiny oceans," I say.

Sylvia picks up my hand. She squeezes it. She doesn't let go until Mum comes, and it's time for me to leave.

SUMMER SEEMS TO HAVE BLASTED IN WHILE I WAS AWAY. Each morning, the sun has belted into my room. Cicadas have lined up on the trees to shout. At the beach, Bump flings himself into the surf like he's a lifesaver and needs to rescue every fool.

The sea has shown off every day—the waves turquoise and glassy, clean and curled, surfers carving lines into the water. Bump has barked and leaped, the sea caught in his mouth.

Mum has found a photography course I can take next year, if I want. It's a pathway to uni, she says. Or not—it's just a course—I don't have to worry about it right now, but it looks good, doesn't it, Biz?

Grace has sent emails I don't read, and a card Mum has propped, unopened, by the cactus in the kitchen. The last time I gave Grace a card was for her birthday. A million years ago, I photoshopped our faces onto hot men's bodies from some fireman's calendar and inside the card I had written, "Putting fires out since 1993."

It didn't make any sense. Grace said she loved it.

Grace said a lot of things back then. We said a lot of things. Our talk made ribbons I would have to squint, now, to see.

It's Christmas next week; how did that happen? The twins keep singing carols and asking how many more sleeps, and does Mum have everything on their present list, along with their birthday list for February? The twins want a jumping castle for their party; they want a hot-air balloon ride; they want ponies. Can they, Mum, can they, can they?

The twins are all laugh and dance and ask and hug and bounce. They're like fairies. Maybe they're not real?

A door slides open, a door slides closed.

Here you are, Biz, says Dad. Says my memory of Dad, says Dad beside my ear, says Dad always.

Look around, Biz.

Look up and breathe.

Mum and I sit on the back veranda after she gets home from work. It's the day after seeing Sylvia. Bump lies at my feet. Actually, he's *on* my feet. When the dog first saw me, the day I came back from hospital, his whole body shook. Tail to nose, trembling and wriggling. Bump kept whining, pushing at my hands, at my legs, at my face, licking and reaching, trying to crawl in.

Mum laughed. "He's lost it." And she cried a bit watching him, because I suppose if Mum could tremble and twitch and push her face into mine, maybe she would.

Mum twirls her wineglass by its stem. It rests on her knee; it's still full from when she poured it. She's busy thinking. Her foot touches mine. She's moved her chair up close, and normally I'd tease her for being sentimental, but tonight, I don't.

We watch the sun slide behind the escarpment. Birds settle into the trees, squabbling over sleeping spots. The air changes before our eyes. It's incandescent, immense. The light has this glow you can't capture on film. You could try. You wouldn't get it.

Some people call this time the gloaming, but I'd call it "the closest to how it feels to float." And if someone wanted me to paint the feeling for them, I'd just put their hand on my chest and say, "Here."

I sit with my hand on Bump's head, rubbing my fingers over his ears.

I'm going to float again. I know it will happen.

This moment will pass. Another one will come. Hard will come—grief and dark and worry and loss. Again. Again. Sooner. Later.

There's a chance I'll float out of it for the rest of my life.

"Is that bad?" I asked Max the psychiatrist on my last day in hospital.

He said, "You know, Biz, it's not the worst thing. The mind does it to protect you. It's a cushion for those moments when things are too much—it's the brain's defense mechanism. You'll work on this, Biz, with your psychologist. You'll figure out when you're doing it, and why. You'll learn not to float completely away." He leaned forward. "I truly believe you'll be able to bring yourself back when you need to."

I'll learn to come home, is what he means, learn to pin myself, here and here. Like maybe Dad tried to with his photos, album after album, placing hope and Mum and me and *the ocean, the first salt kiss of the ocean* onto paper. Then all the years on the end of my bed, Dad telling me who I was, who I am. And now, behind my ribs, the rocks laid there: a pattern of rise, fall, settle, stay.

The light in the yard has begun shifting into blue, into black. A frog burps in the pond by the flowering gum; the dog lifts his head and woofles, and Mum laughs. At least, she makes this hiccupy, half-laugh sound that could be mistaken for everything being okay.

Is everything okay?

That's impossible to say. It's okay now. It's okay now—

But Mum's leaking. She's in tears in the dusky light, squeezing my hand.

"It's too much to ask of a human," Mum says. "Don't you think, Biz?"

I don't know what she means, and I know exactly, so I say, "Yeah."

"I mean, to love someone who lives outside your body, whose life you can't control. You can't hold anything still. You can't be sure anything will be okay. You can't stop the sky from falling."

I look at Mum.

Mum is glass; she's cracked voice and wet eyes. She's trying to walk through the world, and it keeps tilting. How has she stayed up?

"Life does kind of suck," I say. And it's true. Life is impossible, chaotic. It's a maze of sorrow and sunlight; it can't be mapped.

Mum leans against me.

"Yeah, it kind of does," she says.

"Yeah."

"Not always," she adds. "Sometimes."

"Definitely always sometimes, it sucks," I say.

Mum laughs. She looks over the tangle of yard—twisty trees, scrambled grass, shadows shifting.

She takes in a breath. "The thing is, Biz, it's also the best thing I've ever done," she says. "All of it, this, you, the twins, here, now, Dad, me. Really. It's the *best thing I have ever done*."

She rests her head on my shoulder. I lean my head on her head.

We watch the changing light. It keeps moving, it gets deeper, it won't stop changing.

Life is terrible and beautiful, isn't it? It's the best/worst at the exact same time, all possibilities at once.

I guess it's whatever it is when you observe it.

And a second later, it's something else.

Now it's something else again.

Now it's something else.

Mum and I watch the light leave the yard. The twins clatter open the screen door, tumble out, and Dart says, "What's for dinner?"

Billie says, "All we can find are these chick peas!"

They hold up a can each and make faces, and we know what's going to happen next. It's going to be Thai food. It's going to be too much satay and our faces leaning towards each other in the restaurant, the four of us a busy picture in the front window.

Mum and I get up and stretch. The twins run inside to fetch Mum's bag. The last of the light blinks; it eases out from the soft crinkle of the dog's ears, the leaves, the space between us, and moves on.

NEXT MORNING, I SEND A MESSAGE TO JASPER. IT'S SATURDAY. It rained last night while we were sleeping. Everything looks rinsed, like in those ads for dishwashing liquid. It's like the world is pinging—glass against glass, everything spangly, see-through, crystalized.

ME: Hey. *Emoji of a camel.*

He writes back within three minutes (not that I count).

HIM: Hey. *Smiley face. Emoji of a dolphin.*

ME: What are you doing?

HIM: Studying. Ugh. *Crying face.* How's Wagga weather? Hot, or hot?

ME: Um. I'm home.

HIM: Whaaaaaat????????

ME: Yeah.

HIM: Holy shit. I'll be over in sixteen minutes.

ME: Be careful. Don't ride too fast. *Emoji of a sand timer. Emoji of a heart. Emoji of a sandwich.*

o ° o ° o

Sixteen minutes, fifteen,
    fourteen, ten,
    five, four, two, and
    here
    he
    is.

Jasper's hopping off his motorbike, he's taking off his helmet, he sees me standing on the veranda, he's grinning, he's a miracle.

And the twins run out and say, "Jasper!" They're jumping up and down, two wild, bouncing beans.

Mum's at the door too, saying, "Jasper!"

And Jasper's flying up the path like a comet. His grin is like the universe beginning and like atoms splitting and Mum—who's seen love and felt love and been broken and mended by it—sees my face, and gives my arm a squeeze.

"Yeah," she says, and her voice breaks a bit.

And when Jasper and I hug, hard, and he spins me and doesn't let go, the twins leap and scream and Mum can't help but laugh because she knows. How it is. To be in this place, in this moment, under this sun, for as long as you can be, for as long as you get. For as long as you can stay to see what might happen next.

ACKNOWLEDGMENTS

This book would not exist without the enthusiasm, love, and support of many beautiful, good people. I am so full of gratitude, sometimes it's hard to move!

To begin with, a huge thank-you to my agent, Catherine Drayton. You have helped make my book finer, propelled it beautifully into the publishing world, and have been there for every question I've had, no matter how small. I'm so grateful you took me on, Catherine. And thank you, too, to your dedicated and talented assistant, Claire Friedman.

Thank you to my U.S. editor, Jessica Dandino Garrison, at Dial. From the moment I first spoke to you, Jess, I felt instantly at home. You have been insightful, deeply respectful, and visionary about the direction for this book. It has been one of the most rewarding experiences of my life, working with you.

Thank you also to Regina Castillo, for your smart and sensitive editing. Thank you to the people at Dial/Penguin Random House who have championed my book and offered lovely feedback: Lauri Hornik, Nancy Mercado, Ellen Cormier, Christina Colangelo, Bri Lockhart, and Elyse Marshall. To my interiors designer, Cerise Steel, art director, Lily Malcom, and cover designer, Kristie Radwilowicz: Thank you for making my book so beautiful. And thank you to Karolis Strautniekas, for my stunning cover illustration.

Thank you to my Australian editor, Claire Craig at Pan Macmillan, whose vision for my book matched mine perfectly. Thank you so much, Claire, for falling in love with Biz's story and for the work you have done in bringing my book to life. Thank you also to Georgia Douglas, for your close reading, and fantastic catches and fixes.

To my first readers: Each of you gave me wonderful feedback. Thank you to Nancy Huggett, Gracie Alexander, Sophie Miller, and Annie Gilholm Rowland, who each read with such care and then offered beautiful friendship and support throughout my editing journey. To Kit Fox: Thank you for your insights, and your hours of companionship at all the cafés where Biz came to life! To Eric Dunan and Christine Fox: Thank you for loving me and my words so unconditionally. And to Tobias Dunan: You've waited so very patiently to read the final version of this book! *Here it is.*

Thank you to Nina Adams for your Temora information; Biz truly sees so much of it through your eyes. And thank you to Shane Adams—I am sorry if your hometown doesn't get as much love in this book as it deserves!

To Mark Donovan, clinical psychologist and friend, who gave me incredibly valuable information that helped me make Biz's experiences as true and sensitive as possible: Thank you for being a lifesaver, in every sense of the word.

To Paul Templeton, manager of the Mental Health Unit at Wagga Wagga Hospital: I am so very grateful for your help. Thank you for helping me paint a compassionate picture of Biz's experiences, and for being so thorough in your feedback.

Thank you to my talented writing students and the community of writers I have come to know, for your company, kindness, and generosity. I am especially grateful to Margo Lanagan, for your friendship and glorious words, and Kathryn Heyman for helping me see what makes a novel shine. And to my fellow Friday women writers—Chloe Higgins, Hayley Scrivenor, Donna Waters, and Julie Keys—thank you for being in my life!

Thank you to my sister Thomasin, nieces Kate and Emily, and my two beautiful mums, Kathy and Mom. You have believed in me, helped me, and loved me, as long as I have known you. That means the world.

To Mom: A special thank-you for supporting me when I decided not to be a lawyer but decided instead to run away to the U.S. and become a writer! Thank you for inspiring me and for all the things you have done to make me stronger, better, and brighter. You are beautiful to me.

To Eric, Kit, and Tobias, the great loves of my life: You dazzle me, motivate me, and make my days laugh-till-I-cry funny. Thank you for supporting, so absolutely, this writing dream of mine. I could not have done any of this without you. Thank you for your wise company, your kindness and creativity, and for being my lifelines and my friends. Here we are! I love you all so much.

And to my dear Anna Moraová, my person, my friend: You saw the world in ways I had never seen before. You changed my life with your friendship, insight, love for my family, and beautiful heart. I am unbelievably sorry you had to go—cancer will never make sense. But every day, I remember the words you said to me just before you left: *Let your heart not be troubled. But let it be filled with colors.*

I have lived with mental illness my whole life. I carry with me complex PTSD, anxiety disorder, dissociative disorder, and clinical depression. I walk with these things, but they don't define me. I live with, and beyond them. I do my best to speak out and seek help when I need it. To my family, friends, health care providers, and lovely strangers who have sat with me when I've fallen, who have walked beside me when I've begun the climb back to health, who have loved me through all the terrible, wonderful, and everything-in-between moments of my life and given me hope: I am more grateful to you than I can begin to describe.

I am so very glad to still be here. Every day, I do my best to see the colors. I take note. I breathe them in.

REACHING OUT

If you are having a tough time, please reach out. If you need immediate assistance, you can call the National Suicide Prevention Lifeline any time at 1-800-273-8255 or text HOME to 741741 to be connected immediately with a crisis counselor at CrisisTextLine.org. You can also talk to your local health professional or speak to someone you trust. For more information about depression, anxiety, and other mental health issues, you can go to the National Alliance on Mental Illness (NAMI.org), the Crisis Text Line (crisistextline.org), or the Anxiety and Depression Association of America (adaa.org).

Talking has saved me, again and again. It is okay—and you absolutely deserve—to ask for help when things are hard. Remember, lovely human, that you matter very much. You are a miracle of molecules: infinite and extraordinary.

ON SEXUALITY

My family's sexuality is diverse. My two mums, my sister and nieces, my children, my husband and I proudly live inside and right beside the LGBTQ+ community. We love each other to the ends of the earth.

Whoever you are, however you identify—whether you are still figuring out your story, or singing it from the rooftops, or somewhere beautifully in between—here you are, here we are together, all of us deserving to live, love, and be loved, in freedom and equality.

"And love is love is love is love is love is love is love is love cannot be killed or swept aside."

— Lin-Manuel Miranda